NINE BELLS *for a* MAN

NINE BELLS
for a
MAN

PETER UNWIN

Peter Unwin (signature)

SIMON & PIERRE
A MEMBER OF THE DUNDURN GROUP
TORONTO · OXFORD

Copyright © Peter Unwin 2000

All rights reserved. No part of this publication may be reproduced, stored in a retrieval system, or transmitted in any form or by any means, electronic, mechanical, photocopying, recording, or otherwise (except for brief passages for purposes of review) without the prior permission of Dundurn Press. Permission to photocopy should be requested from the Canadian Copyright Licensing Agency.

Editor: Marc Côté
Copy Editor: Don McLeod
Design: Jennifer Scott
Printer: Transcontinental Printing Inc.

Canadian Cataloguing in Publication Data

Unwin, Peter, 1956-
Nine bells for a man

ISBN 0-88924-294-1

I. Title

PS8591.N94N56 2000   C813'.54   C00-930043-0   PR9199.3.U58N56 2000

1 2 3 4 5   04 03 02 01 00

THE CANADA COUNCIL | LE CONSEIL DES ARTS
FOR THE ARTS | DU CANADA
SINCE 1957 | DEPUIS 1957

Canada

We acknowledge the support of the **Canada Council for the Arts**, the **Ontario Arts Council** and, the **Book Publishing Industry Development Program** (BPIDP) for our publishing activities.

Care has been taken to trace the ownership of copyright material used in this book. The author and the publisher welcome any information enabling them to rectify any references or credit in subsequent editions.

J. Kirk Howard, President

Printed and bound in Canada.
Printed on recycled paper.

Dundurn Press
8 Market Street
Suite 200
Toronto, Ontario, Canada
M5E 1M6

Dundurn Press
73 Lime Walk
Headington, Oxford,
England
OX3 7AD

Dundurn Press
2250 Military Road
Tonawanda, New York,
U.S.A. 14150

*The world's a vast stage of excitement
And there's danger everywhere that you go*
                        Ontario temperance hymn, 1912

1

The wind cuts across the water and slashes at them. A slushy membrane of ice laps against their throats, breaks open in the chopping waves, and slides together with a terrible hiss.

A hundred yards off the black spar of a shoreline, clogged with snow and topped by a dark serration of pines, jabs against the night. For a quarter of an hour they have clung to a pine box without uttering a word. Except for the wracking yawns of hypothermia they've ceased making the sounds the others had, the exhalations that turn into screams, arrested shudders that seared out across the lake and then stopped, one after another.

Of the four remaining men one is noticeably older. His skin is the faint, florid colour of rhubarb. A white beard, cut short and assumed by local people to be distinguished, bristles in frozen sprouts from his jaw. Somehow a few strands of it are not frozen yet, and hang down like limp seaweed. "Tilly," he shouts, "Tilly." Tilly is the name of his wife, the woman who has endured him for thirty-seven years. He sobs her name above the waves and into the smothering snow that races into his eyes.

The three others are young men, smoothly shaved, their jaws cleft in a type of determination. At the front end of the box two of them have lashed themselves together at the wrists with a necktie. They dangle, one on each side, while the clods of their hands lie uselessly on top of the box — four pale flapjacks poured onto a cold skillet.

Only minutes earlier they stood in full confidence at the front door of the future and knocked loudly on it. They are athletes, sportsmen, and former playboys. One remains a skeptical bachelor and lives in extravagant Ottawa rooms. They no longer resemble the seasoned commercial travellers they started out as. Black November water slaps their chattering mouths, the same blithe and sugary mouths that sweet-talked a new line of wares for modern companies situated in the heart of the booming city. For what good it did them now, they had borne the confidence of men who travelled and were on easy terms with the world. They had clanged up the black spiral staircases of Montreal bearing imported chocolates for young women named after summer flowers. They had marvelled at the crush of humanity on the platform of Union Station, Toronto. One of them had even proffered a lit match to an extremely continental young lady who smoked cigarettes in plain view. They plied new merchandise made of rubber, hardy new seeds bred in the experimental farm at Ottawa, haying rakes, remedies for coated tongue, tonic water, laxatives, and all manner of labour-saving devices. Their bluff voices boomed among the stooped men of the backwoods, the roughnecks, the rednecks, and the hayseeds who limped from old hatchet wounds — men they so skillfully and cheerfully fleeced. They were colleagues, they worked together, they shared the intrigues of the city and ate in the same dark-paneled restaurant; the Palm Room of the Chateau Laurier, where a supercilious waiter in a glossy vest laid down bowls of soup made from a turtle.

These were city men but they had conscientiously

trained themselves in the ways of the country. The three of them could have written the book on those garrulous, straw-haired fellows with smashed fingers who drank turpentine mixed with brown sugar to cure a cold, who brewed blinding whiskey in stills hidden up on Dohlan's Mountain and smuggled it in saddle horns into the timber camps of Skead, Booth, McLachlin.

The older man had been such a person as this. His life is almost gone from him now, and his screaming has mercifully stopped except for the occasional prophetic outburst, mostly from the Book of Ezekiel. Periodically, he also hollers his wife's name into the teeth of the gale. The last of his utterances has raced to the edge of human endurance and been smothered there. He slumps against the box and makes a final piteous apology.

"I'm no good to you, boys. I'm all done in." He moans these words into the wind, which immediately snaps and unravels them like threads. They are not so much words of shame as of defeat; the heavy, plain words uttered in the proximity of death. He accepts the closeness of it now, the unthinking, final severance from the woman who is his wife, the stark admission that suddenly, as if overnight, he has become too old and too weak to continue with the business of living. It's a new world that has come down and he is old. That's the hard fact of it. He was old and he knew only the old ways. He knew how to make a presentable vinegar from a maple tree. He also knew the exquisite pleasure of a day in 1887 when an Indian trapper handed over to him a seventy-two pound salmon trout in exchange for a quart of whiskey. He'd darkened the whiskey himself, with cherries. These were things he knew; they included the tannic colour of rivers and the orchestrations of cicadas in summer after they emerged from seven years in the mud. He knew soap made from trees, and the taste of a high-bush blackberry served in cream. He was familiar with the sheen on a bear's coat as it came down to rake the blueberries off the rock shores of Kaminiskeg.

Kaminiskeg. The man is drowning in it, and this seems impossible. It was something that happened to little children, like Jeff Coulihan's boy, three years ago. A deep, soggy moan erupts from the man's chest. Such a great many things he knew, that he had known. It had been enough once; should have been enough for his entire life, and for the lives of his children. But it wasn't. Things were getting done now of which he knew nothing at all. Young women were said to be smoking cigarettes in plain view. Of this he knew nothing. He knew his wife's grey hair, assembled on top, held together by an ornate broach made of bone. "I'm no good to you boys, I'm all done in."

With these words he steps aside. He hands the world over to strangers and to younger men. It is their world now, made of automobiles, aeroplanes, thunderous turbines, and the whine and growling of the mills as they chewed a mass of timber up river. It no longer needed an old man who forty years earlier signed the deed to his concession property with an X and had remained an outsider to the written language. He's all done in and there's nothing left for him but to cling to a wooden box, while the lake water turns his flesh inside out, and smothers him.

Across the box a young man clings to the older one, forcing his eyes to stay open and staring dully, fish-like, into the dark. The glinting colour of terror had blazed in his eyes like a bush fire and is extinguished now by the chilling pressure of the water. His young life had seeped from him within moments of hitting the lake, but somehow he is not dead yet. He hangs on to this fact with the same obstinacy that he clings to most things, including the coat of the man across the box. "I am not dead yet," he utters, almost defiantly. His fingers cinch into the fabric like clamps. For all he knows the man inside that coat is dead like the rest of them. It seems to him that death is a physical place all of a sudden, and they are all headed toward it the way one might go to Gananoque, or Kingston, on the train.

The lake cuts through him like a sickle. In the starless evening it is not clear exactly who is wielding it. He hears the steel ringing of wind as it hurls across the water. It comes like shot fired from a gun and crusts on his eyebrows.

A ridge of ice has already formed there. There is no doubt about it; they have got themselves into a damn pickle. The young man watches remotely as his left hand slips from the fellow's coat and falls with a thud on the top of the box.

The box holding them afloat was made of rough pine, a deal box, the boards hewn quick and cheap, nailed together in haste, the sort of box that coffins are shipped across the country in. A bill of lading adorns the side of it, submerged, illegible now; the soaked ink spreads like oil across the parchment. Inside the sheathing of that pine box rests a coffin, lovingly constructed in California mahogany, smoothed and varnished. Four brass handles clap peacefully at the sides, like sentinels.

Within it, nestled into the plush upholstery, the fine stitch work and the general luxury provided to men only when they are dead, rests a young man. He's a commonplace young man except for a fine black suit coat that encases him thickly, and seems oddly tubular, like chimney piping. He is moustached, and from a buttonhole in his jacket hangs a white rose. The petals had detached days ago and lay dry and shrunken on the black lapels. Only the darkened rosehip is left, glaring like a blind eye.

He had once been known for his temper and his ability to bring down mallards on the wing. But mostly for his temper. Now he is back home and equanimous, no longer spoiling for a fight. The frigid lake does not disturb him; he knew its depths once and its pitches, the deep gullies where the trout lurk in summer, the marshes where the ducks skid to a clumsy standstill. He knew even the precise moment when Big John Omanique was at his weakest in an arm wrestle and could be taken. It was said he understood better than anyone, except Darron Staal, how to lunge a horse into a rig and yank the stumps of a pine tree from the fields on the first go.

Nor was the young man entirely ignorant of the world. He'd seen some considerable distance of the west country too; the flat, pineless vacancy of the West. Of course he regretted ever going there. Dirt farming is what it was. Endless fields, in which a man could not even raise a disturbance, let alone crops. He should have listened to his father that day two years ago when the old man looked straight into his eyes and said, "Son, you stay goddam put." Instead, he'd gone out to the west country a living man and come back in a different state altogether.

The man lies in the plush interior of a fine coffin while four dying men and the storms of the world bang against the lid. It's true that he had never known the supercilious air of a vested waiter like some, or the taste of a finely seasoned turtle soup. He did not know the ornate mansions of Buffalo, or the crush of humanity pressed on the platform at Union Station. But in his own reckoning what he had known was much better than any of that, for he had seen Rebecca Chiles, the third daughter of Wallace Chiles, half-undressed in a field of raspberries at twilight after a day of berrying. Her breasts lolled like two perfect puddings exposed for him alone, and her shoulders were more naked than it was possible for any man to know.

2

Yorkton, Saskatchewan, rose like a hasty serving of cups and saucers on a rough board. A rooming house showed on the outskirts, rung by a cluster of shacks. These were trailed closely by Harry Bronfman's hotel, The Balmoral, with its rust red facade, then the beginnings of a hay shed on Topper Avenue, a livery, ironworks, and an advertisement for Nobleman Cigars that nosed its way in cheekily in front of the ever present Dominion Lands Office. All of it was built with imported lumber. The streets themselves remained embryonic; a few broken bits of plank, warped by the cold. A dozen wagons and three black automobiles, one of them listing badly, clung to the land like ravens.

A stain on the earth indicated a type of road, running north out of town toward the settlement of Ebenezer. At several miles came the first sod hut; a blister on the land. It might have stood as a relic of the pioneer age, had not seven people been living it. Following that was the almost prehistoric appearance of an ox, sunk knee deep in a half-frozen slough, staring in astonishment at nothing. Then appeared the rugged indications of a life determined to stay put; houses flung down like dice, black, stout little homes coated in tarpaper. Their frames showed through like the ribs of a starving animal.

Further off on a bluff, broken by an ambitious but leafless cottonwood, stood a farmhouse. A dog circled in front of it, sniffing a stiff, fragrant wind that came down from Lake Athabaska laden with the curious smells of the North. The house rose a story-and-a-half high, covered in batten and painted milk white. Piercing the roof was a fierce, spear-shaped lightning rod. Stairs divided two rooms downstairs and went up to a clutter of bedrooms and storage, the discarded rifle bolts, rusted hinges, bent nails, and loose threads that ravel around a family like old and partially true stories. The cookstove was going, the heating stove in the front room was going, and a thick press of hot air inflated the house like a bladder.

In the kitchen Elizabeth Anne Pachal stood at a table washing the breakfast dishes in a dented tin tub. Beside her on a board waited half a cup of sourdough starter for leavening pancakes. Her brother Herman Brown sat at the kitchen table, cleaning his rifle. It was him who had dented the tub some months ago in a fit of anger. She was aware of a faint, irritating *shush shush* sound as he pumped an oiled cloth up and down the barrel. She preferred that Herman would clean his rifle somewhere else, away from the baby. Moments earlier her daughter had set out on a perilous journey by foot across the kitchen. Near one of her uncle's legs she foundered and fell face-forward onto the floor, where she still lay gamely and without tears, her pink knees scrabbled on the boards.

"You ought to have that rifle outside." The young woman snapped a bead of dishwater back into the tub and looked at her brother. What she saw was the morose look of a fellow who did not have a wife. Some fellows do not survive that, she reasoned. Just like some folks do not survive a change of scenery either. She again felt the heavy suspicion that her brother suffered from both these afflictions.

Elizabeth Anne Pachal had come out to the West three years ago following the receipt of a pleading letter. Her purpose, which she undertook with quiet competence, had been to attend to an aunt who had the creeping rheumatism. But the aunt passed away suddenly in a dark bedroom, shouting the name of a man who had gone up the Cariboo Trail and died there of a perforated ulcer after being kicked by a mule. She had stayed on, temporarily she thought, extending her help to a complex mesh of aunts and uncles. She had already made her decision to return east when Robert proposed to her.

Her brother, Herman Brown, had come out exactly a year later and had not married anyone. He'd not done much of anything but shoot prairie chickens and milk Holsteins, which he did resentfully. Lately he had begun to drive a wagon for Levi Beck. She hoped that might lift him from the funk he had gone down into in the last while. She had gone into it herself for a time; she understood what it meant to see nothing but the sheen of prairie grass, bent double in the wind, to not even see a tree. She'd heard all the stories before. Henrietta Saltcoats liked to tell about a man who got off the train at Melville and spent four hours looking at the wall. He just stood there staring at it until the stationmaster stepped outside and asked what he was all about. "I'm sorry, mister," he said. "But I got to see something! I just got to see something." She had heard the other stories, too, of how the men died, the Galicians, Ruthenians, the Finns, young English fellows even, washed up like driftwood on the prairie. Dead of loneliness and liquor is what they said. Dead for the absence of women was more like it. She wiped her hands dry on a rag and put a finger length of hair back in place behind her ear.

"Kasper, you want more tea?"

Kasper Neibrandt sat in the other room, with the thin pages of a week-old Yorkton newspaper stretched out in front of him. He had a home of his own three-quarters of a mile away on the next section, but his wife was dead, his sons were with the railroad, and Elizabeth Anne was a reassurance to him and a pleasure to look at.

Winnipeg Regulars to Mobilize. This leader of tall black letters put the old man's face into a pucker. It was a particular piece of news that for him displaced the fact that a building permit had been issued to Jay Wood to erect a hay shed on Topper Avenue, or even that a bushel of Number One Northern stood at sixty-six cents. Kasper Neibrandt sat in the front room in the good chair, his head bobbing over the dense columns of words. He owned a wise face, or at least an old one; the riven face of an aging man who knew exactly what sort of festering sinkhole the world was going down into next. In some remote way that Elizabeth Anne did not understand, he was related by blood to her husband through a mysterious agitator said to be rotting in a Czarist jail, and for whom a small prayer was offered up before Sunday meal. "They're getting up the army," he shouted. "They're bringing up the Canadian Army. You hear?"

The young woman stared down into the dishpan and saw a globule of fat floating in the mucky water. She sighed and looked out the window; the quilted darkness of the prairie was still there, still stretching on, still treeless. It seemed to her as though God had pulled back his hand before he had properly finished with the job. He had patted down the land smooth enough alright, left a few prairie tulips, but He had not left a decent hill to look at, and maybe every hundred miles some sort of tree stuck up, a cottonwood or an ash. She sighed. There would come a day when her daughter would see a tree, a proper tree, a whole forest full of red pines like back home. She was concerned that the girl might run from them in terror.

"Herman, you want more tea then?" But her brother did not want more tea, and for his own reasons he wanted no part in the human civilities that accompany tea. It appeared as if he did not want the English language spoken in his direction at all. Or German, either. The only sound that came from that corner of the room came from the small girl who, for no reason, looked delightedly about herself and said either "floegel," or "flu-gull."

From the porch Elizabeth Anne heard the crashing activity of someone wearing extremely large boots. It was the loud, meandering noise of a man more accustomed to having the hummocky earth of the prairies under his feet than any sort of floorboards. Her husband entered with a stack of willow twigs for the stoves.

"I brought in the scantling." He heaved the enormous stack of twigs into the wood box.

"Scantling?" She taunted gently. "That's not scantling, that's twigs."

"Bunting, then," he tried hopefully.

"That's not bunting either. That's twigs."

"I suppose." Her husband looked vaguely disappointed. He had been trying to educate himself in the jargon of timber, for no other reason but to please her. Robert Pachal looked at his wife, and then to the child. It was the soft, adoring gaze of a man who could not believe that either of them was there, right in front of him. It seemed that the shutting of his own eyes might snatch them away forever. He was a man of good muscle, red-haired, bearded, and he was wearing sheepskin. Elizabeth Anne did not approve of sheepskin, though she had got used to it. She refused to wear it herself. She refused to be the stout peasant wife, dressed in sheepskin, and that was final.

"You didn't wear that coat in town?"

"I left it in the wagon," he lied.

He had returned from Yorkton but did not like to come in empty handed to his wife. So he had come in with the scantling instead.

"They're getting up the army at Winnipeg," hollered Kasper Neibrandt from the other room. "You heard that?"

"I heard that in town," returned the young man loudly. He turned with some civility toward his brother-in-law but got no response.

"There's tea," she said.

He'd say yes, she knew it. He'd say yes to anything as

long as it came from her, providing she passed it on to him with her own hands. She looked again over to her brother Herman, who sighted his rifle out the side window. After that she looked at her husband, who returned her gaze uncertainly, showing a warm smile that he erased quickly, as though afraid of being too forward with her, too presumptuous still after two years.

She laughed and turned from him. The effect of his adoration was sometimes too much for her to bear. The responsibility of being beloved — it seemed sacrilegious somehow, but she was not sure how. Privately she suspected her husband to be the most simple thing on earth; a good man. She saw it in the awkward gentleness of his stout body as he stooped to lift the baby. The child wanted none of it and wailed piteously, which alarmed the poor man. He set his daughter back down on the floor like a porcelain figurine.

Elizabeth Anne still found herself surprised by the matter-of-factness of it; that God had sent her a good man. She thought that angels blew trumpets when something like that happened to a woman. But there had been nothing at all. Her uncle had tramped upstairs, knocked on the door. She was still sleeping in the same room her aunt had passed on in. "There's a fellow downstairs wants to marry you. Pachal. He's one of those Pachals," he called through the closed door.

She'd heard the name before. There were Pachals up and down Saskatchewan from Batoche to North Battleford. There were Pachals living in soddies up Carrot River, Pachals living in Regina mansions, and Pachals hunting coyotes at Fort Whoop Up.

"Which one is he?"

Her uncle screwed up his face in a way suggestive of deep thought. In his estimation she had asked a fair enough question, for he nodded and said, "I'll find out for you." The man turned ruefully on the steps and came back a moment later.

"Robert. He says his name's Robert."

She married Robert Pachal in the Baptist church in

Ebenezer with Reverend C. Blaedow presiding. There followed a large celebration with some sixty other Pachals who had appeared out of the woodwork. Music was provided by a one-handed fiddler named Jimmy Conn from Corey County, near Saskatoon. His left hand had been shot away in a hunting accident and to attach the bow to his stump, he borrowed two sealer rings and played all night.

Robert Pachal had been a good man. He was born on Christmas day twenty-four years ago and it had never occurred to Elizabeth Anne that a man of flesh could actually be born on Christmas day. She had known of it happening only once before; a boy back home, Cecil Coulihan, who was seven years old and drowned on the beach at Lake Kaminiskeg. They had his little white body laid out on the beach, while his brother ran through town clutching the drowned boy's clothes, stopping people and shouting, "Cecil got drowned! Cecil got drowned!" as though they ought to be able to fix it. She nursed a small vein of superstition inside her and could not entirely shake the belief that a man born on December 25 must have a drop of Christ's blood in him. Or least more drops than did most men.

Her husband sat meditatively before the mug of tea that she placed in front of him. A wisp of steam, like cigar smoke, drifted from the cup. Pachal felt the liquid burning through the enamel, warming his thick hands. It tasted sugary, the way he liked.

"It's just right," he said. "Just perfect."

She nodded. It seemed impossible for her to do anything that did not leave him grateful. Off in the corner she sensed the dark, scowling presence of her brother. She knew he could not abide any type of cooing between the two of them.

"Don't be putting out any supper for me. I'm going huntin' after." He spoke this like a threat, then grabbed the rifle and turned back for a critical look about the room. He saw a grape-coloured wash of wallpaper, a wadding of white cloth stuffed in the window frames to keep the wind from whistling in, and then an infant on the floor, pink and incomprehensible. He saw a man who feared God beyond what was necessary, a man stricken with foolish love, and a woman who was not his sister anymore. Ten years ago he'd fished the pike with her out at Barren's Creek back home. She had been a girl who wanted to grow up and be a trapper, like Annie the Deer Lady who lived up the Bonnechere and kept a pet deer that slept on the bed with her. She'd wanted to take down geese on the wing, skin rabbits, shoot bears, and not go anywhere without her rifle. He barely recognized what his sister had become these days. She'd become the mother of a baby, and the wife of a man.

Herman Brown turned and went hard out the door.

3

ONE GOOD THING ABOUT THE PRAIRIES — PRAIRIE chickens. This thought formed in Herman's mind as clearly as the call of a woodcock, of which the prairies had none either, or if they did, he had not seen any. The thought formed so clearly in his mind that he felt obliged to speak it out loud.

"There's one good thing about the prairies and that's prairie chickens."

He spoke these words to young Oliver Tunney who sat beside him on the wagon, smudging at two silver runnels of snot that leaked into his moustache.

"What?" responded the young man, slapping the reins attached up front to two drays towing them forward. Like Herman Brown, he was in the employ of the Levi Beck Company. He drove the wagon outside of Yorkton, Saskatchewan, that morning not because of any particular skill as a drayman (he was, by trade, a meat slaughterer), but because Herman Brown preferred to stare morosely at the prairie, and had the habit of jumping off over the side with his hunting rifle and going off to shoot prairie chickens.

They crawled several more prairie inches over the trail until Herman Brown felt compelled, once more, to utter, "Prairie chickens."

"What?"

"Prairie chickens!" Since he hailed from the blue hills in Renfrew County, Ontario, he had every reason in the world to hate the prairies. He spat over the side of the wagon onto the great, unkempt floor of the West.

"You ever et pickerel?"

"What?"

"Pickerel."

"What's that?"

"That's fish."

"Hates fish."

This comment caused Herman Brown to spit once again over the side. What could you say about a place where you had to share a wagon with a fellow who did not like pickerel nor even knew of such a thing? "You think they had any goddam trees in the Garden of Eden either?"

"What?"

Herman Brown shook his head. "Where the hell are we, anyhow?" He was sick of not ever knowing where the hell he was. He did not understand yet that his constant feeling of being lost came about because of the absence of trees, and he had learned, without knowing it, to measure a thing from how far it stood in relation to a tree.

"We're just about over to there."

"To goddam where?" Herman Brown's eastern patience had just about wore out. Things got done different back home, that was for sure.

"To there. To that bluff there."

He looked ahead at what appeared to be a meager amount of dirt, sticking up slightly from another meager amount of dirt. Over him the sky opened sullenly, allowing two cylinders of angled light to crash to the earth.

"Where's that there, anyway?"

"What?" The young man had made a dollar a day hammering spikes on the Grand Trunk spur out near Melville, and he was a good part deaf because of it.

"Well, where's that supposed to be?"

"That," shouted the fellow as though responding in triumph to a schoolroom question, "is where you shot them prairie chickens!"

"Prairie chickens!"

"What?"

"Stop the damn wagon." Herman Brown reached behind to where his rifle lay loose atop the pocked and gleaming surface of the apples. The wagon was packed tight with apple bushels. He grabbed the gun and on the way up got himself a nice red Delaware.

"I'll meet you up the road. I'm goin' to shoot me some more."

He headed out with his apple and his hunting rifle across the bowing grass of the prairie.

Herman Brown marched a hundred yards over the earth and crossed a slough into the tall grass. What the hell am I going to do here, he wondered, then hoisted the rifle to his shoulder and took dead aim at the morning sun. He had the sun in his sights perfectly but did not pull the trigger. The man had no particular desire to see the sun shatter like a china plate and have darkness fold in on the world, with him having been the cause of it, so he lowered his rifle. I am a long way from home, he thought. I have got myself too far from home.

Sleep would have been fine, but Herman Brown wanted no part of sleep. Last night he dreamt the bodies of a million men lying on the prairies. Cannonballs hit all around them and filled the wheat fields with cesspools of water. The concussions from that dream still rang in his ears like circles on a lake when the fish came up to snap a bug. He stared at the sun and saw the same circles turning there in the vast range of the sky. They were turning like the wheels of trains. Those same trains that weren't stopping anymore, for anything.

He scanned the fields for prairie chickens, not caring if he saw any or not. What was a prairie chicken to him anyway. It weren't a partridge like back home, those flecked brown and white creatures that thumped their wings on fallen logs of the forest so a low drumbeat spread out for miles over the bush. It must be some type of grouse. Some type of ruffed grouse. Maybe one of them sharp-tails.

Herman Brown was stalking over the cold prairie, his rifle angled and his knees cocked like two hair triggers, as if he stood again in the softwood forests of eastern Ontario in two feet of snow. He would be waiting for a flushed partridge to clatter its wings together like dried sticks, then lift with its wing tips whipping against the pine trees. But there were no trees. Just this thin little stick of one that Herman Brown didn't know the name of, and was not even worth the felling.

He squatted almost to his haunches and let his back come to rest on the stunted trunk of a willow. His eyes were closed and behind the black film of his eyelids he saw the echoing circles of the sun fade into darkness. He forced himself to see trees, real trees, white pines so thick a man could barely move between them. They stood up against the sky like a torn piece of black fabric.

The young man stared vacantly into all of this. His father was there, too, with a dead buck roped to a wagon, ten miles up the Ottawa River. It was night, they had a tent up. Later they went to a rise by the river, and stood there, staring at the thing.

It was the biggest contraption Herman Brown had ever laid eyes on. On the water, near enough for him to spit on, floated the last great white pine raft of the Hale and Booth Company. It stretched so deep he could not see the far side of it, where it must have rubbed the north shore of the river. It spread out bigger than any town he'd ever seen, including Pembroke, a forest of giant white pine trees, cut down, lashed square together in forty-foot cribs, with those cribs joined, until a mantle of felled trees rippled across the water. "That's a whole damn forest going by," his father said, and the boy knew that it was, that he was privy to a great miracle, and would be privy to great miracles for the rest of his life.

He stood and watched it pass: a city of square-cut pine logs, floating down the fresh water of the river, on its way finally to Portsmouth, and London, lit up like a Saturday night. On it he saw men, living there, casting giant shadows when they moved; tents mounted; shacks with windows hacked out of them. Gold light from the lamps spilling through. Storm lanterns swung in the dark. He saw two bonfires burning high, heard horses snorting, and dark obscene shanty words; the swift, immoral sounds of the French language from the men of Ste. Cecile de Masham. The notes of "Sweet Mountain Smilin' Anne" caterwauled from a fiddle. He saw men dancing out there, their fleet shadows rose and fell through the lamp glow.

It passed under the brittle white stars that had come down out of the dark to have a look at it.

"You won't never see that again," his papa said.

And Herman Brown, and no one else on earth, ever did.

He leaned against the stick of timber that sprouted reluctantly from the ground and placed the cold red apple on his head. It stayed there for a moment, then rolled off down his shoulder and skidded on the dirt. Herman Brown stared at the fallen fruit. It looked as though one of his own eyeballs had rolled out of his head, and now lay gazing, stupidly and fish-like, into the gigantic sky. It recalled to him the eyeball of a young Frenchie from Shawville in the Eastern Townships, rumoured to be pickled in a jar atop the counter of Jack Schenly's tavern in Brudenell back home. He put himself back to that evening two years ago, the boys drinking his health at the Balmoral Hotel; Leonard Marquardt's squeaky voice ringing in his ear: "It's that pepper's eye what sits in a jar on the counter at Jack Schenly's — "

"Well, is it pickled then?"

"Goddam pickled is what it is." The fellows had drunk high wine and beer for the day and whiskey after. Leonard Marquardt put forth his opinions against the West on the grounds that there weren't no goddam trees there.

"There ain't no goddam trees here anymore either," said Pauley Brown, twin of Percy Brown, two of Herman Brown's five brothers. His seven sisters had not been invited to the smash-up.

"There's trees here," said Percy, "if you count hemlocks."

"They don't count for bugger all unless you're making billiard cues," snapped Teddy Hessler. This was the same Teddy Hessler who shot Ray Kultchek in the belly by mistake when they were up Bark Lake deer hunting. Ray Kultchek paddled nearly three miles in his canoe before he bled out and died.

"There ain't no timber anywhere except at the mills. That's where it's all gone." Leonard Marquardt slapped a glass on the table and broke it. "You got these fellers there stood right up to that conveyor, bundling, trimming, sorting, slugging away just like a bunch of goddam oh-tom-a-tons."

"Oh-what?" queried Percy Brown.

"Oh-tom-a-tons."

"I ain't never heard of no goddam oh-tom-a-tons."

"That," explained Leonard Marquardt, "is when a fellow starts acting all liquored-up and he ain't even had no liquor."

"I ain't never heard of no goddam oh-tom-a-tons," threatened Percy Brown, displaying the surly, curdled tenor that sometimes crept into his voice after thirty or forty whiskeys.

Herman Brown had nodded solemnly, even woozily, through his last evening in the East. He belonged to that generation of men who knew what it meant when a gazaboo came down the pike and a fellow was bughouse or jiggerood. He had skidded logs and jammed iron pig's feet into them. He felled and sweated and dragged one end of a crosscut saw though one hundred pine trees a day, twice what his father did when he felled. His father had used a felling axe and could bring down only fifty. He'd manned a donkey engine for pulling loaded sleighs up hill, had worked at sandpiping to save men's lives when it came down the other side, and even operated a Berrienger Brake, but could not learn the thing, even though they said it would prevent so many men from getting killed. He had been forbidden to speak at dinner, sat down with fifty other men who did not speak either for fear of getting sacked. "A fellow talking is a fellow not eating," that's what they said. But the fact was that if they talked at all, it would be about how John Hudder bled to death on account of there was no doctor, how Freddie Liedtke was crushed under a tanker sleigh, and Pete Tomasini had four dollars pay docked to get a tooth pulled and died three days later with his face swelled to the size of a pig's bladder. They'd gripe about how the fellows didn't even get a deal box to be buried in when the typhoid got into the camps, just hauled out in the blankets they died in and pitched into the woods, a spade full of sod tossed over top. And that wasn't right. There was always some fellow wanting to say it wasn't right, wanting the wife to get at least a little something if he got cracked up breaking a jam. They would talk amongst themselves about how the forest of tall pines was going down hard, so there would not be anything left soon for anyone. Not even for making tent pegs.

Herman Brown had got himself good and drunk that night for he was saying to hell with all of it. He would not do it any longer. He would not "go up" for J. R. Booth. He'd starve first. Three months earlier Will Henly had gone over the side of a pointer boat with an anchor cable wrapped around his thigh and that was it. He'd no longer watch men die for fifty cents a day. He would not work for son of a bitch millionaires felling Canadian trees to build the decks of British battleships.

He'd work the corundum mine at Craigmount before he did that. Those mining fellows had said corundum was the hardest mineral in the world next to jewels, which meant they'd need some hard men to dig it out. They'd come to the right place, for there was no shortage of hard men and there was not a jewel among them.

In three days Herman Brown learned he was not any sort of man to be lowered down on a box into a hole in the rock with two thousand other fellows. He was a land man. He would work *on* the land and not under it. So he wrote to his sister asking to come out there to the western plains and help milk cows and grow wheat, and do whatever else they did out there. He missed home though, missed it like hell. Most of all he missed the certainty of being first man to a fight and the first man to a fiddle. He missed the drunken voice of J. T. when he got up on the table and hollered:

> *My name is Johnny Hall*
> *and I'm from Montreal*

Herman Brown talked trees, timber, and punch-ups until midnight, at which point Jason Freeman insisted it wasn't no Frenchie's eye that sat pickled on the counter at Jack Schenly's tavern after all, but an eye belonging to one of Mrs. Cruikshank's pigs. Leonard Marquardt interpreted those as fighting words and reached back and broke Jason Freeman's nose. Pauley Brown hurled Jason Freeman across the billiard table, Percy Brown smashed his brother's head with a chair, Teddy Hessler got sick on the floor, Mrs. Billings came in with an apron on and said she was fed up with the whole bunch of them, and Herman Brown staggered outside and fell into a drainage creek.

Next morning he boarded a train for Yorkton, Saskatchewan.

A wind picked up across the prairie. It was a wind Herman Brown had never heard before, for what was the sound of wind when it had no pine boughs to push through, and no maple leaves to send shushing back and forth? That was the proper sound God made when he breathed across the sky. Back home everyone knew that. Not out here though, here it was just an empty noise, like air getting sucked into a chimney fire.

Herman Brown wanted to hear something meaningful from back home. He wanted to hear John Hudson's ancient lake steamer, the *Mayflower*, snorting and puffing and letting off a shriek of white steam. He wanted to hear the old Polish church at Barry's Bay sounding the matins for the dead, seven bells for a woman, and nine for a man.

He heard a voice then moving across the prairie. It was his own voice, the voice of a stranger in a strange church. Herman Brown had begun to sing the peculiar, remote songs from the lumber camps of Mr. Booth.

We will break the jam on Gerry's Rock
And to Bangor we will steer.

He remembered Armand Prince, who had broke the jam. He'd broke the jam at Big Chute and gone down between the giant sticks. And they had drug him out of there, dead, with his body lolling like a rag doll. Then they erected a cross of two sticks and nailed his caulked boots to a tree.

The words were hardly spoken
When the mass did break and go.

They said Armand Prince had put a man's eyes out with his thumbs during a fight in a Calabogie tavern, but that Jesus Christ had forgiven him and walked side by side with him on the train embankment leading out to Killaloe, right up until the day he was struck by a three-ton stick of waney timber.

Now some of them were willing and some of them were not
For to work on jams on Sunday, they did not think we ought.

For to work on jams on Sunday . . . Herman Brown wondered what day it was. It would be Tuesday then, that was it, Tuesday, November 6, the year of our Lord 1912. It must have been Tuesday as he had milked his sister's cows in the morning, and they were not Jerseys either, like back home, that gave the rich milk, but only Holsteins.

"What's it matter?" spoke Herman Brown into the empty amphitheatre of the western country. For to work the jams on Sunday they did not think we ought. He clutched his rifle like a felling axe, swung it up over his shoulder, and took aim at the sun once more as if to kill it. He listened hard, but heard only silence, until it pounded his ears and he longed to hear anything, even the wet, glucking noise of a prairie chicken as it clapped its way out of the grass to a thin branch. There was not even the sound of that. A single blade of grass touched another.

He started to walk again in circles around the stunted willow. The sound he heard was himself, walking, the noise of an army trampling everything in front of itself. Herman Brown stopped and saw the clouds scudding over top of him like very fast ships. He sighted again, fiercely and accurately, at nothing. The sun felt as cold to him as morning well water against his face. He was not aware if he was crying or not.

4

Oliver Tunney was by trade a meat slaughterer who worked his free hours, as did most men, for Levi Beck. Now with Herman Brown out, he rolled forward an indeterminate distance to a slight rise of dirt that he perceived to be a bluff. There, he stopped the horses, put a wedge of Player's Navy Cut tobacco into a long, straight, Peterson's pipe and, with his gumboots resting on the headboard, began to smoke. He smoked guiltlessly on company time, for his partner was the senior man, and he did not reckon he was responsible for Herman Brown's jumping overboard and going off to shoot prairie chickens. Nor could he rightly go on without him. So he sat with his feet up, smoking Navy Cut, and turned his mind completely to the matter of Hedda Louise Lobzinger.

The matter was serious, and approaching a climax. In five days the Baptist church at Yorkton held its social, and Hedda Louise Lobzinger would have the lunch made, sitting in a black box on a table among the other black boxes that the unwed women of Yorkton placed in front of them. From many long nights of thinking about nothing else, he'd figured her box to contain beans, baked two days in sand, chicken, bread, and a jar of Saskatoon berry jam.

Oliver Tunney concealed himself in a pall of tobacco smoke and imagined, with some precision, what it would be like to pick Saskatoon berries with Hedda Louise Lobzinger. In his mind her father was absent; a crazy son of a bitch with a rifle and a permanent tobacco stain on the right corner of his mouth, like a birthmark. They would go out on to the scraggy dunes of Saskatchewan, to where the Peigan, the Sarcee, and the Blood tribes had been, and pick the purple berry while the sun flamed through the thick gold hair of Hedda Louise, and spilled further down to where it went pale on her neck, for it seemed that Miss Lobzinger must bathe herself in milk before putting her clothes on.

The sure knowledge that the putting on and the taking off of clothes was something Hedda Louise Lobzinger did every day agitated the young man, and he jumped off the wagon and began to pace. "I have got it bad," he thought, although exactly what it was he had bad, he did not know. He tried to place himself again among the Saskatoon berries with the young woman, but was fractured with other visions and anxieties. He remembered Herman Brown going on about how a Saskatoon berry didn't taste like nothing. "The best eating are them blueberries." He'd go on forever about the East, about being back there again and picking blueberries from low bushes off hot rock faces by the lakes.

Oliver Tunney didn't figure anything could taste better than a Saskatoon once it had been roiled up in a vat of jam, and he assumed that Herman Brown was making the thing up about blueberries. Probably there weren't such a thing as any blue berry. Probably the same as with those pickerel fish, too. He was just sick of hearing about the East.

He paced faster now. His pipe was reloaded and he shot scowling looks out to where Herman Brown had got off. Oliver Tunney was in a hurry. He wanted to hear the crack of a rifle shot so they could get back on their way to the crossing. That's all it would take, too. One shot. That fellow had a way with a hunting rifle.

He kicked at something half crusted in the dirt, and then bent to unearth a squashed and empty tin of supplies. The black lines of words were printed on it, those damn words again, and he felt the urge to throw the tin back to the earth. But for the sake of Hedda Louise Lobzinger, he did not.

Oliver Tunney was not a reading man. He was not yet a reading man. For he had intentions. The world was getting filled right up with words, and for that reason he had the intention of being a reading man, soon. But with the social five days away, and Miss Lobzinger's lunch box laid on the table, he was not sure this reading business was something he could get his hands around in five days. He'd been lax in the matter. He had intentions of getting Mrs. Whitton at the boarding house to teach him the facts of reading. She was so expert at the thing herself that she could pick any book she wanted and just set into reading it. She could even read from the back end forward if she wanted.

The young man stared at the printed words on the tin. It seemed obvious that in those black letters were contained the true facts on the winning of a woman's heart. All he had to do was decipher them and that would mean as much as marriage to a woman such as Hedda Louise Lobzinger. Probably it would mean as many damn Saskatoon berries as a man could ever want.

The drayman threw the folded tin back to the earth. The words stared out at him, cryptic and meaningful. He looked about quickly, wanting Herman Brown to shoot the damn chicken and get back here. He was in a state now over the reading issue. Daniel Tilley was a reading man, and he knew Daniel Tilley would be there in five days also wanting to buy the lunch box of Hedda Louise Lobzinger. Not only was Daniel Tilley a reading man, but he'd seen him with a pencil, scratching something down on a board at the crossing, so that meant that he was a writing man as well. It was too much to bear. With all this reading and writing going on, it seemed a woman didn't have a fair chance anymore at picking the right fellow.

He reloaded and lit his pipe for the third time. Maybe there weren't any prairie chickens left. Maybe Herman Brown had shot the last of them. He looked over the pecks of shining apples crowded in the back. There'd be wagons waiting for those apples at the loading dock. He worried about that and felt he should head on alone, without the fellow. But he was reluctant. You didn't move on to some prairie crossing without the fellow you started out with. He took the pipe from his mouth and tapped it once on the wheel. Then he tapped it again and, when he did that, he heard the shot.

The single, foreign sound of a rifle shot scudding across the prairie made Oliver Tunney think of a linen sheet that had got loose off a clothesline and was snapping in the wind. He looked up to where the slough was and half expected to see a white bedsheet floating by. But there was nothing.

"Get up," he said to the horses, and started rolling forward very slowly over the trail. He looked back once to see if Herman Brown was coming yet, the way he did, at half a trot, swinging a dead prairie chicken in his hand, just like an Ottawa playboy with a walking stick. But there was nothing and the young man thought, to hell with him. He can meet up at the crossing like before.

The drayman got to the crossing in one quarter of an hour and put his feet back up on the headboard and waited for Herman Brown. He lit another bowl of Navy Cut and gave a pinch to Peter Saltcoats, whose brother had scratched himself on a wire fence while carrying a pail of milk and died the same day of raging fever. Four other men, one of them was Daniel Tilley, sat around the crossing and did nothing. They smoked and twirled stalks of prairie grass and waited for the Winnipeg train. Their wagons were already lined up for the stacking of the winter apples.

A wind passed in from the land and made Oliver Tunney look out at where he'd come from. He should be close to here by now, he thought. His heart made a quick beat that registered like the sound of Herman Brown's hunting rifle. He stood up on the wagon and looked hard again at where he'd come from.

"Somethin's gone the matter," he shouted. Two men got up and looked out to where the wagon driver was looking. They saw exactly the same thing he did, prairie and prairie scrub, pressed down by sky. It was as if the earth was one of those hummingbirds flattened between the covers of a book that folks sent home to the old countries.

"He shooting chickens?"

"He shot one. He shot one a half hour back."

"Maybe he busted up a leg," said Peter Saltcoats. "Or shot himself in his own foot."

"Waste of that damn rifle of his," supplied Daniel Tilley. Herman Brown owned a 1909 Model .32 Ross sporting rifle with a straight bolt action and a walnut stock. It was much coveted among the men.

"Well, let's go fetch him," Peter Saltcoats got in the wagon. So did Daniel Tilley and one other. The last man stayed back to mind the crossing in case the foreman showed.

Oliver Tunney hurried the wagon out past the low bluff, bent over, face wincing as a dusting of snow came down from the northwest. He stopped the horses.

"That way, out past the slough." The men fanned out and began stomping through the low bush. They met up again in a clearing one hundred yards beyond the slough. Daniel Tilley was already there. The rest of them came up behind him.

"Jesus Christ, our Lord," breathed Peter Saltcoats.

In a half-sitting position with his back pressed against the trunk of a willow tree, was Herman Brown. The Ross sporting rifle lay in his lap. The left side of his face was caved in and caked black from the powder burn. Blood leaked out an opening above his left eye and spread down his shoulder, down his coat length, where it pooled in his lap. His right eye opened and blinked twice, rapidly.

"God damn," breathed the wagon driver. "He's living."

"Get him in the wagon," ordered Daniel Tilley. But the men did not move. The wounded man's lips parted as if he meant to say something, but only a fine spray of spittle and blood issued from them. He looked out slowly, having to angle his head in a wide gesture to take them all in. A grunt came out of him. His eye closed and his head shook from one side to the other. The men moved all together then, and lifted the wounded man by his limbs. They carried him like a shot deer, for one hundred yards, with his head lolling back and forth, until they got to the wagon, where they lay him down gently on a bed of red Delawares and Jonathan Extra Fancy winter apples.

The party rode eight miles into the town of Yorkton with the wounded man alternately moaning and passing off into silence. A half dozen times it seemed the fellow was gone.

"He's finished," said Daniel Tilley.

"He's gone over," breathed Peter Saltcoats.

But Herman Brown had not gone over. His one unmuddied eye opened and he saw sky, leaden as a die press. An exclamation came out of his mouth, weak, indignant. It appeared he wanted a smoke. Daniel Tilley had one left in his pocket, but by the time he got it out, Herman Brown was unconscious again.

It took two hours to reach the outskirts of town, and when they entered it, they did not know if the man was alive or not. Herman Brown did not know either. He felt the hard motion of the wagon jerk him from sleep. That is what he wanted now; to sleep a good long time and to wake without brute labour waiting for him the day long. He also wanted a smoke. But what he wanted most was the damn sky to get away from his face, to either go back, or to lie flat and full on him, for it seemed that when he closed his eyes he'd caught a piece of sky within them, and it fluttered there, like a lady's crinoline beneath his eyelid.

Herman turned his head and saw Yorkton jounce sideways between the rim boards of the wagon. Apples, he thought. I am laying on a bed of apples. He heard a dog bark, he saw a magpie fall down from the elaborate sign over The Yorkton Carriage Works, he saw the jumble of Yorkton, the boards, the boxes, the advertisements for Nobleman Cigars (two for twenty-five cents), he heard the dark crack of an automobile, like rifle fire, and the sound of hammering as the men nailed Yorkton together in time for winter.

The sun came through for a moment. Herman Brown saw it silver and flat, stuck to the sky like a pancake before it went back under the clouds. They are looking to get me a surgeon, he realized, but he knew there was no surgeon. A nurse maybe, at the hospital, maybe someone who knew about the putting on of a bandage. But no surgeon. He wanted to tell them so. He wanted to say *Boys there is no surgeon here, not even one for animals,* but his mouth had got thickened up all of a sudden. Besides, they knew as well as him there weren't no surgeon. Boys, he said, boys, but there was only a gurgling sound that came out from the creak of the wheels, and then not even that.

5

Robert Pachal stood on the platform of the Yorkton train station and examined his watch. A good watch, a gold Hamilton with a lid, but a dear watch, too. His wife had picked it from the Eaton's catalogue without his knowing, and paid for it with the money she brought out with her from the East. She brought twenty-seven dollars in all, wrapped in calico and fitted in the bottom of her suitcase. Almost a year ago she gave the watch to him, Christmas day, the day of his twenty-fourth birthday. The coming together of both those special days in one man is how she justified the expense of it.

Of course her brother was not dead at that point. He'd only just arrived, supposedly to help with the farming, or to get his life out of that mess fellows were always getting into back East. He was not dead yet and the bills for it had not been calculated: the monies for J. W. Christie, embalmer; monies for J. W. Christie, undertaker and coffin-maker; the per-pound freight costs of shipping the body and coffin of Herman Brown one thousand five hundred miles on the railway; the fifty dollars it cost for his own passage. His wife would even have him pay for a berth, too, like one of those remittance fellows. But he wouldn't have it. He'd travel coach. It was three days only, and if a man could not sit up three days on a train there was nothing more to say about him.

Five past seven in the morning. Robert Pachal snapped shut his watch. It was a dear watch and that was all the more reason to make sure it never parted from him. Up the track the locomotive engines pounded hard in their black steel case, like something that wanted out. It would leave right on time, though, and he took satisfaction in knowing this train would leave on time. Somehow the two black hands of his Hamilton watch, moving imperceptibly to 7:10, signalled a perfection the world had not known before. Even his own efforts at farming, at building up Yorkton, and fixing the roof of the Ebenezer German Baptist Church, had something to do with why the trains ran on time. It seemed to him that the whole world was beginning to run on time, and that somehow he was a good part of the reason.

Pachal looked down the platform and saw the dark, polished wagon of the Yorkton Funeral Directors standing a short distance from the rail. The black dray waited, oblivious to death, and snorted funnels of vapour into the cold. Two of Christie's men came forward and pushed the coffin box to the lip of the baggage car, where someone unseen hauled it inside. The gates of the car slammed shut with a steel clatter, and Pachal hurried to the carriage, where he put his hands on the knees of his father who sat rigid against the morning cold.

"Get him into the ground," ordered the old man. "Then you bring yourself back here." Short bursts of vapour whitened from his mouth too, as though he, and even the horses, were imitating the black steaming engine. Robert Pachal was about to speak, but the older Pachal cut him off. "I'll look after her," he said. "And the young one."

"God be with you."

"God be with you, son. *Alles Gutes.*"

The young man turned away, feeling everything more intensely than before; the cold, the jewelled hoarfrost, and the vast wound of red sky that spanned over top of him as he strode across the platform and mounted the train.

Robert Pachal put himself down on a bench and slid tight to the window. He expected the engine to blast a harrowing sound into the dawn before pulling out. But nothing happened. No shrieking whistle, not one single person on the platform waved goodbye to anyone. The train was not so much moving as the platform was slipping away. Beyond the station, he saw the red brickwork of the Balmoral Hotel, the sun behind it like a painted china plate, and then the town of Yorkton was at his back.

He was pulled southeast. The leavened fields hurried up under his eyes, only to stretch even further in front. The crops were off the land now and yellow stubble spread out everywhere, holding the soil on the fields for when the wind blew. It wasn't long ago people didn't understand that, and cut it away. Folks had wised up since then. They had wised a great deal.

Pachal allowed himself to relax in the wooden bench but did not take his eyes from the window. Even with Herman Brown's body in an air-tight coffin resting on the floor of the baggage car, three in front of him, he was as excited as a boy come Christmas time. He was on a train. He was on a steam train, heading east.

He had ridden a train once before; almost twenty-five years ago when his family disembarked at Quebec City and rode Colony Cars two thousand miles to Winnipeg. He was an infant then, sleeping in the arms of his mother. They had made Whitehead and beyond, into Yorkton and out of Yorkton into Ebenezer, looking for an iron survey stake driven into the dirt with a number scratched on it that matched the number on a document belonging to his father. That document entitled him to a hundred acres of God's land, which in half a life had become a full section of six hundred and forty.

Pachal relaxed further into the pine bench. It was as soft to him as his wife's shoulder. He was twenty-five years of age, or would be in little more than a month; his wife was strong, he possessed a daughter not yet two, two hundred and forty acres of Saskatchewan farmland, and he was on a train. "Hitherto hath the Lord helped us," he whispered, as if to slap down the vanity that rose up in him. His eyes were on the land, staring intently at the coulees and the frozen sloughs, at the telegraph poles shaped like perfect crosses. He was now further away from his family than ever before in his life. This realization sobered him, the giddiness in his chest loosened, and as he stared out the window, he began to recite silently, *Remove not the ancient landmarks which their fathers have set . . .*

In the first one hundred miles the train stopped seven times to take on coal. Pachal marvelled. He'd asked so many questions of the stationmaster that if the man had not known him, he would have mistook him for an engineering fellow, instead of a farmer. He was now reasonably versed in the operating of the modern steam train. It was built at the steelyards of New Jersey, pulled five second-hand passenger cars bought from the Rathburns of Deseronto, and possessed the capacity to travel twelve miles before filling up again with coal.

Outside the tufts of dark bush whipped past him. Everything was whipping past. It seemed the world was hurtling ahead too, to a new place where there was nothing men couldn't do. Time fell in great chunks now, and each chunk fell different from the one that landed before. They had already overcome wheat smut by simple bluestoning. And how many short years ago was it that Kasper Neibrandt walked forty-one miles from Saltcoats to Yorkton with a fifty-pound sack of flour on his back after his ox came up sick? "And who was it that carried the ox then?" people wanted to know, and the old man answered, "My hands were full, so I had the wife carry it." There were people said she did carry it, too, and it was not altogether clear she hadn't. They lived in holes in the ground. At his own age, at twenty-five, Kasper Neibrandt dug a hole and he and his wife and children had crawled into it and lived there for three months. They had read a document, written in German, from an immigration agent. It claimed the Saskatchewan winters were warmer, on average, than Florida.

Pachal looked out the window and saw a spread of three or four hundred geese, crossing over. Beneath them, cattle stooped their long necks and cropped the earth as if joined to it at the mouth. The Qu'Appelle River. He saw it spread out forever, dreamlike, in a gold mist. The last section of territory that he knew by heart had trundled past an hour ago. Now the land levelled out, smooth and flat as a billiard table. Only a few stooks of wheat still waited on the plains to be gathered. On a church steeple, far off, he saw a fisted cross. Everywhere the land was laced together with thin stick fences, sat on by magpies, scheming and up to no good, their whites flashing when they swooped away.

The steady rattling of train motion began to seep into Pachal's flesh. He felt his neck stiffening on the one side from his constant and earnest appraisal of the earth. It looked no different from before. Suddenly eight black horses appeared on the plains in the north, galloping as if in terror. For no reason he was aware of, Pachal felt himself smiling. Earlier he had seen a black dog, a lone black dog, miles from anywhere standing on the glassy surface of a frozen pond, chewing at a small toy bear. It seemed to him that the world outside of Ebenezer was not such an intimidating place after all. Mostly it was filled up with animals doing odd things.

He tried fanning his neck from one side to another to loosen the soreness that had crept into it. Across from him, up but one, a murky, suspicious-looking fellow with a scar on his face and the appraising eyes of a bootlegger, had removed his coat and rolled it into a type of pillow, which he stuffed behind his head. Pachal did the same. He removed his wool jacket reluctantly. It was, in his wife's opinion, his finest coat. He folded it tightly, and neatly, and made a cushion of it behind his left ear. But he was not ready for sleep or even relaxation. He was on a train, the world was swooping by, and he would not miss a minute of it. He reached over to the seat where his belongings were, and tugged out his copy of the *Yorkton Enterprise* from beneath his satchel. Pachal was careful to keep it in top shape. It was the testimony he was taking with him to the East; the written and therefore irrefutable proof of what had gone wrong.

It felt sophisticated, even city-like, to be perusing a newspaper while speeding into the East on a train. That's what fellows did now, he assumed. At least prosperous and forward-looking fellows who knew their way about the country. He saw no reason why he shouldn't be one of them. The printed words assembled fleetingly in an ocean of ink, coming and going like taps on a telegraph key. BUILDING IS BEST IN WEST . . . EXCELLENT WATER SUPPLY FOR YORKTON; *Town's Water Comparatively Free of Objectionable Material.* In bold letters it was stated that Yorkton was now in a "leading position," but of what was not specified. In a small banner the newspaper boasted a "sworn circulation of 2,300." This claim was followed by the sudden announcement: *Thirteen aviators were killed in October.* He perused the events of home: new construction in town was still "aeroplaning"; Goddard & Flick had put up an ice house on Haultain Avenue; "Emily Pachal had received a Grade VI mark of 814 of 1,000 obtainable." Only Marjorie Shaw and Evelyn Switzer had done better. Pachal rattled the paper with some smugness for his oldest cousin's daughter. Of course, his own child would be smarter than the bunch of them by an acre. He passed over a lengthy piece on the arrival of the Caledonian Players, and read in earnest what he had read a dozen times already — the reason he was taking the paper with him.

A packed, narrow column enumerated the deaths of the previous week. They were plentiful, as they had been in many other weeks. A heavily loaded wagon had passed over Mr. W. F. Good and broken his neck. A Galician row on Betts Avenue had resulted in Nicola Szpiak getting stoned to death, and another Galician at Springfield had been thrown bodily into a separator while it was operating. Two unnamed Galicians were also thought to have been shot to death in the same incident. It had been a week of wild and drunken Galicians.

Heading up the column was this account:

NUMEROUS FATALITIES THIS WEEK: DRAYMAN KILLED BY RIFLE AND THRESHERMAN KILLED BY BEING RUN OVER

A mysterious accident took place this morning as a result of which Herman Brown, a drayman in the employ of Levi Beck, died in hospital of a gunshot wound at 2:00 p.m.

Mr. Brown, born at Renfrew County, Ontario, and recently arrived in Yorkton, had gone out near a group of bushes for the purpose of hunting prairie chickens. It is thought that in walking over the hummocky ground with the rifle, his foot slipped and the weapon accidentally discharged.

. . . It was thought that in walking over the hummocky ground that . . . Pachal stared glassily at the column of ink, and then turned away. Outside the land was flat and cold. Swathes of snow streaked in odd places, like shaving soap.

There had been responsibilities incumbent on the death of Herman Brown, and Pachal had submitted to one of them eagerly, perhaps too eagerly. He had met with the moustached and vested proprietors of the *Yorkton Enterprise* and provided them with dull details concerning the transportation of the corpse. He knew that in two days the next issue of the paper would be printed and in it was to be a piece concerning himself. Or at least in which he was mentioned. A small piece only, but still, his name would be there, carved in black on white parchment. He closed his eyes and imagined it. The story's headline was enormous, of the size typically reserved to proclaim a Yorkton victory over Regina at football. DEAD MAN'S REMAINS SHIPPED EAST BY COURAGEOUS BROTHER-IN-LAW. He imagined the story unfolding in all of its details. *At great risk and cost to himself, Robert Pachal, husband of Elizabeth Anne and father of Mary Margaret, has agreed to accompany the coffin of his deceased brother-in-law back to the village of Barry's Bay, a dangerous and barely Christian place in the Eastern province of Ontario. Pachal, a devout man, and one widely respected* . . . The piece went on in this manner for several pages, and ended, inexplicably, in a pencil sketch of his wife wearing her wedding dress.

"Winnipeg, next stop is Winnipeg."

Pachal was interrupted from his foray into the newspaper business by the car door opening to show a man in a dark-vested suit. The roar of motion and breakneck speed flooded the car, then vanished. The door shut tight as a seal, the conductor was gone. Only the deep, anguished sound of the whistle was audible, and with each blow a carpet of geese lifted from the earth.

For a few miles a small creek ran alongside the tracks. Pachal scanned it for muskrat hutches. He spotted four, built high, which meant there would be snow, lots of it. There always was when the muskrats built high. It meant a good snow was coming and good snow meant a good runoff. Several sets of tracks duplicated on either side of the train. Far away, grain elevators stuck up out of the land like fat, secular churches. He was entering the city limits.

The train stopped at the Winnipeg station, where Pachal got out and walked the platform. He watched the businessmen and the travelling men as they boarded, and kept his eye out for ladies in the hoopless skirt the newspaper had warned him about. He had read an account saying city women were as naked as Eve, wearing these new skirts. But Pachal but did not see any naked women. It seemed to him the women had on as much clothing as they ought to have for November.

He sat for a moment and smoked a good supply of Hudson's Bay tobacco from a calabash pipe with an amber stem. He bought the day's *Winnipeg Tribune* from a boy, two boiled eggs from another, and kept guard of the baggage car in case the body of Herman Brown might be taken off by mistake.

One hour later, after the train had taken on coal and water, he went back to his seat. The first full feelings of discomfort flared through his body. The bones of his backside ached. A stiffness had got into his neck and ribs. He felt a rhythmic kick as the train started, heard it building momentum as it gathered speed along bridges that spanned either the Red or Assiniboine River, he was not sure which. He knew the Qu'Appelle River, that was all. And then, angling his head to catch sight of the brown, crenellated architecture of Winnipeg, the city was gone from him, and he was on the flatlands again.

He ate the chunk of bread and a winter apple his wife had packed for him. He saved for later a serving of chopped sardines, ham, and pickles, made up from a recipe in the *Canadian Home Cookbook* that he had given her as a gift. Some of it was out of date, she said, and some of it did not apply to the prairies, but she was pleased to have it. It was not always easy for her, coming from the East. He knew that.

Pachal saw that the prairie bush was getting thick, like a beard. The land was full of green trees, bushes really, only slightly taller than what he'd seen before. The West was getting left behind him.

The train plowed east across Manitoba. Pachal's eyes were heavy from all the watching, and all that he was seeing. He forced himself to look once more at the Winnipeg newspaper. VITAL TURKISH DEFENCES ATTACKED. He stared out the window again. Nothing had changed. BRITISH BATTLESHIPS LEFT MALTA TODAY . . . BRITAIN

PREPARES TO LOOSE WARDOGS.

Pachal was tired and allowed his jawbone to press hard on the northern window of the car where the vibrations passed through his face and into his head. There would be war. There would be war and men would kill each other and then it would be over. Pachal did not want to think about it. He turned several pages of the newspaper and forced himself to read studiously a large advertisement in the top corner.

> *The Boys and Girls Factories have started up again with the commencement of the public schools. But you can't build sturdy, robust boys and girls out of books alone. The best food for growing boys and girls is*
> **SHREDDED WHEAT**
> *because it contains all the muscle-making, brain-building elements in the whole wheat made digestible by steam cooking.*
> **(a Canadian food for Canadians)**

Canadians, thought Pachal. He wasn't a Silesian, German-speaking, or Russian anymore. He was Canadian. Everybody was Canadian. It happened overnight. He remembered a small town on the prairie called Pile O' Bones. As a boy he loved that name, would have been proud to live forever in a place called Pile O' Bones. Then he woke up one morning and it wasn't that anymore, it was Regina. "The City of Certainties." He forced his eyes to open and shut and re-examined the paper. He would talk to his wife about this shredded wheat business. They would get Mary Margaret on to it as soon as possible.

No Truth to Rumour that Winnipeg Regulars Mobilized. Pachal turned the page again. There would be war. Like Neibrandt and his father had said. In one year, maybe two, a man would be afraid to speak German in the town of Yorkton and would keep it to himself, to his own house and his own family. The pastors in Ebenezer and Rhein and Yorkton would not give service in German either. They would throw stones at you in the towns of Yorkton, Melville, Regina, even if you had busted up the land with a stick and lived with unweaned babies in a hole. That is what would happen.

Pachal felt himself hurtling into the scrubby evergreens. Strands of green triangles pointed up at the sky. He was disappointed to not be among the big trees yet, the great pines. But they were coming; pines that grew taller than a church steeple and built the houses and even the navies of England. He would be there soon, in the East. Maybe he was already in the East. He had half expected to see an enormous sign that spelled out, EAST.

A longing to be home passed through his entire body. He'd strayed too far away from it.

Pachal stood up and walked the length of the car, through it into the next one. The thought occurred to him that if he were to turn around and walk far enough the other way, backwards through the cars, he could walk all the way back to Yorkton.

Many of the passengers were asleep. The carriage fluttered with their breathing. A few attempted to curl uncomfortably against folded coats and wrappers. Four gentlemen crowded close together and passed a flask between them. They talked of war. That's all anyone talked of anymore. "The world would see . . .," uttered one, thickly, with menace, "then the world would see." What would the world see? Pachal wondered. Ahead of him sounded the laughter of a young woman. A clutter of gallants gathered round her and he was forced to squeeze against the seats to get by. Cigarette and cigar smoke accented the sodden pall of pipe tobacco. He passed an Indian man wearing a stove-pipe hat and red scarf, staring ahead at nothing. He could have been dead for all Pachal knew.

Pachal pushed open the coach door and met the rushing force of darkness, ice cold, slapping hard into his face, brimming his eyes with tears. The abrasive, burning taste of soot pricked his mouth. He wobbled across a metal grid, got his free fingers on the cold handle of the next door, yanked it down and was pitched heavily into the adjoining car. An infant, wrapped in a blanket, slept on the floor and he stepped over it carefully. Someone, a man, was sermonizing with a stranger across the aisle. "Corn," he insisted. "Corn is all hoeing; you cannot have corn without hoeing . . ." Pachal nodded mutely in agreement. At least some folks were still talking sense. Most of the lamps in the car had been dimmed, but the heat was still close and thick on his neck.

At last he entered the baggage car. A lamp burned there, and it was much colder, refreshing to him. In the middle of the car, away from the suitcases and parcels, the deal coffin box glinted in the light. A cast of scarlet reflected along the side of it, reminding him of the dawn sky, hours ago at the Yorkton Station. Without thinking, he put his boot up on the box, feeling the cramped muscles of his leg loosen like a strip of whang leather. He had an image of himself as he might see on a calendar, placing his boot on a prize buck he'd brought down with a clean rifle shot. Quickly, ashamedly, he stepped off.

Have mercy on the soul of this man, prayed Pachal, for he was the brother of my wife; a hard man, a drinking man, who had left the timber fields of Ontario because he would not work for thieving millionaires. That's what he called them, thieving millionaires. He had left them behind alright. But he found instead only the day-long drudgery of labouring, did not have a wife, and died foolishly. Have mercy on him. And have mercy on us all. Amen.

Pachal rooted in his coat pocket for several of the dead man's items. He felt the old timepiece found on Herman Brown's body. It no longer ran, stopped at 7:28. He considered winding it, but did not. It was about as useful now as a bachelor with a pig. Three coins belonging to the dead man were also in his pocket. Pachal pulled one out and rubbed it idly against his thumb. It was not an actual coin, just the private money minted by Levi Beck, the man who had hired Herman Brown, the man who was glad enough to take Harry Bronfman's money, but insisted he would not see a Jew elected dog-catcher, let alone mayor of Yorkton. The coins were stamped "Levi Beck — One Dollar." He paid his men with them. They were good at any store the Becks owned, and some they didn't.

Pachal squeezed the coin in his hand and returned it to his pocket, along with the watch. He felt the train underfoot, mimicking the surge of his own life. He was heading east, travelling to a place where corruption was dealt out in the form of credit for western farmers, of rooms in high buildings, where fires raged across the territory and turned the structures of men into ashes. It was the East and it spoke of greed, of lazy men on remittance, of women who wore skirts that revealed their ankles, and even of men like Herman Brown whose easterness waited inside of him like a fatal seed, a flaw in his character.

Pachal stared at the box containing his brother-in-law and experienced the solemn weight of returning a dead man to his home. He took some pride in what he was doing, for it rooted him in the obligations the living owe to the dead. He felt protected by the action. "Brother," he whispered with all the feeling he could muster; they had quarrelled and not been close. Only his regard for his own wife had kept them civil.

Robert Pachal left the baggage car and returned to his seat. The lamps were lit and the soft amber shadow of coal oil filled the passages. Outside the train windows the night pressed Bible black against the glass, and the land shuttered by dimly, without tangible form. He saw his face reflected in the blue window-pane when he put himself up close to peer out. There, that same face came to join him on the other side; his own face, a neat beard, red hair, dark eyes, but the flesh was the vaporous flesh of a reflection, as though that man, who floated in the dark, was not well fed, was forced to peer desperately into the warm carriages at what he could never have for himself. Pachal wondered if Herman Brown had felt that way, when he sat in their house with them at night, under the lamps, with Mary Margaret playing on the parlour rug and his sister tatting lace by lamplight.

He closed his eyes and ruminated about ghosts and what a ghost could never have. A daughter, a wife, probably it was substance that a ghost could never have. That's what *he* possessed; substance, a man of flesh. Pachal drew his coat around himself and took one more look at his other self, the ghost in the cold dark with the empty face looking back at him and seeming afraid. That is my face, he thought, if I'd stayed a bachelor all my life.

He stared back and saw beyond his own reflection, behind it, into the black land where different shades of darkness fought among themselves for territory. Was it water out there? Rock? He had no idea where he was anymore. Rat's Portage? Minaki? What were these places?

Heat from the steam pipes pressed against him like a sodden cloth. His eyes shut and remained shut, even through the unpunctuated wail of the train's whistle that cried out to the surroundings.

The train hurtled through northwestern Ontario with the night stretching over top; cold, flushed with stars, brilliant in the absent moon. A trapper with the gamey grease of muskrat fat on his fingers stood in the doorway of a shack and watched the train thunder by. He felt no kinship with it. It was his considered opinion that no good would ever come of a train. On a rock-face a deer stood still and marvelled at the blindness of the thing. Three raccoons wavered left, right, uncertain whether to cross. The machine dragged the length of its body through the rock, lighting up the dark. Then it was gone, without caution, smashing into the night.

6

When Pachal awoke it was early morning and he was among rocks. He had never seen rocks before. Now they erupted from the land; single rocks the size of ox carts, rock outcroppings and rock faces bigger than barns. He saw tiny skiffs of snow unmelted in the crevices of rocks, angular and straight rocks, as if a man had sculpted them with a chisel; black rocks big as tarpaper shacks. Rocks hurtled alongside the train, and heaved up like enormous waves, the surface of them covered in green and orange fungus as if a carpet had been laid over top.

The Shield, thought Pachal. I am in the Shield of Ontario. He sat square to the window and watched entire hills made of rocks. Behind them rose the distant, misted outcroppings made of more rocks. Mountains, he wondered? To him they were as big as mountains. He claimed them, for himself, as mountains.

Sporadically a soupish swamp slid past the windows, with the colour faded out of it, lying soft between the rocks, flat and uneventful, like the prairies. Somehow the swamps looked like prairies to him, with the horizons of them all framed by small granite mountains.

Then the land dropped away. It was not there anymore. The earth had dropped fifty feet below to where a black creek scribbled on the surface. The train slowed to a walking pace and he saw the square timber of the trestle on which it now rumbled. He saw more timber assembled together in this one gridwork than he had ever seen in his life. He also saw that the dawn had just lifted from this place, the last clinging vapours still floated up and thinned into nothing. Three thundering whistles blew from the front. But no one seemed to hear. Even the small trees that grew out of the rocks did not acknowledge it. It seemed they were made of rocks themselves. No birds lifted. Nothing.

At that point the water appeared. For a few moments, a few clatters of train wheels, Pachal didn't recognize it as water. It wasn't a creek, or a pond, or slough, or river. It was a flat plain of black fluid, chipped across the surface where the wind lapped it and showed the underbellies of countless waves, small and silver as aspen leaves. In front of it the water seeped and cascaded through the rocks as though the rocks were a field of melting ice.

Pachal stared out the window. He had known cattle to fall down and die for a lack of water. He'd seen families walk away like stick figures across the cracking earth. Now out that window he saw more water than the world could ever need. It lay there like sheer wealth, without sign of habitation or irrigation or even anything to irrigate. Water among rocks. He had not imagined so much water lay upon the earth. His wife had spoken of it; words describing steamboats, canoes, swimming, fishing, trout that schooled at the bottom of enormous lakes. But he never imagined water like this. It spoke to him of the East somehow, of wealth hoarded, of wealth beyond necessity, and of greed; as though somehow men had conspired to keep water hidden here for their own selfish purposes.

He wondered how could you take the measure of a man if he had this much water to work with. It would take a man's life in a whole different direction. Pachal's father had once planted one hundred and fifty acres of Russian Ladoga wheat, and after a dry season of one hundred and twenty-five days it grew six inches from the earth. "We'll get down on our knees," the man said, and young Pachal had gone to his knees to pray, but his father said, "not to pray, son. To pick the seed."

Pachal shook his head, bewildered and vaguely indignant. Surely it was the lack of water that caused Red Fife wheat to get crossed with Hard Red Calcutta in the first place? It wasn't what a man had that showed his mark, it was what he didn't have, what he could do when he had nothing at all. Not even water.

He watched nameless, uninhabited lakes slip past him. The water sat cold and dark as gun barrels. In a remote part of himself he was frightened by it, as though those granite lakes had no bottom at all and the surface was the blank eye of fear. He saw the water stretching down to Hell, where the drowned men tumbled for all eternity.

The train continued to rattle with rhythmic hard clacks across the North. There was a challenge for a man here, but he did not comprehend it; it wasn't his. It wasn't the challenge of flat earth, of dirt and dust without water.

Pachal reached down to the floor and picked up the newspaper, fallen during the night. He read carefully the small letters on the folded section: *CNR Switchman Killed In Trainyard* — *Veritably cut in two and ground to pieces.* Directly beneath it: *Boys Drowned in Farm Slough* — *Supposed that they ventured out on thin ice while after ducks.* Pachal shuddered and imagined his own God-given daughter drowned in a slough. Drowned. He was suddenly terrified by the thought.

The dark lakes flew across the window. Up front of him a man coughed violently. A few benches beyond that a young man and woman stirred beneath their coats, slow and pleased in the warmth of each other. From somewhere an infant uttered its first, exploratory gurgle. Thickly, out the back, floated the burnt, rich smell of coffee and sausages, the smell of kitchens in winter. Pachal was comforted by it, amused even, that men should attempt to fry sausages and brew coffee while piloting gigantic engines at high speeds between lakes and granite mountains. He removed a section of corn bread from his satchel and began to gnaw on it.

At Nakina the engine veered south, like the helpless point of a compass. The endless waters rushed up to meet them, the deep black lakes whose names, when spoken at all, were spoken in the Cree language, or in the tongue of trainmen. Pachal rose and started forward, stumbling, clanging open the steel doors between the carriages. He entered the baggage car and stared around him for no reason he could remember, then tottered out. Herman Brown lay as he had left him. Still dead. Three days now. Pachal was relieved that the mortal stench of death had not come to claim him yet. He'd paid extra to Christie for that, to build the coffin airtight. It was cold there in that baggage car, too, and that had helped.

The young man stepped the length of the train. He knew quietly that his task was a noble one, unselfish, that it shone through him, and people could see it. In this idea he was brought up short by a man in a grey suit. The fellow lounged unpleasantly on the bench and took his sweet time before drawing his legs up to allow Pachal to go by. He wondered about such a man, of his church, and whether he belonged to any church at all. Maybe a man like that was better off writing home to England and asking for more money, in order to fix himself up with a sleeping berth. To soothe himself, Pachal visualized the sweep of his two-hundred-and-forty-acre section. He had left that all behind to transport the body of a relative, at his own cost, half way across a continent so that he might be buried like a Christian. Surely that entitled him to something, but he did not know what.

Pachal continued down the carriage and felt the cold enclose him as he stepped out of one car and into the next one. The cooking smells tugged at him like a rein. He would get a bite then, fried scrapple and some coffee.

A steward in a white jacket led him to a seat in the dining car. Pachal saw at once that he would be getting no fried scrapple in such a place as this one.

"I'll just be having a coffee," he ventured, "and maybe a biscuit." The steward flashed a pained expression and retreated. Pachal seated himself against the window as the bush trampled unendingly across the glass. Rusted slashes swirled in the woods along the shores of lakes, vacant black. Everything was shattered as though wolves had brought down a deer. He'd seen that once in the low brush north of Yorkton; that is what it looked like here. Except for the size, which was impossible. Acres of broken sticks, black and dead, as though a savage hand had ripped at the earth and left only rock and dirt, made bloody by bark chips. . . .

"What do you make of that then, brother?"

7

THE MAN STOOD INTENTLY AT PACHAL'S SIDE BEFORE sitting down to face him. He had on working clothes, a tie tucked between the buttons of his shirt, suspenders, with a store-bought coat over that. Licks of grey hair rose like wheat stooks on his head before disappearing into his hat. Hard, veined grooves, like dried creek beds, wavered along his face. It was the face of a drinking man, Pachal thought.

"That there is the work a' timbermen. Only I don't call 'em timbermen no more. They're not fit for that word, see?" He wiped the back of a hand across his face. "I call 'em shit. Human pieces of shit, if you want the truth of it." The man had a tic, a nervous way with his chin that kept it bobbing, as if a fly was tormenting him. A few loose beads of saliva had formed permanently on his bottom lip. "I worked in it eleven years, working for the king of the shit, Mr. J. R. Booth." There was garrulous phlegm in the stranger's voice, and Pachel heard "*Booze.*" *Jayer Booze.*

The man held up his arm as if to shake hands, but did not extend it, just held it. Pachal saw the stump of one finger recessed like the eye of a potato, missing at the second knuckle, two others cut clean away at the palm. The thumb was smashed beyond recognition.

"Timbermen . . . Eleven years. Took every piece a tree there was out the Ottawa, and now look at 'em. Comin' after sticks." He lifted his chin at the window. "Sticks. The good timber ain't nowhere around here no more."

The fellow lapsed into a fuming quiet. Pachal felt it incumbent on him to say something. He did not know what to say about timber. He knew that twigs were not scantling, or bunting either. But aside from that he did not know a grounder from a Saginaw, or a skyman from a big blue butt. His knowledge consisted of poplar poles used to hold up a sod hut. He also possessed a fleeting image of the old stockade the militia put up outside Yorkton to fight Riel's Indians. No Indians showed, and people tore it down for firewood, including his father who rode back a cart of it for the stove. They burned it all but one stick, which his father kept for twenty-one years, as history, he said. He kept it until the winter in ought six, the year the cows froze solid, and his mother forced him to toss it into the stove along with anything else that burned. That was the only time anything useful ever came of history, she said.

With all of those trees out there flashing by it seemed to Pachal that a few good men ought to be able to put together a dozen stockades in no time at all.

"That appears fair enough timber," he ventured.

"You would say that, see, if you were a western man. A western man would say that, brother. A western fellow like you from Winnipeg, right?"

"No sir."

"Esterhazy?"

"Yorkton," said Pachal. "Ebenezer. I have a section there."

"Yorkton? Then you would know Mr. Isaiah Tilley, has a boy somewhat your age."

"I have heard of the farming Tilleys, yes."

"Well, they was the mining Tilleys in Cobalt till it caved in. I was that myself, see. A mining man. A mining man, after donating half a goddam hand to Mr. Booth. A half hand and half a brother too. Cut in half by a brake cable at the Sproule timber camp, for which his wife was given a half sack a flour. One half sack a flour for a widow woman with five children and one hundred acres of farming to look after. He fired half the axemen, see? Booth did it, for wanting half a wage. Brought in those striking stevedores from Montreal and paid 'em less too. Now look at it. They got rid of the horses, is what they done, and they bring that machinery into the bush and that frigs everything. That's what's frigging the country, is those goddam machines. They got nowhere to hide do they?"

"Pardon me?"

"The trees, I mean. They got nowhere to hide. I seen how it works. I seen beech trees up Christian Island so big you can't feed them into the sawmill. There ain't no sawmill in the goddam Dominion big enough to cut them."

Pachal made a somewhat polite and inquisitive arch of his eyebrows. He could not imagine such a tree and had a faint sense he was getting played.

"What they do with those beech trees see," the man dropped his voice down to a hushed, conspiratorial whisper, "is first they drill a hole in the side, after that they stuff the dynamite in the drill hole and blow those damn trunks to smithereens. Once they done that they float the big chunks across the harbour to where the mills are. Imagine that, hay? They're blowing out trees like a goddam silver mine."

The man coughed, a harsh, liquidy sort of cough. "There's nowhere to hide out there, son."

Pachal obliged by looking out the window. The slash spread far back from the tracks to the woods, devastated and strewn like the torn carcass of an animal, with course clumps of fur ripped from it. Single thin pines jutted up from a mass of felled wood, and the ground lay black, exposed, with veins of snow tracing it. He presumed a fire had ripped through here. But it was not a fire. It was something else. It looked like pure rage. Rage stoked with whiskey until the white fury lashed out.

At that moment the train tossed itself under a black encroachment of rock. Pachal sat civilly, facing the foul-mouthed, spirituous fellow who had failed at timbering. In the darkness the grim outline of his face looked as though it belonged to a man who had failed at mining, too. There was all manner of fellows on a train, thought Pachal, ladies as well. They all sat still in their own lives, as if in a chair they'd carried on board with them, but everyone was in motion, too, moving at great speed. It was a time of great movement across the country; Pachal felt that he was part of it, that he was entitled to be part of it as well. He'd made a go of it, the life given to him was intact and spreading, like the span of the railway. Many years ago it was broken in two by an ocean. He'd lived a squalling baby for two months in a turned over ox cart, spent half his boyhood in a sod hut built at the cost of one dollar and eighty-seven cents, which was the total expense of a glass window-pane and a pair of hinges. He remembered the warmth of that soddie in winter, the coolness of it in summer, how the water percolated through the thatchings of the roof after the rain. Neibrandt called it "having running water in every room." His mother said it rained one full day longer inside than it did out. But she said that only when the new place was built, west of Ebenezer on the slightest bluff of land, next to the fat willow that got hit by lightning, a stone's throw from the muskrat creek.

Pachal wished suddenly that he had a cigar. He felt the urge to pose in the sumptuous manner of the cigar smoker; to puff up one of those enormous foot-long specials that Mr. Van Horne had custom-made for him once the doctor cut him back to three a day.

Outside the train the nameless interior of bush, rock, and muskeg tumbled across the horizon formed by the bottom window-sill. They were now north of Superior, where the train lines had sunk in the mud time and time again, some of them. That's what he'd read, back home in the newspaper.

The waiter brought Pachal another coffee and a sweetcake. Across from him the man did not make an order. He had the air of someone focused, but not entirely sure on what. Pachal had seen such faces on the other men who failed, dirt farmers and wolfers who came with nothing, got off the train at nowhere, and left with less than what they came with. "Those folks," Neibrandt said, "who figured they could tickle the prairie and it would giggle up a fortune." He had seen it especially six years ago in every face he looked at, the 1906 winter, the bad one, when the blue snow came down and the animals froze up solid and everything alive or dead had a solid coat of hoarfrost growing from it.

"You ever seen a cow froze solid?" Robert Pachal blurted out this question into the hard face of his companion. They were blunt words, he knew, but he had not spoken to another person in nearly a day and a half. Fortunately he'd picked a topic close to the fellow's heart, for he came back at once.

"You mean upright? You mean standing up and froze?"

"Upright."

"Well now . . ." The man put his mind to this question with some relish. "I don't believe I have. Not upright. I have seen a froze cow derail a train though. Outside Depot Harbour, killed five men." He glared at Pachal with unmistakable pride.

Pachal nodded. It was a grave nod. He trusted it was the nod of a man who appeared familiar with the workings of the world, or at least cows that had froze up solid. A man somewhat experienced with the ins and outs of travel, and the hearing of stories. As an infant he'd been transported half way around the world in a jumble of mules, wagons, trains, cattleboats, and more trains. He had huddled sleeping or crying in a clamorous Immigration Centre, but he'd not travelled beyond that except to go twenty miles to the swamp for cordwood, and twenty miles back. When he thought of travel, it meant pulling up the family and moving somewhere else because of drought, or locusts. It meant starting over. Like the Doukhobors. He'd seen the Dukes set out with dogs and draft animals, walking west to where the mountains were supposed to be, to start over, on account of a disagreement with the government. Travelling for the luxury of it was something he did not understand. But the exchange of stories, the hearing from different men what they knew, that was something different, even helpful. Pachal situated himself back home with a fine cigar. He was telling people he'd met a man who'd seen a frozen cow derail a freight train and kill five men. That would get some heads shaking. That was something he could tell to Mary Margaret when she was grown up.

"No, I have never seen a cow froze upright. But I'll tell you this. I have seen a team a horses disappear under the mud and not get back out. Took place on a loggin' line near Golden. Two grey Percherons foaled at Ottawa, cost a fortune, went under that mud in less than a minute, thank you. They'd gone in to pull out a *auto-goddam-mobeel*. It's those machines what's friggin' the whole country."

Pachal nodded. He'd not seen anything like that. But he had seen the winter of 1906, the year of the famous blue snow, when the first blizzard came hard on November 5, and the range cattle were already dying by December. It was the year of the carrion spring, when the snow thawed and the cattle ballooned with rot and lay dead to the horizon in all directions; hanging from the low trees, some of them. Horses, too, up in trees, dead. He had wondered at one time how winter could do that.

A silence blew up between the two men. They had drifted each apiece into the vast territory of their own lives. Pachal looked a ways down the car at three women drinking tea, an older woman, chaperone maybe, and two young ones wearing pretty hats, with hair that spilled down in great plaits. The older one was talking.

"Duluth. We were on the train to Duluth. I had on my Hudson's Bay fur coat, genuine beaver, with a fox collar . . ." One of the young ones crinkled her nose, made a movement of her lips on the sly to her young companion. Pachal realized she was speaking with her face. He had seen that before in women, how they spoke a different language among themselves, an eyebrow got raised and that meant something to another woman. A bottom lip got bit, a row of white teeth showed like crinoline under a skirt, and that meant something else. He had no idea of the grammar of it, or what it was about. It was a language that went in and not out, he figured that much. It had something to do with what went on behind the eyes and beneath the skin. Even when his wife spoke to him she seemed to speak only half a language. It seemed that words were something man-made for the purpose of getting things done, like learning a pamphlet on how to seed Manitoba No. One Hard. She only bothered with it in the first place to keep a man happy, like cooing at a dumb beast. Pachal did not have extensive knowledge of the language of women. He would have liked to know a part of it anyway, for his wife's sake, but didn't. The language he knew lay in front of the face, not behind it, lay out there beyond the glass eyeballs of the train.

Looking out through the window he realized he did not know that particular language very much either. What could be the purpose of land like this, he wondered. He'd heard that Indians grew corn here as many as a thousand years ago, but it could not have been here. Not right here, that was certain. Only rocks grew here. Rocks and water, and you could not plant on either of them.

"What is it you're going East for then?"

Something broke off in Pachal's mind, like a twig. He'd started to think of his wife; the fact that it was her brother back there. Whatever that meant to her took place inside her, in a place he did not know of. He regrouped into a facsimile of solemnity, even nonchalance.

"I'm taking a coffin back. My wife's brother. He's getting interred at a place called Schutt, Ontario. I'm taking him first to the village of Barry's Bay."

"A young fella?" His companion started, suddenly curious, then relapsed into silence.

"A hunting mishap," said Pachal. "He was killed in a hunting mishap."

The man nodded and lifted the stoppered jar of whiskey from beneath the table where he was hiding it. "You'd want a drink then?"

"No, sir, I do not take of spirits." Pachal heard something overly severe in his manner and added quietly, "I am not a drinking man."

The stranger took a solid belt from the jar and then left it in plain view on the table. "Nor me, brother. I'm not a drinking man either. I would be, mind. If they let me. But they won't. I'm what they call a Blind Pigger. You heard what a Blind Pigger is?"

No, he had not heard that.

"Well, your Blind Pigger is a fellow opposed to the Local Option. He is a drinking man who wishes to remain one, only cannot, on account of people would rather have him drink wood alcohol by stealth than good whiskey at the open bar."

"I'm in favour of banishing the bar," said Pachal. "I mean, I won't tolerate such drinking that a woman can't walk the streets of some towns without getting exposed to rudeness. I read that in the newspaper back home." Pachal felt some heat under his collar and was tempted to tell about Freddy Belmont out in Corey Township; Mr. Belmont got stood drinks at the bar, came home every night, and beat his wife with a three-foot length of strapping. Finally some men tied him to a fence rail, smeared tar on him, and tossed him in a ditch. That's what it took, though, and then some. Pachal restrained himself and said nothing. He had not come East to tell black stories of the West.

The stranger put the jar to his lips again and drank full from it. He slugged slowly, absently, as though he had no awareness of the action. "Blind Pigger," he repeated, sedately out the window. It seemed as if this condemnation came from the land itself. "You see, that's what I am. I was a Blind Pigger out your way too, brother. Regina . . . Bassano, Winnipeg. I was living in that whiskey strip there in Winnipeg, you know?

Every morning Constable Logan come by, put you in his wheelbarrow, and takes you down the jail. I had a few rides in that wheelbarrow alright. I also come to in Ginger Snooks wagon with a dozen other piggers, all on their way down to city hall. Snooks was a Hebrew, see? He charged the city a dollar a piece for every man he collected off the street. That was Winnipeg." Winnipeg! Just the sound of it made him thirsty. "I'd sit there at the Stock Exchange Hotel when the boys finished work at the packing plant. I tell you they got off the streetcar at Arlington, hit the road at a dead run to cash their cheques at the bar. I mean a dead run, too. And Bassano," he went on, "I'll tell you about Bassano. In Bassano you can *hear* the drinkers before you even see town. It's true. I was a Blind Pigger in Bassano for awhile, then Capreol till the Local Option came in, a Blind Pigger in Cobalt and a Blind Pigger in Timmins, too. So I'm heading down to Hamilton to work the foundry, that's good work there, brother."

    The man took another short plug on his bottle and watched the hard, wooded rockfield clatter in front of his face. Indian land that's what it was. That's all it was fit for. He put his nose to the glass window and held it steady there. A line of whiskey smouldered in his throat and he swallowed hard on it. It was not apparent anymore in which direction he was travelling; up or down, whether he was moving into the bush, or the city. The city probably. Before that it was the silver mine in Cobalt, the nickel works at Timmins, and before that the Algonquin forest, felling white pines for Mr. Goddam Booth and eating pork fat for breakfast. The days of sowbelly and bannock, of making train lines out of tree trunks. Of pile driving, of, of . . . All the train lines of his life were merging into one; west out of the timber fields, north to Capreol, where he got off stinking drunk and realized he was in the wrong place. He recalled blurrily the town of Biscotasing, when the transcontinental came through, a half-Indian town made up of timber yards. He'd met up with some fine fellows and drank hard. They had a concoction there of pure alcohol and port wine stirred up in a tin pail. Moose milk, they called it. He could not say what exactly he'd done in Bisco except he'd bothered a man's wife in a raspberry patch and found it necessary to leave the place in a hurry.

He poured another line of Canadian Whiskey into his mouth. It was fair stuff, Hudson's Bay Company, eight dollars a pail. The conductor sold it from behind the water-closet door for a dollar a half-pint. He felt the tight familiar warmth pull on his lips and begin to glow behind his skin. The scenery now was most agreeable to him; long narrow lakes with thick bush teeming on the shores like fox fur against a woman's neck. It was something, alright. He felt his head nod toward it, heavy with goodwill and proprietorship, as if the land belonged to him. And why shouldn't it? He had staked a claim to it, at least to an isolated hunter's camp with a rack of buck antlers nailed above the entrance. A lousy rack of buck antlers. Suddenly he was angry. He was angry because of buck antlers and because Mr. Walter Keegstra, Sr., of Whitney, Ontario, had not seen fit to put up his first daughter to him in marriage. Mr. Walter Keegstra, Sr., could go frig himself then. He'd wasted no more time on the man, had gone straight into the bush for the Booth Company with a crew of five and took down two hundred pines a day. They took down trees like the world would never see again. One hundred and eighty footers, straight as a plumb line and so fat you could cut a four-foot board out of it. Four foot, good board too, working board. In ten years try to tell a man you'd cut a stack of boards four-foot-wide from a tree. He'd call you a liar.

Another slip of whiskey burned his mouth. In truth he preferred brandy, Gillman's brandy. It improved mightily the taste of lake water and it burned different somehow. It seemed to him a powerful injustice that he was drinking Hudson's Bay Company whiskey instead of Gillman's brandy, like a gentleman. It was an irritation, like goddam buck antlers and black flies, like the goddam seat he sat in, made to irritate a man and that's all. It felt now that he was standing still. The bush was moving, not him. It was flying away from him crazily, to get away from a god awful fire. That's what it was. There would be a bush fire coming. There was even a bush fire in *him*, and it was consuming him bad. It would not surprise him one bit if it were the goddam stinking devil himself deciding to put up a shanty in his guts.

"You ever seen a fire, brother, a good fire?" He threw this out to Pachal, like a challenge.

"I have seen a grass fire once, a bad one. We got some wet sacks on it and put it down."

The man wanted to spit. Wet sacks! He was getting sick of young fellows, riding trains, living good. Getting motored all about in autogoddammobeels and aviating devices. Looked like a span of drays and mud road wasn't good enough anymore for playboys.

"Wet sacks was it? Got yourselfs some wet sacks, then. Put out the fire did you? Let me tell you, brother, there's one thing a fire wants and that's wood. I expect you know that."

"That's something that doesn't change much from one place or another." This was as close to wryness as Robert Pachal would allow himself to get.

"You're right there, see. Only where you come from there ain't no wood. Where I come from there ain't nothing but. That's what folks have is wood. Enough wood so you can take an axe and put up a house to stand one hunnerd and fifty years. One thing take that house down is fire. And that's what takes it down too, fire. You heard of the great fire of nineteen oh three?"

"I have, in fact. My wife — "

"Well then . . . I was not much older than you, lived outside Whitney picking stones daybreak to dark for one half dollar a day. That's where it come from. Off the Whitney side, from the west, moving east. It was out of hand early. Starts to run up trees, see, jumps from one tree to another. That's your crown fire, and that's not something to get put out with a wet sack. That's when you're in some trouble, when you got a crown fire cause that's a jumping fire, don't care about a crick or river being in between. Just gives a jump over top. Once it done that it burns down again, down the trunk to the bush floor. And that's a bad thing, because of Mr. Booth and his timbermen. Remember now, a crew of five takes down two hunnerd pines a day. You got seven thousand skilled fellows taking down the sticks, and they're taking out but a half, because they're squaring them off. Half that tree stays behind on the bush floor. So what you have is a tinderbox, the whole goddam land's a tinderbox. It starts to move east into Whitney there, eight miles an hour, seventy miles across, shaped like a horseshoe, flames going up one hunnerd and fifty feet. Half the country's on fire. There's a rock cliff glowing like a coal. Imagine that, a hunnerd foot high, solid rock, glowing like a coal! The earth itself, I'm talking dirt son, raw dirt coming on fire! Folks swum horses into the lake with them, and they stood there, horses, men, moose. There was moose standing up next to you, and birds landing on fellows' shoulders. Those wagons that got pulled in got melted right off. Just spokes left sticking up. Everywhere you look, wild animals, running pell-mell through town; deer, bear, fishers, foxes . . ."

The man leaned forward across the table as if he was about to grab Pachal by the throat. "The goddam dirt itself was on fire, see!" Then, as suddenly, he slumped his shoulders to the back of the bench. "We did not see the sun for six weeks after." He wiped a sudden gush of saliva from his bottom lip.

Out the corner of his eye Pachal saw the chaperone usher her three young charges out of the car, flouncing and indignant. She cast a fierce look in their direction, but the blind pigger paid no attention. Evidently he was not finished yet.

"Yer great Ottawa Fire, son, that was a real fire. Started up in Alphonse Kirouac's place on the Chaudière, swept straight across the Ottawa, and that ain't no crick there, we're not talking about no little crick. Swept right across the river, burnt the whole goddam city down, Hull, too. You got twelve thousand people living in tents after that one boy, yessir."

This prospect seemed pleasing to the man. The bitter recollection of his own life had left him with a satisfying vision of teetotallers and timber merchants having their flesh licked in the flames of an endless inferno. The flames were wracking the world alright, hellfire was consuming the sons of bitches, and he was drinking goddam conductor's liquor from a jar. "None of that ain't nothing now to what it used to be either, no sir. I'll tell you, son, you ever heard of the Great Miramichi Fire of '25?"

No, it turned out that for the life of him Robert Pachal could not recall the Great Miramichi Fire of '25.

"Well, it was just the greatest goddam fire in the history of the world, that's all. The most dreadful conflagration in the history of the friggin' world! Five hunnerd people dead in that fire. Back then, brother, there weren't five hunnerd people in the country. Stretched seventy miles on either side of the Miramichi River and threw flames two hunnerd feet into the air . . ." Pachal was aware of other passengers in the car staring at them, coolly. "The winds from that fire, son, I'm telling you, those winds got up so high that salmon were sucked out the frigging river and flung into trees. We're talking fish hanging from goddam trees!"

Pachal fitted himself back onto his bench in the coach, safe there from the sour exhalations of drinking men, and the endless fires that seemed to rage back and forth across the country. Thankfully, a rain came down now, washing the scabs of snow from the land. Runnels of water, shaped like tongues, heaved one after another down the window. Outside a fog scrim tried to rise up from the land that clung to it as black as rags. The long howl of a train whistle pierced his ears and then the blackness came, like the blowing out of a lamp. He was versed in the ways of trains now, but that did not stop him from sucking involuntarily, and holding his breath. He could not get familiar with being inside rock, even for half a minute. The blackness pressed against him as though his eyes were shut hard, but he kept his head angled against the glass, fascinated by the tight black hole that showed, when they hurtled out. It was not even round. The men had just picked away at it with axes in every which direction, slamming pickaxes against granite for as long as it took to cut a hole through a half mile of rock. It was something.

He watched the last three coaches spit out from the opening, like cherry pits, and then breathed easier. Boreal, unremitting woods paced evenly against the train. The trunks of trees glistened with rain water. Pachal was lulled by it, bored, fancied himself back home already, telling about fires that blotted out the sun for six weeks, prized Percherons screaming as the spring mud sucked them under. There was nothing like a spirituous man for telling stories, that was true. Still, Pachal thanked God for not making him one. He knew what it could do to a man — the fellows hustling off to the red brick enclosure of Harry Bronfman's Balmoral Hotel in Yorkton to stand with their foot up on a brass bar, and thumbs in vest pockets, hands around a glass of whiskey. And this getting done with the crop still standing on the field and winter already piling up. No, sir, he was glad for the Local Option. Liquor was destroying the place. It was no wonder that people would veto it. It was like Mr. W. S. Pierce, the writing man for the *Yorkton Enterprise* had put in the paper, one that Reverend Blaedow liked to quote from the pulpit, "A sober town means more buildings, more food, and more boots." You could not argue with that. You could not argue with more boots.

The train had stopped at some unknown siding, taking on water and anthracite. On the platform Pachal spied an Indian boy. His chin was upraised and grinning, as if he had knowledge of something that the world did not. The rain thrummed off the boy's hat, then they were gone again; a short kick, puffs of vapour spewed out between the carriages. He was accustomed to it now, the rhythmic long and short cough of a steam engine.

Robert Pachal got his aching body up from the bench and walked into the baggage car, once more. Light streamed from two small portholes, and he saw the arrangement of things was different now, from the getting on and off at whistle stops. A new alligator valise stood against the wall where previously had been a tumble of smoked hams. The coffin box rested square and untouched in the centre.

He took his pipe out of his jacket and struck a match against the hull of the carriage. His pipe was made from a calabash pit, and curved to smoke cool. He had not smoked at all prior to his marriage to Miss Brown, when she presented him with the pipe and four ounces of Navy Cut. "I have never heard of a fellow not smoking," she said. She would not have such a thing. So Pachal sucked the smooth stem of the pipe, and felt the idle contentment of tobacco. It was a sin, but it was not a sin like the imbibing of liquor, it was not a mortal sin, and he was satisfied to watch the smoke fold heavily to the roof.

8

He edged his face sideways, reaching for the tresses of his wife's hair. Something was hounding him, something big and metallic, with a dull single eye that gathered speed as it thundered over the land, moving one step faster than him. He was terrified of it. It was something he wanted nothing to do with right now. What he needed now was rest. He needed the warm comfort of his wife sleeping next to him, the heat of her body seeping through flannelette. Pachal wondered where she was, and realized with a pleasure that washed against him like bath water, that she must be up, tending to the baby. Relieved, he thought no more of it.

At that moment the determined clanging of a bell penetrated his dream and he woke up. His wife was not with him. No one was with him. He tried to imagine what she was doing at the moment, asleep, probably, or she was up tending the baby. Whatever she was doing it was taking place more than a thousand miles away. He grabbed at his own coat instinctively, and looked around. Something felt wrong; a vast, unreturnable distance had wedged itself between him and his own life. He saw himself plunked down into the middle of it, a vaporous thing like a room filled up with smoke after the stove damper got jammed. He was drowning in it. No, he was not drowning. He was just . . .

Robert Pachal realized he was awake, he was settled in the steaming compartment of a machine, hurtling through the darkness of a strange land. He felt his heart pounding. Sweat, thick as a rope, clung against his neck. A film of condensation had formed on the train windows. He reached for the glass and wiped a section of it clean with his forearm. Slowly his breathing came back, regular and tempered. He was on a train, that's all it was. He felt the steady vibrations, heard the endless *ru-ku-ku* . . . *ru-ku-ku*. The turning of steel wheels.

He'd been asleep and dreamt of an Indian man, or was it his brother-in-law? Some ferocious machine, like a train, but not a train, moved across the country, uprooting trees. Terrified horses fled in front of it, nostrils flaring, steam pelting out in two white columns. His wife was in his dream, too. She had beckoned to him and given him a package. The package was empty, but that seemed entirely without significance. It was a remarkable gift, the one he had always wanted, and he buried it under his shirt, against his body.

Pachal felt his heart distantly beating against his rib cage. He put his forehead against the cool glass of the window and let it calm him. It relieved him that the other Robert Pachal was not there anymore. The ghost was gone; he no longer freeloaded on the outside of the train window, making every move that Pachal made. Not enough light came from the lamps, his view outside was no longer blocked by his own reflection.

The train drifted slowly through the dark toward North Bay, a place he did not know. On the wall in the club car hung a framed map; Pachal had studied it carefully, but the countless names of places defeated him — from Hornepayne to Hearst, from Pagwa to Pickle River. He remembered only the shape of Ontario as a distorted boot getting pulled onto a very fat leg. He was going down into the ankle of it somewhere, the thin part, halfway between a town called Sudbury and Ottawa, the capital. He had made a vow to Kasper Neibrandt that he would take a small side trip there to the parliament buildings to straighten out Mr. Borden in regards to the issue of the dreadnoughts. "Explain to him that we do not need any more battleships for the prairies." Pachal agreed to take up the matter with the mighty statesman, but he would not be taking any side trips to the capital. He would get himself straight home following the funeral. Already too much distance had been put between himself and that house — Pachal saw it standing on a slight bluff of land surrounded by the tan fields. It looked incredibly flimsy and vulnerable, as though even a slight wind might knock it down.

He had not conceived it possible to get so far away from his wife and from the child that she had borne. He felt apprehensive about it. It was possible for a man to stray too far into the bush. He could attempt to do one good thing, only by doing that he would by necessity neglect the other. It could get so that when a man tried to return to the woman he loved, it was no longer possible; the distance had become too great.

Through the window he watched the black terrain of Upper Canada fly west, away from him. The land was different here, it was changed now. The repeated open blackness of the lakes gave over to something more compressed. The hills were gentler. Twice he saw the soft yellow lamplight of a dwelling set back from the track. People were living in these places now. Somehow the land had become fit for living in. He felt the reassuring warmth of human habitation. The blackness did not crouch so intensely. Tilled fields raced by in the blackness, he saw the lights of living people, up late for some reason, although he could not think why a man would be up at this hour except for wasting lamp oil.

Pachal flipped open his watch and saw it was coming on to two o'clock in the morning. His body was swollen with fatigue and cramping. Only his own exhaustion cushioned him against the relentless clacking of hard wheels. He tried to remember the last point at which he'd known his bearings, but couldn't, unless it was Winnipeg. Probably it was Winnipeg. Now he was in the dark, drifting across the Dominion. It surprised him to see just how much darkness there was still to go around, how desolate it was. It was a loneliness held together from the blackness outside.

The train swung suddenly left on a curved section of line. The meagre headlight flashed though the ragged bush, lying shallow at the foot of the trees, casting the bottom half of the trunks a dull silver. The white beam seemed a paltry thing, weak and without conviction, as though it did not possess enough strength to penetrate the dark. It jumped back immediately as the rails straightened, leaving only the darkness of the bush and the night sky.

For all its tonnage, its steaming and shrieking and burning of anthracite, it felt as though the great black machine had become flimsy. There was no more strength to it than a birch bark Indian canoe stuck together with pine sap. It was a good thing the track was made of steel, Pachal reasoned, laid down and bolted solid to the earth. At least that way they would not go off it, wandering like a lost man in the woods, turning stupidly in circles.

Pachal wrapped his arms around himself and stared out the window. Somewhere a match flared and he saw his face again, briefly, on the glass coming to meet him. The face was pale and blue with a shadow cutting straight across it; the eyes open wide and knowing, like the eyes of a prophet.

He looked into the window, as though somehow the thought had articulated itself there. My brother-in-law shot himself in the head, with his own hunting rifle. The words leapt audibly into Pachal's mind and rattled there like empty rolling stock on a rough line. That is what happened; it was suddenly undeniable to him. Herman Brown had looked into a dark crevice of his life and could not go into it. He could not step back either. Pachal knew these thoughts from before. It was such thinking that came from loose talk and drinking fellows, from slack-jawed employees of Levi Beck who found pool-playing time even at harvest. Now it was all written clearly on the sad, tired eyes of that other one, the ghost who hung pinned to the outside glass, and poured these thoughts into his head, just as the water got poured from water towers into the tanks of the locomotive. Pachal stared at his quavering, untouchable reflection, which had appeared suddenly in front of him with the lighting of a nearby lamp. He saw the winding cracks and furrows of train travel and tiredness grown like prairie dirt around his eyes. Suicide. That is what those two eyes spoke to him. *Suicide.*

His reflection disappeared but the word still rang precisely in Pachal's ears. It was a word that carried images of dead Finnish boys and young Galicians, washed up each spring on the prairie. Dead from sheer loneliness is what people said. Dead from hunger. Dead from the absence of women is what his wife said. *Suicide.* Pachal was breathless, and shaken. It seemed the train had yanked him into another layer of complexity. A new dimension of complexity now stretched between himself and the sky. Only moments earlier there had been just air for him to breathe. Now there were men shot dead with their own hunting rifles.

It was suddenly obvious that Herman Brown had put his sporting rifle to his temple and pulled the trigger, just like some of Levi Beck's men said. It seemed to Pachal that he knew why, too, could see how Herman Brown had cried out from a place where a man is not heard. He cried for a living wage, and for the senseless death of his fellows; the Saltcoats boy who scratched himself on a fence. An *eyelash* of a scratch they said, and dead before the sun came up. Herman had shot himself for that and for the blue shadow that crossed the snow in the mutilated bush. Farm boys, just children, who crossed the ice on a mirey prairie slough to throw stones at a duck, and then were dead.

He was dead because of Renny Blandin's son, who had a board give out on his wagon when he tried to mount, fell to the earth where his frighted horse jerked a wheel across his skull and killed him. Twenty-three years old. He was alive, a man, a young man, in the fullness of being a man. Maybe he had a wife, a child, a hundred, two hundred acres that his father had "proved up" on. There was a country in front of him because he'd pulled it out of the dirt with his fingernails. He'd greased axles with ox droppings and dead frogs, and maybe had driven in an automobile twenty-five miles from Yorkton to Melville and had done it in half a day. This he did because he was alive. Then, in the time it took to blink, he was not. He tugged at a fence and it left a cut on his thumb the size of an eyelash. He took a .32 Ross sporting rifle across the hummocky ground to shoot prairie chickens . . .

Pachal watched the thick darkness clip alongside the train and felt the earth turning underneath him, faster, faster. He was six weeks from his twenty-fifth birthday, only three years younger than Herman Brown had been. He thought of his brother-in-law, resting now in an airless coffin alongside the suitcases of complete strangers. He would return Herman to the town of his birth. He would meet his wife's family. He would present them with a lock of his daughter's hair tied up in a braid of prairie grass that his wife had purchased from an Indian woman, wrapped now in a fold of paper pressed to his chest. He would go straight back, treat himself to a fine meal in the dining car, and get out of this place. On the map it appeared in the shape of a foppish boot on a fat man's leg. Home. That's where he needed to go. The one place a man had a right to be.

Pachal felt his toes curl against his boots. They had a will of their own and stretched themselves out, as though by doing so they might feel the density of his own farmland underfoot. He had not placed his feet down on solid earth for two days, only on the carpeted floor of the carriage, held up, he knew, by fast moving steel wheels, in turn, once more separated from the earth by an endless track of steel. It didn't feel proper to have his feet resting on man-made things instead of the earth they were meant for.

He pondered getting up, but decided better of it. What he needed was to sleep and to stay asleep. He'd change trains in the morning, twice he would change trains, then arrive in a place called Barry's Bay. He needed sleep, he needed to keep that sleep bottled up inside him. There would be preparations, and further travelling by wagons. There would be hand shaking and the always confusing business of talking to strangers who somehow, by law, were his family now. It was a strange thing.

Pachal closed his eyes and floated in his own tiredness. He saw himself bobbing like a cork on the vast blackness of the night. His eyes opened for no reason except to prove to himself that the night still existed out there, and he was still travelling through it. Bush, and the shadows of bush, stood up against a dark sky. There was nothing peeking through the darkness, not even stars. He stared up, looking for a trace of the northern lights. The Reverend C. Blaedow had once called the phenomenon the Archangels of God. But tonight the angels were not visible. He saw only a dark vault.

Pachal tried to whistle. Back home there'd been a Swampy Cree who claimed you could make the northern lights come out by simply whistling. *"If you want to see the northern lights, eh, what you do is whistle. You just whistle."* He'd said this as though offering up a piece of wisdom. Again Pachal put his lips together and tried whistling for the lights, but nothing came. He was not a good whistler. After another try he managed to push out some wilting half notes that sounded like the shrieking dry axles of a Red River cart.

His eyes followed the monotonous dark. At once something appeared before him; apparitions driven by wind, a flash of dirty white, then sharp, drawn-back faces. He saw animals hurtling alongside the train. They vanished in the bush, then came back again, pummeling forward. He counted three, four, five . . . Wolves!

Pachal straightened in fear against the window. He was in the undeniable presence of wolves. Their dark forms hugged the ground, folding and unfolding as they hurtled across the earth. They seemed to exist in motion only, to exalt in a passion of movement. *Timber wolves!* Pachal felt a deep Christian hatred rising inside him. For a moment he sensed the terrifying presence of the Devil when he takes the form of an animal. Years before, he had heard the impossible, demonic wail that came from them. He knew the sound they made. It was not a sound intended for this world; not the distant baying of coyotes, a sound so familiar that Reinhart Schlesinger's parrot had taken to mimicking it. This was something else again.

The creatures tore alongside the train pursuing it in the sheer abandon of running. They ran relentlessly, the way that evil follows a man through his life, separated only by a transparent sheet of glass window, or the timing of a prayer. For a moment the wolves seemed actually to wait for the train to catch them, and bolted again. Pachal followed the hurtling shapes as they dove into darkness; their eyes penetrated the night. I need a rifle, he thought, a rifle, to dislodge the window and exterminate the creatures that waited everywhere in the trunks of trees and under the surface of old moss. His wife's safety and the well-being of his baby daughter depended on it. The land was not safe for a woman or for a girl child. It was swept over still by wolves. Eastern wolves. Pachal felt the blood-calling to make land safe for a woman and children, to rid the country of what waited in its spaces, those huge spaces of Canada, where only the Red Man and the animals had learned to suffer the darkness.

There was nothing he could do; just a man sitting on a wood bench in an eastbound train, stark still in his own helplessness. Then the animals were gone. A single phantasm veered straight up away from the train and disappeared into the bush, like smoke sucked up a chimney.

Pachal cast about the dark carriage for other witnesses to what he had seen. But there were none, only the mingled broken snoring of men, and the heat of sleeping bodies. He was entirely alone. The wolves had appeared for him deliberately and for no one else. No other witnesses. That's how the Lord worked, thought Pachal. The manner in which He tells of His ways.

He tried to sweep these thoughts from his mind, there was nothing to them, only fear and the temptation of the Devil, the vanity of believing that mortal flesh could know the telling of the Lord's ways. He was safe, that was all he needed to know. He was on an eastbound train crossing down into peninsular Ontario. The body of his brother-in-law rested safely in the baggage car, encased in a good coffin, made by a skilled craftsman. He would make sure it got to its burial ground. He was already making sure.

The thumping in Pachal's chest softened. The train penetrated further and further into the muffling night. He felt his eyes close hard. He was back home again in a close room, the stoves fired fragrantly with apple wood. He loved apples, loved the tree even more. He felt the prairieman's fondness for the apple tree, the first tree in the first garden. He loved most of all the sweet smell when it burned in the stoves; his wife, his mother, aunts, other women gathered in the house to tat the lace, the floor so densely covered with white fabrics and cuttings that even the dog didn't dare step across it, but lay immobile on a woven rug.

Pachal dropped softly back to sleep. He dreamt of a steady fire that moved through the forests of central Canada, warming him, drawing a colourful quilt behind his family. He began to snore, the thick involuntary rasp of a resting man. His right cheek trembled on his shoulder.

The engine and its six wooden carriages drilled furiously into the dark. Over top of everything a bright oval eye blinked on the side of the night. A green light shot downward like a skein of silk, shimmered, then raced back up in red and white shafts, dancing behind the ragged tops of the pines. The colours pulsated against the dark, shrank, and swirled again like brush strokes painted on a canvas of stretched blackness.

9

Pachal awoke on the final day of his journey in the brilliant sun of the Ottawa Valley. Immediately he saw the wide river proceeding without haste, its flecked surface cracked with shadows. He roused, stung by the light, and shook the fractured remnants of sleep and dreaming from his head. He felt, strangely, as if he had arrived back at home already. It was the farm pastures that did it; standing clear and cultivated to the river's edge. He felt a special nearness to his wife now; he was very close. Out the window he saw the land that gave birth to her.

The train slowed and announced itself to the town with a short bellow, followed by a long, indignant one. Pachal heard the high raking noise of the engine bells being rung after that. A church steeple on the shore pointed pristinely in the sun's glare. The air glowed blue and taut, casting an outline against the trees.

Pachal craned his neck against the window and stared westward up the great river. He saw where it lost itself in hills and the occasional black covering of forest, the dark triangles of the pines. The river pulsed with certainty, broad and worn. Many centuries of carrying people and cargo on its back had pacified it, like an ox, to its duty.

An old childhood memory conjured itself in his mind; a map tacked to the wall of a classroom back home. He attempted to situate himself on that old map. He was there, a red pin on a long gash of blue water heading east —

— PEMBROKE.

The word appeared stencilled in black letters on a narrow fingerboard sign that flitted by the window. Next to it he read 38.4- 30. Pachal no longer tried to comprehend these numbers. They belonged to the unfathomable, mystic numerology of trainmen and he accepted them as beyond his understanding, like stars.

He had arrived, finally, in the East, was now about to stand on solid ground at a place called Pembroke. He was about to switch trains and take a short dogleg southwest in a brilliant pre-winter sun to return Herman Brown to the earth; to his very own earth. He would be forgiven there, too. Pachal was certain of it. Forgive him God. He offered this prayer to the window as the river chugged away, beyond it. Forgive us all, he added.

As they neared the town of Pembroke, Pachal saw the Ottawa spread flat as a prairie section. He tried to imagine it filled with logs, from one side to the other, the way Herman Brown told it on those nights back home when the glint of story-telling had been in his eyes, and the smell of liquor on his breath. The train slowed into a broken rocking. Already the young man lifted to his feet in anticipation. Under his seat lay the *Winnipeg Tribune*, two days defunct. He'd read every word in it, forgotten every word, and read every word again. In Europe a country was on its knees in terror. In Britain the wardogs roared against their chains. In official circles the situation was considered precarious. Two children had broken through the ice of a prairie slough, also precarious, and died in the low water. He remembered that the Manitoba exhibit, at the Dry

Farming Congress held in Lethbridge, had won a solid silver tea set. Somewhere in the tiny countries of Europe the first man in the history of warfare had died from the sky while operating a motorized flying machine. That is how they would die, thought Pachal. Aiming their machines at the sun. They would aim everything at the sun, even while the harvest needed tending on earth. He had no doubt others would die that way too, crashing and blazing from the sky like injured dragonflies.

Pachal felt the exhaustion swirling inside him, and tried to concentrate on where he was. Pembroke. It was some town or other. The train jolted to a smoking standstill; he saw wagons stationing themselves below the telegraph lines that drooped gloomily over top. Behind these things the river coursed toward a place that could not be seen.

The train was stopped. Pachal rose, excited, but kept his manners and let the others get off before him. Three ladies were swept up into the arms of other ladies waiting on the platform. He heard the thrilling rustle of skirts and crinolines.

Then he was off the train. He stood on the hard, cold dirt of the East. He felt the earth under his feet, packed hard with rock and roots.

Slowly he began to scan the faces as though he expected to find his wife among them. It seemed plausible that her having tread similar ground for all those years would cause her to resemble these women too. And they did some. But mostly it was the faces of men, gruff faces, familiar dark eyes, winged with moustaches, threatening to lift them off from the turbulent station. "*Why Hilda, harnt you growed* —" He pulled away. The men looked vaguely like Herman Brown, back when he was living.

The door to the baggage car slid open and people gathered there to have their luggage handed to them. A rough deal coffin box came out and tottered forward into the arms of two men who slid it carelessly on to a flat wagon. Pachal stepped forward.

"I'm looking after that."

The men fastened the box with quick downward snaps of their arms.

"What is it you're lookin' after?" One of them stared hard and blank at Pachal, the eyes narrowed. He couldn't tell if the man was being insolent or helpful. He put his arm out to the box to hold it still, and demonstrate his ownership.

"Steady. Watch your hand!" The trainman, standing inside the car, hollered this. Pachal looked up into the yawning black of the opened luggage area as another pine box came plunging out. This too was heaved onto the shoulders of the same men who stacked it on top the last one. Again they threw straps over it.

A third box came out and tottered on the lip of the car. Pachal steadied it as well. Somehow overnight the land had become plentiful with the dead. The new ones had slipped in anonymously next to Herman Brown. Miners, he speculated, suffocated by rock dust. Or timbermen crushed by trees. Pachal smoothed flat the bill of lading, a Form 19, nailed to the coffin box. *Departs Yorkton 7:28 A.M. Arrives Barry's Bay via Pembroke/Golden Lake.* He held the box steady and wondered what to do next.

Before he could worry about this, it was taken care of; a flat wagon backed up expertly in the place of the one that pulled away. The box containing Herman Brown's coffin was slid on, banging harder than Pachal thought it ought to under the circumstances. The teamster had on a black round hat a half head too small for him. He coughed, held a rough fist to his pocked nose, and threw heavy ropes over the box before climbing up front onto a sagging board. The man jerked his chin to the space next to him.

"Pembroke Southern?"

"Yes, that's right. Pembroke Southern. To Barry's Bay?" Pachal enunciated clearly. He would not get lost at this point.

"Got to get into Golden, first, son. Golden Lake."

"Yes. Golden Lake, and then Barry's Bay?"

"But firsts you hit Golden Lake see. On the train."

"Yes. And from there to Barry's Bay. Westbound?"

"From Golden, sure. But firsts you got to gets to Golden."

"Right," Pachal nodded.

He mounted beside the teamster and they were off. The horse leaned into the harness, the two men jounced on a plank board, the coffin box skidded once to the right, and held.

Under stunning light they wheeled slowly down the river road. It was a light Pachal had never seen before, silver and heatless, spilling from a sky he'd never seen either; clamped like a glass bowl, fitted tight to the earth, and circular. On the hardened mudflats by the river young boys, dark as shadows, piled slabs of timber, rhythmically, without interruption, as if they had done this their entire lives. Behind them mill hands moved in and out the black doorways of mill shacks. The lumber astonished Pachal. Mighty piles of it stood at attention, stacked, drying in the yards. It was harvested here like wheat back home.

They turned up to the town centre, clopping loudly over the hard road. Some fine white stone buildings graced the streets, along with the tarpaper shacks. A giant angular palace commanded the town from a height of land. The teamster saw Pachal staring at it.

"Booth's Mansion," he supplied.

Pachal nodded, as though this meant something special to him. He eyed the house from top to bottom. He had never seen so many gables stuck to a place. White veranda-work projected all over, more windows than a man could ever look out of. Convoluted peaked roofs with lightning rods and weathervanes jutted from a half-dozen corners. What type of life went on in there? Pachal laughed curtly. It was not so much the laugh of something funny, but as though part of him had been offended. The driver looked over, and looked away.

"Booth's Mansion," he repeated. "One of them anyhow."

The massive baronial structure jolted out of Pachal's view; he turned to stare at it. It didn't seem rooted here, did not belong to this part of the world at all. What could it possibly have to do with those small shadows of men who worked at the bottom of the hill, stacking timber? It didn't belong here, he thought. The doors wanted to swing open on somewhere else, the packed streets of London, England, or a European capital somewhere where the streets were massed with carved buildings, draped in money.

Pachal shook his head. He remembered clearly that first winter in his own house. He had wakened in the early morning to find a three-foot snowdrift inside the place. He had to shovel snow out before he could leave home. This made him laugh again, for no reason he could fathom. It got so cold that night the cat crawled into the oven.

"Tch, tch," said the teamster, then, "giddap. Tch." The man drew his tongue along a sparse moustache, stained blonde with tobacco. Beyond his left ear the river glinted blue as though sapphires had been loosed on the surface.

They headed through the centre of town on their way to the station of the Pembroke Southern. A gang of smartly-dressed vagabonds wearing thigh-length jackets and black hats stood against the wall of a building, thumbs in pockets, their dangling watch chains catching a few shards of sunlight. They were serious full-time smoking men; Pachal watched a spume of tobacco smoke assembling over them like thunderheads. One nodded at the driver, who shook his head and looked ruefully at Pachal.

"They're not much for workin', hay? But they're buggers for the fun." He withdrew a piece of broom straw from his vest, ran it through his pipe, then heaved it over the side like an arrow. Pachal watched him accomplish this task with dexterous precision, the reins fixed between his knees, whistling throughout, a mournful tune that Pachal was unfamiliar with.

"Yes, sir. You don't listen to no tale they tell around here, son. Can tell you a lie in serial those boys. They'll tell it to you in goddam serial." The driver spit thoughtfully over the side. "They come about it honest enough, though." Somehow he'd ground up a heap of tobacco in the palm of one hand and filled a crooked pipe with it. He offered a backward nod to the men on the street, then got his pipe lit with a long straw match he conjured out from someplace in his vest. "I mind I was like that myself one time. I'd get myself good and rory-eyed a few nights. But the Woman would not have it, so I took the Gold Cure. Took the cure, and so I do not get rory-eyed no more, no sir. Got me a homestead at Clay Bank on the White Lake Road on the Madawasky River near Wallace's Bridge three miles east of Arnprior."

The man nodded his open face proudly, puffed the stem of his pipe, and jammed it up deep in the back of his mouth where it somehow did no damage to his speaking. He considered explaining how Wallace's Bridge was not so much a bridge as a floating bridge, a scow, rowed over by Henry Wallace. To get his attention it was necessary to holler across the river or shoot a rifle in the air; the problem was that Henry Wallace had been stone deaf for twenty-five years, and did not see so well either. The driver possessed a deep reservoir of such stories, some of which were true, in principle anyway. He had amassed a collection of characters as well; some had glass eyes, others wood legs; a particular dew-eyed woman from Bytown had a heart made of gold. He told another story instead. They galloped inside him, like horses.

"My papa was Red Jack," he started. "John Red-Pack-Jack from Pakenham they called him, died right there." He slowed in front of a large stone house and pointed. "Dropped dead," he boasted. "Dropped dead right there in the street from eating canned salmon. Tch, tch, giddap."

The horse moved steadfastly at the same speed.

"Yes, sir, that's where papa died. He was on the way to the dance. Only had one leg, you know? Lost himself a leg in McLachlin's Number Two mill. That was a fine mill, oh boy, Number Two, for taking off a fella's arms and legs. They gave him a wood one. They've got stacks of them in the back there. He had a wood leg, yes sir, but he could dance like hell."

Pachal turned from the teamster and pulled his coat around himself. Drunk or sober they were a talking people, these easterners. there was no one like an easterner for spewing out the words. He looked about the town, as if searching for an explanation for why easterners talked so much. Several black automobiles stood in disarray around the train yards. He saw trees, and the stumps of trees; stripped trees and stacked timber, the carting to and fro of cut logs. He saw horses sorrel and chestnut, grey and black. A haggard raven threw itself from a telegraph pole to a church roof. He tried to take in the multitude of this new place where he found himself. Each thing out here had its own word that went along with it. Each day there were more things, more devices, more machines, more people, too; all of which meant more words and more mouths for them to come out of. They had more things here alright, from ornate wall mirrors to watch chains. They had more money, too. It seemed sensible that all those extra things required extra words to go along with them.

Pachal was not completely satisfied with this explanation. It remained a mystery to him; the constant speaking of words between people. His wife would say to him, "Mary Margaret is feeling poor." "What is the matter?" "Don't know." "Well then, we'll get the doctor." "The doctor ain't here, he's at Melville giving a baby." "Well then, we'll get Mrs. Langer to come by." And that was it. You went to sleep and you rested yourself for the next day's work.

Pachal let out a breath. His wife was a thousand miles away from him. He found this intolerable, almost incomprehensible. He began to remember, with some discomfort, the wordless manner in which he had courted her. He had followed her out of the church one night and stayed a respectable, even fearful, ways back. She knew he was there, though. And he knew that she knew. He hung back anyway until she went into the house, then he stood outside a moment mute as a peasant, before going home to lie awake in bed. That night he was tortured by a mix of feelings, muddied together like soil and water and stuck to his own skin as though it were never coming off. It wasn't all torture exactly, there was some sweetness in it. Next week, after the playing of the Reverend's gramophone, he followed her home again. When she went into her uncle's house, he waited outside until the lamp came on upstairs. In his own mind that was a signal that some action was necessary, and in he went. It could not have been five minutes later he came back out again. Everything was taken care of. The deal was done. They were getting married. Her guardian uncle said yes; he'd not said no, anyway. He'd gone up the stairs, come back down, gone back up again, come down, and that was it. A cigar was offered but Pachal was not yet a smoking man, and he awkwardly declined it.

Sitting next to the teamster Pachal could not recall for sure whether he'd spoken any other word in that room beyond the six or seven it takes to ask a man if he might marry his niece. He regretted that now, intensely, and shamefully. He should have offered up some fine words, like a statesman; words with Reverend C. Blaedow's silver shine to them. But he didn't. He got out of there fast, with his heart slamming.

On the buckboard Pachal vowed that he would put a change to all that. He'd get home and make speech come out of him like music from the throat of a songbird. He saw himself at table, telling stories to great effect; travelling stories that a man gets to know when he goes racing halfway across the country.

He huddled low against a wind that came swiftly down the road. The teamster was suddenly quiet. Behind him, Herman Brown was also quiet. All Pachal heard was the creaking of the wagon and the steady *clop clop* of a shoed horse. Somewhere far off bells were dinning.

At a station on the outskirts of town the coffin box was placed in a train car. When that was done Pachal slept for a short time slumped on a bench up close to the stove, snoring. The pitch of a steam whistle roused him and he boarded the new train like a sleepwalker. The engine was noticeably smaller this time, black, glistening like a colt. Within minutes the train began to funnel south down the

Canadian Atlantic line from Pembroke. It screamed once, exultantly, and broke loose across the land.

Pachal sat smoking his pipe in the thick comfort of a horse-haired lounge chair. He was in one of those fancy eastern trains now, with mahogany panels on the walls, and gaslights. He was hungry. His wife had told him he would find children selling foods at the platform, skipping alongside the train, offering up fruit and tapioca through the open windows. He hoped to see children bolting breathless beside the black machine, selling hard-boiled eggs and gooseberries for a penny. But things must have changed since she came out, because there had been no one around. It was November twelfth and cold, the fruit was all picked and eaten, canned, or else drying in root cellars around the country. Instead he'd seen a few horses stood hoof to hoof with clattering autos. He had seen a few hard and stately women dressed in black, displaying hands that had clung a lifetime of frosted mornings to the teats of cows, aimed rifles at bears, and opened black hymnaries to the birth and nativity of a country.

Eastern Ontario rolled by the window, cold and stump-ridden. Pachal stared passively at it; a lone pine whipped by, a white pine he presumed, though there was nothing white about it. Herman had told him the whiteness lay on the inside. "White once you cut it open," he said. The branches reached up like arms, beseeching heaven. He was getting close now. He felt the excitement mounting in his stomach.

Across the fields black snakeboard fences zigzagged a path to the trees. Farms made of squared logs jutted from the earth, stout and low, surrounded by sturdy outbuildings. The land was parcelled out and claimed. People had set their lives upon it. It was getting worked, even down to the very stones that erupted in the fields. The place was littered with them like a massive graveyard. Pachal's wife insisted it was lightning that cast them out from the dirt; every time lightning crashed across the sky those white stones heaved through the skin of the earth. Her own mother had insisted on it, and she believed it, too. Pachal could not convince her otherwise. He told her how the shifting of the temperatures, from winter into spring closed the land and opened it, like pudding, shoving the rocks upward. But she would not have it. She looked at him as if he belonged in a home for incurables. Staring at the countless loose rocks that lay on the earth, Pachal was not sure himself anymore.

In the first car the luggage lay piled like a stack of books. To one side rested the coffin box, sedate as stone, barely vibrating in the rhythmic kick of the train's motion. Four wooden pews spanned the back half of the carriage where the passengers sat, keeping an eye on the luggage. Two ladies held the front seat, side by side, without speaking. A child sprang up and down the aisle, banging his hat against his knee.

"I sar a dead man up in the clouds. Didn't I, mar?"

"You didn't see no such thing." His mother trailed behind, trying to corral him into one of the seats. Out the window Pachal saw a hundred-mile heap of clouds tumbling in together like herded animals.

"Last time, he got himself stuck a half hour in the water closet. They had to go stop the train. Imagine, stopping a train for a half hour. Just six years old and he stopped a whole train already." The young mother could barely conceal her pride in the boy.

"I sar a dead man in the clouds, mar." The child jumped to his feet and glued his face to the window. "Lookit, there's a dead man!"

Pachal turned and found to his alarm that the young boy was staring directly into his face. He turned quickly and forced himself to examine the clouds, as if looking for the dead man. All he saw was the dark underbelly of bad weather coming in from the west. The sky above him remained stretched open and blue, closing fast.

"You didn't see no dead man, Thomas, keep yourself quiet."

"Maybe it was the Kaiser that boy saw." A restless fellow up front turned back to say this. He was a commercial traveller of some sort; a sample case rested tight against his seat, a few words stencilled on it in white paint. When Pachal tried to discern them, his own exhaustion caught up with him. His eyes closed, a flash of ragged light cut across the black, and he actually did see a dead man. He saw Herman Brown before Mr. Christie had gone to work on him. The contours of the wound seared across a young man's bewildered face.

Pachal forced his eyes open and looked into the sky. A mass of clouds piled up unstoppably in the west. They consisted now of the faces of a thousand men, but he couldn't tell if they were living or otherwise. He returned his gaze to the interior of the train, and pictured it filled with soldiers, legs wrapped tight in puttees, nodding, half asleep as they hurried off to some ravaged place of war, at Mafeking perhaps. His eyes remained closed and only opened at the hard-clacking jerk of the train.

He was numb with fatigue. Half a country had sped under his body. When his eyes shut he saw prairie fields swell up and drop in a scattering of dark lakes. A rim of ragged pines sloped and rose like the bristles on a dog's back. Rocks punctuated the dark, imbedded on the inside of his eyelids. He fell suddenly on a thin sheen of ice formed in the November cold — the earth gave out from under him. A .32 Ross sporting rifle discharged and spewed flame from its muzzle. The bullet sped across the Dominion of Canada and entered Pachal's throat. He opened his mouth to shout, but what came out was the piercing blast of the engine whistle, jolting him wide awake.

"Golden Lake."

Out the window a town flung itself against a plain of lake water, black as roof tiles, glinting in the cold. A few clapboard buildings leaned crookedly, like teeth. The train bucked, and grudgingly stopped. A stillness jelled the interior of the carriage. Two seats up the commercial traveller hoisted his sample case across his lap and spoke with authority to the ladies in front.

"I hear Carswell is not sending men up the bush this year."

The older of the women was taken back a moment by the man's audacity, but then forgave him, for she came back eagerly.

"There's no more trees for 'em is there?" she uttered with finality. It appeared she had dispensed with the man once and for all, but she turned back in his direction with some vehemence. "You explain it to me. We're sending cigarettes to China and playing golf on Sunday, yet we can't send our own men up the bush for Carswell? You explain that to me."

The traveller had flourished somewhat in the woman's attention, and conversed now in a measured and philosophical tone. "Well, you know what those timber fellows are like. They'll cling to whatever filthy pig they can as long as they get a piece-a-pork to chew on." The woman seemed to agree heartily with the sentiment.

Pachal turned away to examine the lakefront. Stacks of cut lumber towered to the heights of telegraph poles. Behind them he read grainy yellow letters on a sign: GOLDEN LAKE LUMBER CO. Despite the stacked lumber the mill yard was empty, ghostly. Only a raven stood cold on the ground.

The train rolled backward for a span before clanging to a stop. Pachal stepped out and felt the earth spreading underneath his feet; the air cold, sharp, foreign. He sucked gladly at it, examining the opaque blurring of the tracks to the west where the final stop waited him, Barry's Bay. He'd get a meal there. An intense vision of food assembled in front of him; white plates, a scattering of gulls.

The westbound train shunted slowly down a spur and stopped. Pachal was obliged to stand off the tracks, his view of the Pembroke Southern now eclipsed. He heard the clanking of a carriage door which meant the luggage was getting transferred over, and he passed up front between the two locomotives to give a hand. But again the box was taken care of; bobbing lazily on the shoulders of four anonymous pallbearers, who shifted it from one carriage across the short space to the other. Who were these four men, he wondered? Silent, respectful in their anonymity. Then it was done.

Herman Brown was back among his people. Even the box he lay in was being handled with gentleness.

A sigh released from Pachal's lungs. The thing was finally done; he'd brought his wife's brother from the open prairies to a cramped, covered-up space by the water's edge. He'd boarded the train in Yorkton, Saskatchewan, in a clear, red dawn, after coming home to a warm bed, having slept with his chest against his wife's back and the child curled against her while the wind groaned through the house. It felt like years had passed since then. He missed it already, missed the safeness of it. It was the only safety he knew; the pressing of warm bodies together so that no grief or pain or worrying could enter in between them.

Pachal fastened his coat against the wind. Down the merging tracks the sky disappeared into a blue covering of pines. Somewhere out there, after the final few steps of his journey, he would sleep in a warm, proper bed in the same house his wife was born in. In his mind he saw himself fussed over by seven sisters. A quantity of brothers regarded him with respect from a short ways off. Why shouldn't they regard him with respect? He'd borne his cargo half way round the world.

The train panted uphill through the trees. On the blanched surface of the earth the ageing stumps broke through like a crop of weeds. Pachal did not see how a man could remove a single stump of that size, without it taking up half of his life to do it. Between those stumps the lakes spattered everywhere — sparkling puddles.

Forty minutes later the machine stopped in the hills of a village called Killaloe Station to take on water. Up front the commercial traveller stood up dramatically before the ladies, gave a slow, theatrical bow, and sang throatily:

> We'ez on our way for picnic day,
> where the sky is sweet and blue,
> so when we gets drunk on the old Grand Trunk,
> throw us off at Killaloe!

"Throw us off at Killaloe," shouted the child. Beside him his mother clapped devoutly.

The engine shrilled.

Robert Pachal put his forehead to the glass as the hills dropped away.

10

It wasn't sun that streamed into his eyes. The sun had sunk into a massed heap of sky, hanging like a parasol over top of him. It was not the immense sky of back home either, turning like a wheel.

He squinted into the silver sheen leaking from the belly of the clouds. It was just the last quick hour of light that allowed him to see the hills. They bolted up all around him, squeezed the sky into a handful of silver, gloved loosely by trees pressing from the sides.

The sweet smell of sawed wood wafted like perfume. Thick strands of it poured into Pachal's nostrils. He breathed the unmistakable smell of trees cut in massive numbers, the fragrance of sawed lumber. Beyond that smell he felt only a cold hunger press against his stomach like a steel rail.

Robert Pachal stood on a golden carpet of sawdust that whirled up and scurried across the tracks in a low northeasterly wind. On three sides a solid wall of timber cut off his view. Stout, hewn logs stretched as far as he could make out, jammed together like sows in a pen. Beyond that he saw an indication of cleared land, the white flecks of tree stumps, a grey stain of lake water, and a string of telegraph poles. They loomed like crucifixes, exiting crookedly into the trees.

He saw nothing for certain; not the open lay of land like back home, unsecretive as a naked man. Instead he saw land in front of land, hills in front of hills veering off in sudden angles, trees concealing trees. The convulsions of this new earth dizzied him. He was fatigued and hungry, staring at a silver bowl of sky, turned over and lowered down on a village called Barry's Bay, in the province of Ontario. He saw nothing at all beyond that bowl, and he did not trust it; the endless concealment of hills and eastern forest. It seemed certain that the blue, creviced shadows of the bush were packed with strangers, or with wild bears and men who wanted only to flim flam any fellow who was foolish enough to arrive from some place far away. Pachal lifted up his suitcase from the earth. They will not flim flam me, he resolved. He had not come all this way from Ebenezer, Saskatchewan, to end up buffaloed by some eastern sharper.

The coffin box lay on an unhitched wagon on the platform between train and station. The black, stout figures of men, dressed against the cold, bent like nails against the wind, jerked by and paid no attention to it. He decided to leave it there, unattended, for the time being. It ought to be safe. No one would steal the body of his wife's brother, not here, in the land where he was born. Back home Pachal knew of some folks who might rip the planks off for firewood. But it was doubtful they would rip the planks off for firewood here. He saw that there was no shortage of firewood about. It lay in the street, like nuggets of gold, just waiting to be picked up for the burning.

He crossed the tracks toward the rough, battened face of the Balmoral Hotel, which stood opposite the train station. The sign reassured him somehow, as though this squat wooden construction was the twin brother of the

Balmoral Hotel that loomed against the horizon of Yorkton, Saskatchewan. It seemed possible to Pachal that he might go inside and demand an interview with Harry Bronfman himself; or even Levi Beck, and thrash out the matter of the filtration plant for the Yorkton water supply. Or the Schools issue.

Despite the cold a half dozen commercial men had gamely spread their goods on the tables and were now in the process of packing up; cedar shingles, watches, rows of Hood's pill bottles, and yards of cashmere hose already whipping in the wind. A few men and ladies sidled by in the practiced, condescending manner of people who never buy anything.

Pachal removed his hat and entered the hotel. At once the thick heat from the cookstoves wafted against him. Ham. That's what it was. He smelled the hominess of ham and turkey and the white starchy thickness of potatoes as they thumped together in a vat of boiling water.

"You're a friggin' liar, Murphy, you never worked no pilin' gang with Omanique . . ." The voices poured out above the swinging doors to his right. Quickly they mingled in with the tobacco smoke that unfolded like swamp gas along the walls. He recognized the old smell of shag tobacco; the coarseness of it made him draw breath.

"I mind big Omanique wouldn't work with no feller like you."

"Ah yer fulla wheat you!"

The doors swung open momentarily and Pachal was exposed to a roomful of drunken timbermen. He breathed the close odour of malt and metal polish. He saw faces clad in fur, some toothless, some bearing the bruises of old frostbites, mouths glinting with gold, almost all of them buried in the mottled foam of beers and stout glasses topped with whiskey. He determined then and there not to enter. He did not see how there was a need for him or any other man to go into such a place, unless he was a soldier for the Salvation Army.

He turned away and saw a number of doorways gaping around him in all directions. One led up a steep narrow staircase to the rooms on the second floor. He felt the warmth rolling down from up there, flooding in with the gauzy light from a window at the end of the upper hall. It was a woman's warmth that came through. The work of a woman's hands was all over the place up there, making it warm and liveable. To the right of the staircase, a dark room checkered with red and white tiles yawned emptily; a half dozen round tables waited inside, surrounded by chairs, rickety, crooked chairs, as if the weight of men had proved too much for them.

Pachal turned left to face another room that opened on to an even larger one behind. Healthy flames snapped from a massive stone fireplace at the back. At the rear of the first room a glass case jutted from the darkness, topped with an ornate metal cash register. He approached cautiously in the near darkness, feeling like an intruder, or at least a man uninvited. On the glass case Pachal saw a pen, an inkpot and, upside down, a thick ledger, he craned his neck deceitfully to read:

> *Nov. 10.......... JC Hudson .25*
> *Nov. 10..........T. Delaney .25*
> *Nov. 11.......... JC Hudson .25*
> *Nov. 11..........T. Delaney .25*

Unsure what to do, he backed off from the counter and turned self-consciously to examine a framed photograph on the wall. *The Barry's Bay Baseball Club 1910 Ottawa Valley Champions.* Nine uniformed men and one shady-looking fellow in a black suit — the manager presumably, stared out at him.

"That is Chas Murray in the front, the short fellow with the moustache."

A small, aproned woman with a tray strapped around her midsection passed swiftly in and out of Pachal's vision. Before he could speak, she came back from the far room, without the tray this time, holding a broom instead.

"Them boys are for baseball for dinner, supper, and breakfast. They were champions, you understand. Champions of baseball. Champions among men." She said this with some apparent mockery.

Pachal brought his hat closer to himself and rattled it slightly against his chest, to reinforce to the woman that he had actually removed it from his head. She paid no attention to him.

"A room is two dollars fifty. Dinner is a quarter."

"Dinner," he said. "I'm just wanting dinner."

"You can have ham. That's all what I have left is ham. Good ham. It's from out Mrs. Cruickshank's place. That's where the best pigs are."

"Yes, ham." Pachal rummaged desperately for some conversation to make with her.

On the wall behind her back hung a long wooden sign: *We Know This Hotel Is On The Bum — What About Yourself?* He glanced at it, while behind him came a roaring whiskey laugh that cackled out from the tavern. The woman kept up her sweeping behind the counter and paid no attention to it. He did not believe he'd ever seen a woman as small as her. She was light as feathers, her grey hair bundled up around her head, wearing a grey frock covered up with a grey apron. It was a wonder she was not smashed to pieces by the sheer noise made by those drinking fellows. It had increased now to a thundering conflagration.

"You are a dishabilitated son of a bitch and a liar!"

Pachal expected a ruckus to break out in the tavern at any moment. Instead, a wash of rough laughter rose from the place. The woman leaned the broom against the wall and made a *tsking* sound.

"Oh, well," she sighed, "I mind when Bunker Joe Hefferty and Rickety Pete got going. Big Bob Foy had just drunk the bad liquor and died up The Swisha you see . . . Oh, they had some foine discussions in those days. As long as they weren't murderin' one another." She smiled, more to herself than him.

She had fallen back into a reverie of men with irrefutable nicknames. Forty years earlier they had directed meaningful and intense stares at her. She wore a blue summer dress on the grounds at Costello's racetrack in Brudenell. Woodpeckers cried from the trees, the sun nestled on her, she was a young woman. She was ready for the soft and gigantic battles of love. Her heart flew upward on the fans of angels . . .

The woman placed her hands on the glass counter and examined them in wonderment. Where in the world had those liver spots all come from? And how was it the weather back then was finer by a piece than it ever was today?

Pachal did not know how to proceed. "I have a coffin," he stammered. "On the landing at the station . . . It's safe there? It's in a box."

The woman gave this some thought.

"Is anyone in it?" she demanded brusquely.

Pachal blushed. "My brother-in-law. My wife's brother." He felt more comfortable phrasing it that way.

"I figure he's safe there as any other place. Don't see why no one should go stealing him."

"No . . ." A feeling of foolishness warmed Pachal's neck, followed by a boyish urge to unburden himself to her, to someone. "Herman Brown is who it is. He is from here, from near Palmer Rapids."

"There is Browns at Boulter, too, you know. There's Browns and Bruns and Boehmes all over."

"Schutt. He is from Schutt, in the hills near —" Pachal clutched about, trying to remember the name of the place. The East was full of foreign names, Scottish ones in particular. They held no meaning for him. "Combermere," he said finally. "I am taking him to Combermere."

The woman seemed not to register this, but then added sagely, "That would be Madelaine Boehme. Married a Brown, had thirteen children. He belongs to that patch then does he?"

"Elizabeth Anne Brown is my wife." Pachal went on eagerly. Now the connection was established, he would not be stopped. "We have two hundred and forty acres of dairy on a section out of Yorkton, Saskatchewan, on the prairies. Two hundred forty," he repeated, as if this explained everything. "My papa proved up eight years ago."

"It must be a far distance," mused the woman. "I've never known of it. I might of *heard* of it now. A course I never been there."

Pachal nodded. "No," he said, diplomatically. Finally, he felt himself to have arrived in some way; at least his body was established in this new place. Herman's coffin lay outside in the cold, protected by a rough pine box. He himself stood hard, and big-footed on the thick timber floor of a hotel that bore the same name as the hotel back home. His suitcase, the hem of his coat, the exterior of his hands were here with him. Even his own shadow leapt from the wall and finally joined him in some satisfactory way.

None of this appeared to mean much to the woman who went back to the broom and worked it fiercely into the crevices where the walls met floor.

"It's a shame now you missed the boat, the *Mayflower*. Up for the season, see? That road is a bad one on to Combermere. It's awful bad."

Pachal nodded. "I am to telephone to William Boehme of Combermere, and he will arrange it. He'll make the arrangements for me."

The woman nodded in return. She seemed to think this was as it should be.

"You tell William to get that *Mayflower* brought up here. I've got paying customers for that boat. Mrs. McWhirter upstairs, and Stewart will not have her on that road, I know that. It's not fit for her. There's those commercial fellows too, the four of them."

"Yes," Pachal was all business now, as if he understood everything. He felt encouraged by what he was hearing. He would operate the telephone machine and bring news of paying customers. Prosperity would follow him in, like a bird, from the West.

"You have a machine here?"

The woman put her broom against the wall and went smartly into the lobby. "It is in that closet there." She indicated a narrow wooden cubicle with a folding door. "Give it a whirl. On the right."

Pachal approached the wall cautiously. The truth was that he had never operated a telephone machine before, although he had seen one functioning in the Yorkton Post Office, and Reverend C. Blaedow kept one in his parlour on a table next to a phonograph machine, shining in a box of polished mahogany. It was Pachal's assumption that mahogany allowed for the most efficient release of the electrical fluid and therefore made the best telephones.

Inside the closet the planks showed the colour of brass, and pressed his broad shoulders. They must be making men smaller, he thought. The floor of the booth felt soft, uneven, scraped away by the tread of previous telephonists. The door swivelled shut obliquely on a V-shaped pin. He was crushed by it, and pressed further against the oak walls, hardly able to breathe.

In front of his eyes he saw, in elaborate script, *J. Hennyman Sept 19, 1909*, carved deep into the wood. Sweat pulsed on the side of his face. J. Hennyman? What kind of name was Hennyman? Had he died here, in this wood box, killed by the telephone? Pachal had a sudden, claustrophobic fear that when he lifted the device, smallpox and scarlet fever would pour out of the wire into his own mouth. Like it had in Montreal . . . He wiped sweat from the side of his face and reminded himself it was not true. The telephone company put an end to that; claimed there was no hollow centre to the wire for smallpox to slide through. He'd read it in the newspapers some time ago. It was all cleared up. There was nothing to worry about anymore.

Pachal attempted to pull open the door and let some air in. The panels caved inward, forcing him even tighter to the wall; the only air that entered came freighted with the voices of the timber crew who continued to bellow at each other from behind the doors.

"I'm telling yeh big John Omanique never worked no goddam stinkin' pilin' gang with the likes a goddam stinkin' you!"

He swivelled and confronted the device; a magneto wall

phone with two silver bells staring at him. The mouthpiece drooped forward like the bloated nose of a drunkard. Pachal lifted a black, wired cone and attached the piece to his ear. He assumed he would hear instantly the voices of the Dominion murmuring with business and trade, busy as dawn birds. Instead he heard the shush of his own blood, the watery silence of a lake lapping in his ear.

"*That goddam Omanique feller ain't no saint, mind —*"

He tried to squeeze the door shut to keep the noise out, but it wouldn't comply. The last thing he wanted was the foul language of drinking men to spread out through the telephone wire, with him being responsible for it.

"*It weren't him what killed that pepper anyhow —*"

He felt the cold handle on his flesh and cranked it. Nothing happened; the quick grinding of gears, then the same liquid blackness. Suddenly the black evaporated and he heard a voice break through.

"This is Paddy O'Brien here, Combermere exchange. Who is it yer looking for then? Who is it?"

"Who is it?" Pachal shouted back, confused. He tried to project his voice eighteen miles to the next town but it did not seem humanly possible to yell that loud. "Who is it?" He pressed the black funnel hard against his ear, worried that the voice had disappeared into the ink, and would never come back out again.

"*It weren't Omanique, that's fer goddam sure; he just put the feller's eye out —*"

Pachal pressed the palm of his right hand over his free ear, to try and keep the noise from shooting into the machine. "Is someone there?"

The voice came back at him immediately.

"You stop that shouting, mind? We have the conductors up at Blackfish so you stop your shouting. I can hear you plenty. This is not a megaphone son, it's a telephone. You understand? I'm Paddy O'Brien and who is it you're wanting after?"

Pachal unscrewed his voice a notch and tried to speak evenly. "Boehme, William Boehme." He pursed his lips shut to give time for the words to travel there. Probably they travelled at least the speed of birds; eagles, at full flight, looping through the black cables in the treetops to Combermere. He imagined his words shooting like birds to an unknown place. He figured they ought to be able to travel that fast anyway, and waited some time for them to get there.

"Willy Baum? In Schutt? Is that who?" The sound crackled at him.

"I beg your pardon?" A shout from the bar room had clouded Pachal's hearing.

"*Daillaire is the pepper alright. Cracked up at Slate Falls —*"

"William Boehme." Pachal kept to the German pronunciation. "Buh-ma," he floundered, "William!"

"Willy Baum?"

"Of Schutt."

"Schutt?"

The words came out of the darkness like silver shavings, Pachal could not grasp on to them.

"*It weren't that pepper yer talking about Mack. It were that cookie from Shawville.*"

"*Today's my goddam birthday is what I'm telling yer —*"

Pachal heard a distinct popping noise, like a rifle shot, followed by a swimming silence of black water. Then a voice said evenly,

"This is William Boehme talking, who is it I'm speaking to?"

He heard a sudden grace in the voice that dismantled the shouting and the vexatious goings-on around him. The cursing from the bar room dipped obligingly, and Pachal heard the far-away howling of a train whistle. From the corner he saw the tiny woman again shoot like a pigeon through the hallway.

"I am Pachal, Robert Pachal." He felt himself crushed ridiculously in the telephone box, announcing his arrival into a drunkard's black nose. "Of Saskatchewan," he added, substantially, as if that told the whole story of who he was.

"We're related by marriage, son, aren't we? It's my

pleasure. Lizzy then, she's in proper health?"

"She is, yes." Pachal felt in the steady grip of a disembodied paterfamilias. It was William Boehme he was speaking to, the brother of his wife's father, one of five. A tailor; his mother had taken a legendary walk, pregnant, from a place called Farrell's Landing on the Ottawa River, a hundred miles west along the Opeongo Line. Her sister had homesteaded the Huron Tract and once helped an Indian woman give birth to twins while descending the Saugeen River on a raft. He knew the shreds of these stories from his wife, but they had all seemed fantastical to him.

Now he sensed that the man he was talking to was made of stone, that he had erupted from the ground at the clash of a great lightning bolt.

"And the little girl?"

"Mary Margaret is strong. Like her mother."

"Herman Brown? You brung him back all right?"

"Yes, sir, he's on the siding by the train stop. I'm told the road —"

"No, no, you will not get a coffin down that road. I'll have the *Mayflower* brung up. It's down for the year, but I think Jack will do that. Jack Hudson, he's captain, he'll do that for me. We'll get that boy down here and have him buried mid-week."

"Yes, sir, he needs to be put in the earth." Immediately Pachal regretted saying this. He fumbled for some way to explain that Herman Brown had been packed into a good box, that good money had been paid to J. W. Christie to have the thing done properly. "He has a fine coffin," Pachal tried, indecisively. A brief, shimmering silence filled the earpiece.

"*Omanique put that friggin' pepper's eye out with his finger —*"

He stooped closer to the black nose of the telephonic machine and tried to shut out the cursing words with his own. "There are some drinking men . . . in the tavern."

"You bet your life on that. That'll be the McLachlin crew. You stay clear of those boys, they'll be on a rip for a week."

"There is also other folks, paying customers. For the captain. Four commercial fellows . . . There's an old woman."

"I'll tell that to Hudson. We'll have that boat up for six o'clock, at the wharf by the Polish church there, for six o'clock. You get yourself a wagon from the livery and — "

"*It's that pepper's eye what sits in a jar on the counter at Jack Schenly's* — "

"Pickled?"

"*Goddam pickled.*"

"You hear me? Six o'clock, I'll be on it, with Paddy, you talked to Paddy on the telephone before me, he runs the telephone out here. I'll bring him out with me, and this other fellow, Murphy. We'll get Herman back down here tonight, son. You have yourself a good meal from Mrs. Billings. You have the ham there son, she makes it just right. I shall see you then shortly after that."

Pachal heard that same rifle shot again. The shimmering stars filled the blackness in his ear. Cut off, alone, he extricated himself from the telephone closet and stood like a burglar in the dim lobby of the Balmoral Hotel.

The floor rumbled from another train plowing in from the west. Out the window Pachal watched it loose itself, shaking and rattling to an eerie stop. Flat rolling cars were stacked high with countless trees, headless, without limbs. He saw tree trunks out there as thick as a sod hut.

"*You let the egg-sucking bog-trotter sing them verses and I wull hava phart on yeh.*" This voice came throaty with intemperance from the far room, followed by the bangs of fists on wood tables, cracking out from the darkness.

Robert Pachal stared at the coffin box lying on a wagon by the train station. He shut his eyes as the drunken, erratic singing of a man's voice quavered behind him:

> *The world is round and runs on wheels*
> *Death is a thing what everyone feels.*

11

Given her druthers, Mrs. McWhirter preferred to wake up to the dawn chorus of birds vibrating through the pines, and for a lingering moment she thought she had. Two muted columns of sun penetrated the window, with the birdsong blowing in from behind it. But in fact she did not hear anything at all. Above her stretched a board ceiling painted milk white, grey shadows where the grooved boards fit together. She wondered where she was. A bell tolled, clanged once and flattened across a large surface of water, then tolled again; the distinct B sharp of the Polish church bell at Barry's Bay. That's where she was. She knew it now; she was in the Billings's place, the Balmoral Hotel, in Barry's Bay, and someone had died.

Mrs. McWhirter listened as another chime flung itself across Lake Kaminiskeg. And then another. She imagined each chime rippling across the lake as though the wind was pushing hard against it. Seven. She counted seven bells, the seventh faded into the distance like the caw of a raven. It was a woman then. A woman who had died. But who? She could not think who the woman was. It must have been some infant girl. She did not know with certainty whether they rang the passing bell for an infant girl or not. Besides, it could have been a man. It might have been nine bells that rang and she woke up only on the third ringing. Probably that's what it was, for she could not think of a single woman who had died lately. Probably it was for Jonush Ritza then, who had gone up for McLachlin and been killed in a felling accident.

Mrs. McWhirter removed herself from the bed carefully. She did not want any mishap this close to home. Her two hickory canes leaned against the bed table, but she would not be needing them at the moment. She would just rest up a short while on the bed, her feet touching lightly on the thick rug, until she was more fully collected.

In this position she examined the wallpaper, a fine pattern. The close, clustered flowers of a lilac tree burst in purple across the walls. It was faded now so the lilacs had more the pale colour of wild phlox, but it was a cheerful thing for a person to be looking at, and she felt cheered by it.

Carefully she brought herself up to her feet and moved several steps closer to the window. She was close enough to see the reflection of her face in the glass, close enough to be displeased by it. She saw a face that might as well have belonged to someone else. It was folded in on itself these days in countless, unexpected ways, soft and pliable, like pastry. An old face. Somehow that had happened to her. She was eighty years old, a cripple, and now given over to a slow and pleasant mumbling, to herself for the most part.

Mrs. McWhirter made it to the window and braced herself against the frame. Below her the timber lay stacked against the town; black trunks and cut board piled ten feet high rung the land from one side to the other. Off by the hills the burner heaved a smudge of black smoke against the sky. That old burner was going at those mill scraps all the time now, in a furious hurry, like everything else these days.

Twenty-four hours a day the smoke erupted from it, wavering constantly like a loose thread in the clouds. She stared at the embankment of timber, and the activity taking place around it. Four times each day the trains came to take it out from here. Four times in, four times out. Mrs. McWhirter saw her head shake of its own accord in the glass. What could the world want with such amounts of timber? Where was it going? What was the great hurry? And how was it, with the world wanting no end of timber, that the Golden Lake Lumber Company was shut down and her grandsons would not be going up the headwaters for Mr. Booth this winter? Not for Skead either, or McLachlin. Instead they had to move off to places in the north that a Christian person had never heard of, places called Cobalt and Haileybury, New Liskeard and South Porcupine. Mining towns. They were sending men north to dig the rock out.

Mrs. McWhirter stilled herself against the window frame. It was a new world that had come of a sudden, and things were done different now. Things got done in an office far away by writing a word down on a sheet of paper, or speaking another word through a telephonic machine. There was no sense to it. Men were going about saying the trees were all but gone. That's what the men said, that you could not find a standing purchase left up between here and Ottawa. "Crooked trees make straight dollars. Cut 'em down, boys." That was the cry over at McLachlin's, and that's the way it was.

That's all they ever said anymore. And somehow fellows were still getting rich at it, too; she knew the Vankoughnet boy had seen a lake with ninety thousand cut logs on it, no brand on them either. Just floating there all together like stolen cattle.

Things had become different, alright. It wasn't like before when Richard and Thomas fished pickereen on Barren's Creek. Then, you just lit up torches in the front of the scow and speared the teeming fish under a sickle moon. Why should things change from that? Why ever? Of course, she was not a woman for eating pike in the first place. She preferred the pickerel to the pickereen. Still . . . that's how it was then; you measured your fish by the barrel.

Two floors beneath her the chickadees flittered hungrily across the dirt. The entire surface of the earth was picked clean. Even the birds could find nothing. It was no wonder they were sending men below it, underneath the rock to get at that, too. That's how it was.

She turned from the window and faced the printed lilacs scattered up and down the wall of the room. Beneath her the warped floor slanted comfortably downward from one end to the other. Someone had made sure that dried flowers were put in a vase on the bedtable, and she appreciated that; black-eyed suzies, purple clover, she had a fondness for daisies in particular.

A weak, contented sigh released itself from her body. *I have been a few places, alright.* She had, and she was proud of it. Many years ago she had gone sixty miles to Eganville where she boarded two nights to take the Entrance exam for nurses. And she would have, too. Would have taken the Entrance, but she got sick for home. It was a strain on the family as well, the boarding money, so she came back and did not take the Entrance.

She turned once more to the window. Should have took the Entrance, she thought, should have got on with the nursing, for I have always been good for the nursing. It was true that when her sister got the pleurisy she kept fresh mustard on her front and back, till it went away. But she did not get on with the nursing; she gathered beaver hay for the cows instead, did butchering in September, piled fieldstones on the stone boat in spring, strained milk quarts in a shortening tin, and one unforgettable day in the field, she looked up and saw the miraculous apparition of the Virgin Mary spread across the sky above the settlement of Fort Stewart, Ontario.

Mrs. McWhirter remained in room number 8 in the Balmoral Hotel and passed the time. She arranged dried flowers and let her memories shift across her like water. She lay down. She got up. She put a brush through her white hair. She saw a raven align itself to the earth. She moved imperceptibly around the room. She had regrets; she thought of Jay Prince, who had been young once with a broad fine back, who had worked on a piler gang, and had died. She regretted that she was not one of the miracles of Ste. Anne de Beaupré, like Constance Beirnaki, who had gone there and hung up her crutches and come back with a single cane. Of course, later she'd lost her two boys in a house fire and was given now to roaming in the streets and talking about the baby Jesus to complete strangers. But still, that was a holy place there, across the river on the French side.

The woman shut her eyes. Every place was holy, she knew that. This was a holy place too, the Balmoral Hotel. Holy as hell, as her husband used to say, seeing how the crippled men came on crutches to the tavern and by late night they did not need crutches at all. They went home dancing. That was the truth, too, although Mrs. McWhirter was hard against the drinking of spirits. She was hard against the drinking of spirits and she was hard against the playing of cards for money.

For where did it ever lead to?

The woman opened her eyes and took a slow breath. It led to evil and to killing, that's what it did. Like Jack Tomasini and his wife, just down the street. They had shot that poor brother of his. First they beat him with a spade, and then they shot him. Shot him dead like an animal. Just down the street, too, where the children swim. He had been going hard on to the wife. That's what people said; going hard on to the young wife, and for that they shot him. After that the police had come; for the first time in living memory there were police constables in the village of Barry's Bay, and they held Jack Tomasini prisoner, right here, in the Balmoral for one full day. Then they took him down to Kingston and hanged him up like a poisoned wolf, and it was on account of drinking, too. That she was sure of.

The shrill of the Canadian Atlantic, westbound, drew her back to the window where she watched it creep into town. Black steam hedged over the trees and then the train was in, squeezing through the stacks of lumber and coming to a clanking, disconsolate stop in front of the hotel. Immediately a commercial traveller leapt from it with his suitcase and began to set up his wares on the display tables. The westbound out of Ottawa. She watched it huff on the steel rails, black, ornate with chrome, constrained, as if mighty cables held it tight there. It looked to her as if that black machine was in a hurry to bolt forward into the future, the same future that waited up ahead on the shining tracks, and kept trying to move in closer every day. That was a foolish train then, she thought.

Mrs. McWhirter stood at the window and watched the action galvanize around the locomotive. Children rushed up yelling, begging the engineer to pull the whistle chain. Three wagons rolled solemnly to the baggage car. A funnel slid down from the water tower, water foamed from it into the sides of the engine. A rough coffin box was disgorged from the first carriage. Mrs. McWhirter wondered if that was him; the dead man that the bell ringing had been for. Probably it was just some poor fellow who had gone to the West or to the North and come back dead. That's what happened to you when you did that. God put you in some place for a reason, she reckoned. And it was not for you to be going somewhere else.

She stared, not quite in focus, at a young man who came out from the carriage to oversee the laying of the coffin box on a wagon. He stood tall and stout with red hair showing under his hat — hair the colour of chanterelles, when they grew fat beneath the pines. A fine-looking fellow. Young, too. She always had an eye for a young man. He looked not much different from her husband when she saw him dance the chicken reel with Martin O'Grady and take first prize at Cormac. That's a fellow who can dance, she reasoned, and watched as he looked uncertainly about the town.

Mrs. McWhirter felt her eyes close. She was tired again. Always tired. I have worked too hard in my life, she thought. The woman picked her way carefully back to the bed, wishing that the train was able to go all the way to Combermere. It was a hard road to Combermere. It was too hard for an old woman. But it did not go to Combermere. It went to Madawaska, to Whitney, to places further west, through the Algonquin.

She went back to the bed and lay in it. I will go to sleep. I will sleep until they call me for the coach. Then I will be in Combermere tonight and home tomorrow. She closed her eyes and was asleep.

The bells of the angelus rang from the church in the Polish settlement across the bay, and woke Mrs. McWhirter for the second time. She heard them clearly over the water, the predictable deep bass chimes. They are ringing for me, she thought, on account of my entering into heaven. It made her feel awkward to have such a fuss getting made of her. For some reason she was standing in a mighty snow, the Deep Snow of sixty-nine that brought the roofs down, but it was not cold. She was not cold in the slightest. The bells rang low, deeper, and slower, like the Edison gramophone winding down. I'm dreaming, she realized, and then she slipped out of it and heard the hard, impatient banging on the door.

"You can come in." She was surprised by the sound of her own voice, having barely spoken an audible word since Golden Lake, a day and a half earlier when she visited her grandsons.

The door creaked inward; a fellow bent timidly into the room, and then ducked his head back again when he saw her on the bed.

"Excuse me, ma'am." There was low, conspiratorial whispering behind the door but she did not hear it.

"Are we leaving then?" She recognized the fellow from before; he was the coach driver. Stewart, his name was Stewart. Or Herbert. She felt a sudden, irrational fear that the coach had left, that something unforeseeable had gone wrong. The world had gone off its tracks and she would not get home, ever.

The maid entered abruptly from behind the door. She was a young Polish woman entrusted to fry up Mr. Billings's steaks every morning. A sad white pallor festooned on her cheeks as though the pastry flour refused any longer to be wiped from them. She gave a shy nod, followed by a half curtsy.

"Is boot, ma'am. Boot!" Suddenly her English collapsed and she could not think what to say next. Instead, she turned back to the driver who moved awkwardly into the doorway. He held his cap in both hands and stared at the ceiling, like a gentleman.

"You'll be taking the steamboat, ma'am. It's coming up from Combermere. Hudson's boat, the *Mayflower*, it's coming up."

The woman looked at him, blankly. What boat? Of course she was not taking any boat. She was going by coach to Combermere.

"Road is bad, yes? For you is bad." The maid offered this in a sudden upsurge of confidence in regards to her English. She was making fair enough progress. Only once had Mr. Billings called her a damn Polack. That one morning when she got the steak wrong, and overcooked it.

The driver moved hesitantly, another step into the room.

"I will not take you in the coach, ma'am, on account of you being a cripple. You'll get broke up on that road, see? Broke right up. I come on it yesterday, ma'am. It ain't a fit road for a cripple. It will break you up."

"You take boot," interjected the maid cheerfully.

"That's right, ma'am, you take the steamer, the *Mayflower*, it's coming up to get that dead fellow."

"What dead fellow?" Mrs. McWhirter looked hard at the man. This was an entirely new wrinkle on the matter. She had a firm and personal interest in the dead now, and sensed, almost in a panic, that someone had managed to pass over without her learning of it.

"That Brown boy. It's one of those Brown fellows, ma'am."

"Well, is it the Boulter Browns or the Schutt Browns?" she demanded.

"The Schutt Browns, ma'am. One of the fellows shot himself up hunting, on the prairies. That's what I heard, anyway, from Mrs. Billings. They're bringing up the boat from Combermere."

"I'm taking the boat?"

"Yes, ma'am, the *Mayflower*."

"I'm fond of the train," she said. "I do like the train." In fact, she adored the train. That was the way for an old woman. With her back resting on the maroon horsehair —

"Yes, ma'am, but — "

"Oh, there's no train. There is no train to *Cumbermere*." She seemed to utter this as a warning to them.

"No, ma'am." A silence followed. Mrs. McWhirter was momentarily caught up in a gauzy veil suspended in front of her eyes.

"I won't be getting on any boat with a drinking man," she emphasized this threat with a jab of her index finger. "I will not be ridden about by drunken sailors."

The teamster looked once to the Polish girl, and from her to the ceiling.

"Oh, no, ma'am. She's a fine boat. That's Mr. Hudson's boat, there. He's the reeve," he added as if this solved everything. "Mr. John Hudson, the reeve, ma'am. Reeve of Radcliffe. He would not allow foolery on the *Mayflower*."

The driver did not know what to do with his eyes, so he pointed them at his hat, and revolved it limply in his hands. He had just told an enormous lie to a very old woman, and was ashamed for it. The fact was that fellows got themselves exceptionally drunk on that boat. Two years ago the entire Barry's Bay Baseball Club, after beating Brudenell in the Valley Championships, got aboard the *Mayflower* and went on such a rip that not one man was standing when she came back in. Chas Murray had jumped overboard and was found a day later in a tree, and somehow Mickey Dohlan had set himself on fire. The boat had also sank twice, at least once. The other time it nearly went over in the wind with the

Monsignor on board, and last year she grounded on a sand bank in three feet of water in the Narrows. They had ladies on board that day, three of them, and it was a scandal. It was rare you put a lady aboard the *Mayflower*.

The coachman knew all the sordid details of the *Mayflower*, but he also knew it was eighteen miles by road from Barry's Bay to Combermere, that the fall mud was frozen like rocks, and that the wagon box would scrape and bump the top of that road all the way there. He'd be hauling down axes and swede saws to cut branches off the road each time the wind blew. Twelve hours it took, and every inch was a hole that could crack a person in two. It would be a crime to take an old cripple woman down that road. Even Walter Ilnisky could barely take that ride and he was just a peg-leg. Younger, too.

"It's a good boat, ma'am. It's not three hours on the water, and it's his hotel you'll be staying at, the Hudson House, in Combermere there. The captain, he runs the Hudson House, so he'll be looking after you."

Mrs. McWhirter stared through the window into the clouds. "I suppose I can paddle my own canoe." She nodded at the man and tried to conjure all the places she had been at, but there were too many and all she remembered was the white, massive sky that pressed on the mountaintops of Fort Stewart where she lived. It wasn't that sky at all anymore. It was another sky, she was at Barry's Bay, Ontario, in the Dominion of Canada, looking out the window of Josh Billings's place and there were now so many skies in her long life that they rested one atop another like pages in a book. Too many, she thought, too many pages. But then she was sitting in the grass for the first time at the Tannahill concerts on the Gleniffen Braes, a child staring up into the stern faces of men, and the soft sky that showed beyond them.

"I will have myself a bath," she said. But the room was empty now and Mrs. McWhirter decided she would not have a bath. It was too much botheration. She would have another sleep. Then she would eat dinner downstairs before taking that damn boat to Combermere.

12

A DRINK WOULD HAVE BEEN MONUMENTAL, A SIMPLE HALF glass of Gillman's, or even house whiskey, warm as tea. Instead John Hudson reached out and banged his knuckles on the window. Outside in the yard, the boy was too wrapped up in his own stupid thoughts to hear him, or at least to pay any attention to him. All he did was bring the axe down again with a dull whack against the chopping block. Hudson noted grudgingly that a substantial heap of pine slabs had grown up out there in the last half hour. He was not a lazy fellow, he was just stupid that was all. He was not much for hearing either, when he didn't want to.

John Hudson stomped hard across the fresh pine floor that glistened in his empty dining room, and hurled open the door. The door was also brand new, he'd paid five dollars for it from the Devine Brothers at the sash and door factory in Killaloe. Somehow it fit too loose in the frame, for when the wind caught hold of it, it nearly shattered against the outside wall.

"Tommy!" The axe fell again. "Tommy!" he hollered. This time the boy's slow, peering eyes aimed themselves at him like the eyes of a pine martin. Hudson had several theories, some of them quite elaborate, on what it was that made a bastard child slower than one birthed in the Christian manner. Properly speaking, the boy, Tommy Delaney, was not a bastard. In his wife's eyes he'd been elevated to the position of orphan, which is how she phrased it. She had generously killed off both parents in the black diphtheria of 1898. For his part Hudson was still convinced the boy was spawned in the hold of a cholera ship packed with famine Irish on the hoof from County Sligo, or God knows where else.

His wife was in the habit of cleaning up the dirtiest ragamuffins in Upper Canada and presenting them like angels to the world. It was something he resented in her, but he grudgingly respected her for it, too. That's the way it was with women, he figured. The issue was either half white, or half black, depending on how you looked at it. It fell to women to civilize the place, is how Hudson looked at it. Once the men had taken all the trees down and shot the bears and bobcats, and put names to places, then it was time for women to lay on the civilizing touch. He visualized this as the spread of a white lace table cloth on a rough groaning board. It was a womanly sort of thing and Hudson was not sure if he approved or disapproved. It made him think of Ben Haggerty who was cleaning the flues up the Bonnechere River when a loose log shot by and crushed his skull. He'd been hauled out of there dead, and while the boys carried his body down the main street of Renfrew, Mrs. Burdock ran out her front door and draped a linen sheet over him. You'd have thought she was waiting there behind that door for just that purpose; for putting clean linen over the bloodied carcasses of men, so they could not be gaped at by boys and girls or even by the indifferent face of God Almighty.

Hudson attempted a whistle, and gave it up. Of course, a man could get too much civilizing. He could get way too much of it. The whole trick was to balance the thing.

As far as Hudson was concerned his wife had proved herself to be quite suited to the task. At least she was wise enough to bite her tongue instead of asking him to sign a pledge card. She also lived under the comforting illusion that the boy, Tommy Delaney, had rooms at Mrs. Hennesy's boarding house in Barry's Bay. Hudson did not have the heart to disabuse her of the notion. The truth was that the little bastard was sleeping on a rucksack, midships on the *Mayflower*, up next to the boiler.

"You get them slabs on her!" he hollered.

The boy looked at him indecipherably.

"Put the slabs onboard, we're taking her up the Bay."

"The Bay?" echoed young Delaney.

"Up to Barry's Bay. You fill the box up. We'll burn a good patch coming back against that wind."

"Coming back?"

You could beat some of these youngsters with a stick, thought Hudson, and still be no better off than before.

"We're going up to get a dead man, and bring him back here, with passengers, too. Herman Brown's boy. Herman, Jr. You remember Herman Brown, Jr., the sportsman? You hear me?"

If the boy did, he did not indicate it. Hudson peered tiredly over the jagged tree line and saw the clouds come in, black as ravens, their bellies packed thick with snow. They'd get up there fast enough, with that wind behind her . . . but coming back. He knew from experience that by nightfall the wind would go down some. Typically the wind went down — except sometimes it did not go down. In which case he'd need that boiler steaming like hell just to get through the teeth of it. He did not fancy being in those Narrows with a wind, in mid-November, not on the *Mayflower*. It was a time when a man should be at home, having some drink.

Hudson glanced suspiciously over at the old clapboard paddle wheeler. She bucked slightly in her hawsers, and groaned. Nothing better than a shoebox really, especially when it came to navigating in wind. In his mind he had a vivid, sickening picture of them having to put off in pitching water at Parcher's Point, the *Mayflower* stove in on the rocks, and everyone standing in the cold wanting their money back. People just did not understand the complexities of being a steamboat magnate. That was half the problem right there. People did not understand. Tree cutters is all they were around here. Tree cutters and rock farmers.

Hudson stepped back and examined the stark, empty hall of his new hotel. In the process he anticipated a teacup full of whiskey proceeding down his throat in three professional gulps. Where the hell were those paying customers anymore? He wanted to know. Used to be, in the old place before the fire took it down, that the McLachlin crews and Booth's boys danced the floor to pieces, and then ordered up no end of ham and beans. In those days that kitchen stove was fired up all the time, and bad whiskey splashed into men's throats like water down Slate Falls. Every riverman's pocket bulged with a Chicago roll just waiting to be taken off him. Now there was only an Irish bastard boy and an empty dining room. It was on account of the train, he thought. It was because that damn train went west to St. Anthony's Mill, the company town at Whitney, taking the last sticks of Algonquin timber into Barry's Bay, and every other little hayseed sawmill village, like Killaloe. He remembered a day when the roads were black with timbermen, two hundred teams of men, like the Prussian army on manoeuvres; every livery stage, every wagon, every hotel room rented out, and every store open till ten o'clock at night. That whole road to Tramore *black* with horses taking men up the headwaters. Now look at it. It was the train, that goddam train.

John Hudson considered his own conflicted feelings about the train. After all, those fellows would not get to Killaloe in the first place if it weren't for the train. Furthermore, if they ran the line down to Combermere who would ever need the *Mayflower* to cargo corundum from the Craigmount mine down the York River to Bancroft? That damn train could have him ruined in a night. You could go to sleep a man of means, and when you woke up you were ruined.

Hudson put a brake on himself and tried to give it up to the Lord. "You are given too much to worrying," is what his wife said. "Let the Lord take care of it." Fine for her to say, being who she was. That was something else; him and her being married for nine years now. It was one thing for an Episcopal Methodist to marry up with a Wesleyan Methodist, or a Scotch Anglican to go out in a buggy with a German Baptist, but you marry up a devout Roman Catholic with a low church Protestant who had a taste for the poteen and it was a miracle you had any sort of marriage at all.

Hudson took a dose of encouragement from this. It was a miracle, and it sat like a trophy in a vault in which he kept the rest of his miracles. It was in these assembled miracles that he estimated his total worth as a man. They included a small share of stock certificates in the steamer *Oceanic Persia*, which struck an ice floe and sank off Labrador; two tracts of timbering rights on the Madawaska on ground that had not been cut since 1857; and his documentation amounting to thirty dollars yearly for representing Radcliffe township as reeve. Alongside that he counted the deeds to the same Hudson House he stood in now, built on the same old foundation as the one his father built twenty years back. His father had built the old hotel on a grant of freeland, only it burned to the stumps in the 1910 fire.

Hudson was fond of visualizing his entire worth as a man. He would need every penny of it, too, now that the squared pine market was shot to hell. He could forget about McLachlin's boys doing any dancing anymore. Men were out there cutting hemlocks now, hemlocks, no thicker than a stove pipe. Ten years ago who would have believed that men would be sent into the bush to cut hemlocks?

Hudson went nervously to the window, and glanced without purpose at the *Mayflower*. She lapped freely, up and down, in the pitch of the Madawaska River. Her black tin funnel gaped against the trees. Hudson shook his head. Men were leaving. Every day they were clearing out of here and heading up to Cochrane, Cobalt, Swastika, digging for gold and silver instead of timber.

"Tommy," he threw the front door open again. A heap of pine slabs, brown as tobacco stains, flowed up over the chopping block. "Take the barrow. You take the barrow and put them slabs on her. You get that boiler fired for four o'clock." The boy swung his head and went for the wheelbarrow.

I'll be helping him myself soon, thought Hudson, with my own bare hands. He felt the old familiar longing for a good whiskey, firing along the length of his throat. Behind him, across the floor, stood two dozen neatly arranged bottles of good drinking liquor on glass shelves. Evasively he packed his mind with sobering calculations; two hours up to the Bay, three hours back. He could see already the disapproving face of Will Boehme reflected in every one of the windowpanes of the pilothouse as he steamed up to Barry's Bay. Paddy wouldn't mind. Paddy'd have a slug himself, or maybe a dozen. So would that friend of his, Bill Murphy from Rockingham, the poet, a man who reportedly read the Hebrew Bible with the aid of a lexicon. You never knew if he'd signed up with Chapter 151 of the Temperance League, or gone into a black Fenian rage and was getting set to blockade himself with a bottle in the coal shed, hollering "No surrender" to imaginary agents of His Majesty's Government.

The Paddy O'Brien hotel and telephone exchange occupied a section back from his own, directly across the river on the west side of the Madawaska. Hudson stared at it and wondered enviously if the two of them were in there right now having a drink and getting that pretty Lipetskie girl to work the telephone. He imagined the whiskered face of Paddy O'Brien, a flaming pink colour, while he and Rockingham Bill Murphy sang the songs of the old country and tossed a green bottle of Irish back and forth. He felt a powerful urge to rush over there and sit down on the sofa chair, and sing those damn songs with them if he had to. One good-sized drink before the trip to keep that wind off. That's all he needed. Of course, he'd be wanting another one after that. That was the trick of the whole damn thing; that other one that came after the other one that came after the first one. No, this time he'd hold off. He'd savour it more for having exercised the discipline.

Under no circumstances did he want himself crashing the *Mayflower* into the wharf at Barry's Bay, while those farmers shook their heads. He was sick of goddam farmers shaking their heads in a way that came from conversing with cows and old-timers for their whole lives. No, he would not go into town with whiskey on his breath, it was not worth it. He would not have Mrs. Billings or anyone else *tsk tsking* at him. He'd be sober Jack Hudson, Jack this and Jack that, the way folks liked it. He would be the distinguished reeve of Radcliffe Township, proprietor of the Hudson House, owner and operator of the *Mayflower*, and the most popular man to pick a prize-winning pastry at the Craigmount picnic.

Hudson turned his back on the shelves of flirtatious liquor and escaped from the hotel. He would catch Aaron directly out in the field, away from that wife of his, and give him the news. For some reason the woman had gone cold on Hudson lately. Probably it was the matter of those twenty-seven dollars that had not worked out to Aaron's liking.

He stuffed his hands into the pockets of his trousers to keep the wind off, and began to walk. Aaron Parcher was his acting captain and pilot. As far as Hudson was concerned he'd take Aaron Parcher as pilot over any of the local men who went up the Nile to save Chinese Gordon. Of course it peeved him that he was quitting. Any day now he'd be taking his wife and family out west to Kirkland Lake. The man had got his hands on some big acreage out there, for a decent price, too. Hudson felt an inbred respect for any man who'd got his hands on a big acreage at a decent price. He was bitter, though, to be losing him.

The sun came out for a brief while from behind a press of grey sky, and lay down a path between the stumps. Off to the left the river curled like a snake through the estuary and the dark islands. Hudson did not appreciate the look of it. He did not care for water in any manifestation at all, and today in particular the cold seemed determined to leap out of it, like a partridge. The wind didn't help either. He hunched his shoulders up to keep a fresh blast off his neck, and lay his big feet forward on the earth.

The trail led down the point by the Parcher farm. Hudson walked, head bowed between the black branches of the choke cherries, stripped now, so they stuck out like darkened bones. Somehow he saw them stir, twenty-five paces ahead of him. He did not have good sight anymore, he was rather dim-eyed, like a wolf. But like a wolf, he had a fierce perspicacity for seeing things in motion, and when those bare branches started shivering, he stopped short at once.

In his chest came the thudding, familiar fear of being in close proximity to a bear. He was in no mood for a bear. He was in no mood for any entanglements with another bear, not with the *Mayflower* being put back in service for a final late season run, and paying customers already lining up for him at the Balmoral.

"Get away!" He hollered. His forty-seven-year-old voice carried the authoritative edge of a whiskey burr, and resonated with ten years of oratorical flourishes learned and perfected in the county seat at Pembroke. It was there, in the midst of acrimony, that he had cleared his throat on the issue of the water flues at Renfrew, and whether or not they should be improved upon. He had explicated cleanly and closed off with those memorable words, *"If you saw as many dead horses, dead cows, dead hogs, dead dogs, and dead deer floating about in that water as I have, you would feel squeamish about drinking from it, even through a damn filter."* Coming home on the train Tommy Prince called it the best goddam speech ever given in the Dominion, and that same year the Bonnechere waterworks went up at Renfrew. When it came to speechifying, there were those who held John Hudson to be a cut above.

He remained fixed in the usual, heart-ringing stance of someone about to have a set-to with a bear; legs locked, motionless in the frozen mud of a wagon rut. The branches clacked, trepidatiously. At that moment a body emerged from the low brush; a boy, a young lad wielding an antiquated .22 rifle, crouched over, peering from one side to the other in the trained manner of a professional marksman.

"Howard Parcher. You put down that gun."

The boy swivelled toward him but fortunately did not swing the rifle about with him. "Shoulder that damn musket," barked Hudson.

The boy clapped the rifle barrel clumsily to his left shoulder.

"Yes, sir. Sorry, Mr. Hudson." He stood erect, vaguely cadet-like in the cold, but could not contain a frightened, backward look to the bushes. The branches of the chokecherries wavered again, and out crawled Silas, Jr., armed with a pointed stick.

"Stand down."

The child bolted up next to his brother, and then held up, timidly, two bloodied ground squirrels looped together by the tails, like a scarlet handkerchief.

"We was huntin' squirls."

"I can see that." Hudson, in the main, did not approve of children. He had capitulated to one himself; Edward, age eight, but on the whole they were not much good, and they were prone to dying. Four years ago his friend, Charlie Hanrahan, the cooper, had gone to the doctor to see about one of his boys, then went across the road to the coffinmaker for another. When that was done he went back to the doctor, who told him it was the black diphtheria and he better cross the street again to have seven more coffins made to go with the one he had. Eight of nine Hanrahans killed by black diphtheria in less than five days, and now Charlie Hanrahan was a stick of man, waiting in the cold for the tavern to open. As far as Hudson was concerned there were enough things that could go wrong without that sort of thing happening. There were enough things for fretting over.

Nor did he approve of children banging about in the bush with a rifle, either.

"You might a shot somebody, other than that damn squirrel. How did you kill that thing, boy? With a stick?"

"No, sir, I shot him dead."

"It was a Prussian," said Silas.

"He thinks it was the Kaiser, sir."

Hudson spat. It was nothing but a poor little animal that, likely as not, was eating out of their own hands when they bashed its head in with a rock. Hudson was all for the killing of animals; he felt in his heart the stern moral obligation to do so, but still, he did not like to witness them lying there, with that look frozen on their faces, as if they had been caught doing something shameful.

"Either you put that thing in the dirt, or you feed it to the hawks, because it ain't no good to anyone anymore."

"Yes, sir, Mr. Hudson."

The younger boy, Silas, pushed his chin down glumly. He had whacked that fat old German Kaiser to death with a stick, and now he was not to be admired for it in any way.

Hudson pulled his coat tight around himself. Another slanting wind came in at him from the western depths of the lake.

"Where's Aaron? Up the smokehouse?"

The boys nodded.

"You tell him to get over to the wharf. We're taking the *Mayflower* up the Bay. Four o'clock now. Don't you forget. What time?"

"Four o'clock!" shouted the boys.

"You tell him one of Herman Brown's boys is lying in a coffin up in Barry's Bay and he's been shot to pieces. He's been kilt, you hear me? Now get!"

The boys swivelled together on a pin, and bolted.

"He's been kilt, you hear, kilt!"

Hudson turned face first into the wind, while the children fled home.

13

J OE HARPER, COMMERCIAL TRAVELLER FOR THE CONSOLIDated Rubber Company of Ottawa, sprang up from the lobby chair with a letter in his hand. *Dear Nellie*, it read, *I have given up on my plans to travel by train to Altmonte. I do not figure on it being profitable trying to sell shoes to hayseeds in Altmonte where they would just as soon go barefoot or otherwise swing through the trees like monkeys.* He did not see how Lord Tennyson himself could have phrased it much better than that. The letter was signed with love and affection, and if it got out on the eastbound train to Ottawa, his wife would have a good chance of reading it in bed tonight.

Harper marched into the lobby in search of Mrs. Billings, but she was not to be found. Impulsively, he threw open the swinging doors of the tap room and haughtily surveyed the smoking inferno of drunken timbermen. He was a tall, thin man, and from his height he saw men seated in chairs, men standing on tables, and men lying on the floor. Swirls of tobacco smoke circled upward as if from a battlefield. Some long-standing dispute was taking place about a young French Canadian's eye, and whether it sat pickled in a jar at Jack Schenly's tavern up at Brudenell. "Well I wouldn't say it was if it goddam wasn't would I?" snarled one of the men. Harper had the distinct sensation that the dispute could go on for some time.

Mrs. Billings was not in here either. He turned and went back into the lobby, tapping his three page missive into the smoothness of his palm. He took pride in the smoothness of his hands, the clipped cleanliness of his nails, without a specimen of dirt underneath. It was not unusual for him to shake two dozen hands a day.

I am very glad now that you persuaded me to take my heavy coat (she had presented him with a Hudson's Bay buffalo robe with a fox fur collar on the occasion of their first anniversary, a month ago) *for I have met up with Messrs. Peverly and Bothwell as well as John Imlach, the bachelor, who you thought handsome, though not so handsome as me. We are travelling by coach through to Combermere where I look forward to at least some sort of business. That steamboat the* Mayflower *that I told you about is now docked for the season at Combermere, so we are forced to take the stage. If you had not told me to bring my good coat, it is sure I would be frozen up on the ride.*

Obviously Mrs. Billings had vanished somewhere in the wooden labyrinths of the Balmoral Hotel, either up those stairs, or down into the bowels of the place to chip something out from the root cellar. Harper elected to step out and deliver the letter to the stationmaster himself.

Outside it was cold, an erratic snow came down, dissolving into shining sweat against the black skin of the Canadian Atlantic locomotive. The machine puffed on the tracks, weighted down by the stacked trunks of severed pines that towered from the carriages attached to it.

A distance off, on the hotel side of the landing, a coffin box lay on a wagon. It was a melancholy sight, and Harper lingered over it. A dead man in a pine box in the falling snow on a train siding at Barry's Bay, Ontario. What could be more wretched than that? A shiver ran down his back.

He turned and wiggled his fingers reassuringly around the envelope in his hand, which would soon be on its way to his very own wife. *I remain your loving husband.* He could almost see her in the Alden Apartments, in Ottawa, running a porcelain brush through her hair.

Harper shuddered at the blunt fact of being dead. He had been very close to it once in the Carp River in 1907 on a canoeing expedition. He was a twenty-three-year-old bachelor fishing for rainbow trout with a party of five. In truth they were drinking rye whiskey by the jug and finally the canoe went over. Harper, unable to swim, choked in the warm water, felt himself going dark with the onslaught of death. Eventually he was hauled out onto the pebbled shore where he saw the sky, white and mucous-like, as if he were seeing it through the eyes of a fish. That was five years ago. He was a married man now, a valued traveller for the Consolidated Rubber Company. He did not take a drop of rye whiskey unless he had to for business, or thirst dictated. He still could not swim a stroke.

Stepping inside the station, Harper gave the wizened clerk there his letter. The man turned without a word, shoved it into a wall of cubicles, then went back secretively to whatever other work he did. Joe Harper hustled back across the platform to the hotel, squeezing his shoulders against the cold. He gave one final look back at the coffin box, and saw, advancing from the livery, a man and boy leading a placid mare. The man's shoulders were bent with exhaustion; reddish hair flung out from beneath a foreign-looking hat. He looked a regular hayseed from somewhere far away, Harper thought. The boy quickly hitched the wagon to the rigging of the horse and stood there, waiting for a gratuity that came only awkwardly, after the man executed much patting and rooting about in his pockets.

Joe Harper sprang into the steaming dining room of the Balmoral Hotel, and scanned the place. There was nothing he did slowly. Each and every one of his motions was that of a machine, finely oiled and wound tight. It was the way the men of the Consolidated Rubber Company carried themselves, and it was the way of the world, too. It was clear that a man like Joe Harper had no time to waste on rubbernecking. Not these days, when life bolted on its way fast as electricity, and threatened to leave you behind, stuck in a rock like an old fossil.

The heat from the room buffeted his face. In the kitchen, the big stove — a Forest Beauty from the Imbleau Foundry in Renfrew, Harper had dealings with them — was stoked up and spread heat through the place like flowing lava. Sheets of warmth blew out from the kitchen. Carried in its wake was the Polish girl, then Mrs. Billings, both laden with plates. The entire room seemed in motion, like a clock opened up at the back. From across the lobby drifted the roar of a timber crew, fading and incoherent.

"Joseph Harper!" This confident bellow came from the mouth of a man named Gordon Peverly. He sat in the corner alongside Mr. John Imlach, the two of them collectively putting forth a great fog of tobacco smoke. Harper went there, scraped a chair up to the table, and sat down.

"You had better write Nellie another one a them billydoos," instructed Peverly. "We're going by steamboat after all."

Gordon Peverly — a smooth-faced, avuncular twenty-seven-year old — had about him the stature of someone older and overfed. In fact the man was an athlete of some renown, at least formerly, in the clubs of Ottawa and Montreal. He travelled now for the Corticelli Silk Co. of Ottawa, possessed an extensive understanding of ladies' corsetry, a wide-ranging expertise in silk ties in particular, and wore blossoming from his neck the most radiant cravat that Harper had ever seen. Privately he conducted a small, thriving trade in Dr. Morse India Root Pills, which he sold as a cure for coated tongue, constipation, biliousness, and torpid liver.

"I suppose Captain Hudson has got himself on the cure then?" This came from the extremely thin lips of John Imlach, a quiet, cynical man with an angular, wrinkled face that, inexplicably and to the chagrin of Gordon Peverly, was considered attractive by women. Imlach resided in a fine, high-ceilinged bachelor apartment on Thornton Street in Ottawa where he was prone to hosting parties that, in the recent past, had received some veiled criticism from the Moral Purity League. He travelled for the General Supply Co., and possessed a growing reputation as an extremely sophisticated man. He had lately sat with a young woman in the Palm Room of the Chateau Laurier who, calmly, in the continental manner, lit a cigarette and smoked it in plain view. The incident was written up the next day in the Ottawa papers under the banner "*Brazen Lady Lights Up.*" His ambition in life was to be rich. His best friend was Joseph Harper, who secretly envied him for having a monied family. Harper's own parents were both dead and buried in a decaying graveyard outside of Kilburn, east of Arnprior.

"Whether he is on the cure or no has nothing to do with it." Gordon Peverly cleared some room in front of him for Mrs. Billings, who arrived with two steaming plates of food that she slid expertly, like spinning tops, before them. The men eyed the mashed potatoes piled like snow banks, and the steaming meat.

"What is it you're having," she demanded, "ham or ham?"

"Well . . ." Harper drew pensively at his chin. "What is it you recommend?"

"Ham," said the woman. "I recommend ham."

"Give him the ham," suggested Imlach.

"The ham is not bad," intoned Gordon Peverly. "You can't go wrong with the ham."

"Perhaps I'll have the ham then," said Harper.

Mrs. Billings flew out under a wafting wave of heat from the kitchen. She wore a line of perspiration on her top lip, and considered it her personal duty never to crack a smile before those fellows. She wanted to make it clear that she did not have time to chew the rag with the likes of travelling men. She had a world to keep in order. An entire world. And it was coming apart at the seams.

"It's not the cure," resumed Gordon Peverly. "It's the price of a ticket. That's what's brought that boat out again."

There was a nod of general agreement. A trip on the *Mayflower* cost one dollar fifty each way, and even a child was charged fifty cents. Both these sums were acknowledged as a form of robbery. A full plate of Mrs. Billings's ham with all fixings came to exactly twenty-five cents. Given that, there seemed no other explanation except that John Hudson was a criminal. People said he owned a heart made of stone. How else could he rob a man of one dollar fifty to catch pneumonia pressed against a boiler while the wind came off the lake through the open hull, because he was too cheap to get doors put on her?

"It is not just us getting fleeced either." Gordon Peverly indicated the activity in the corner. A white-haired woman, propped up on two walking sticks, was having herself settled into a chair by the Polish girl. The matriarch gazed about the room in a queenly, but ill-focused manner, then settled slowly into stillness. "She's getting on, too."

"Looks like she needs propping up with some of those India Root Pills of yours," suggested John Imlach.

Peverly let the remark slide. "There's a dead man, too," he said calmly. "It's bad luck to sail with a dead man."

"That's right," Harper joined. "His coffin's out there in that box on the siding. It's out there getting snowed on right now."

John Imlach slid what looked to be a full portion of piping pink ham into his mouth and managed somehow to dispose of it with a minimum of chewing.

"Maybe he gets half price for being dead," he speculated.

"He'll be family of some sort, that dead man." Peverly lowered his voice. "They're all family of some sort around here." He fixed his attention on the snow bank of mashed potatoes that was receding quickly across his plate. "A Brown . . .," he managed between mouthfuls.

"The Boulter Browns?" Harper had sold a shipment of wading boots to E. W. Brown of Boulter not more than a year ago.

A full mouth prevented Peverly from responding right away. Finally his dabbed his bottom lip with a linen napkin, and shook his head.

"Palmer Rapids. The Schutt Browns, I believe. From the hills. Shot dead on some sort of hunting expedition out West. That is what the good lady told me. Isn't that right, dear?"

At that very moment Mrs. Billings reappeared out of the smoking mists of the kitchen and deposited Harper's plate down in front of him.

"You save your breath for cooling your porridge," she advised, and retreated back into the kitchen where an arrangement of pots and pans clashed like a full orchestra.

"So we're putting off with a dead man and an old cripple woman," said Harper, before tucking into his ham.

It was then that Scotty Bothwell entered, carrying a sample case and a loose sack. The sample case contained various sets of flatware cutlery imported from Sheffield, England. The sack contained a dozen beets. He steamed straight toward his three friends in the corner, and let the case drop with a clank on the pine floor.

"Gentlemen." He put his hand affectionately on Peverly's shoulder, and revealed an ostentatious garnet on his ring finger. He was best man at Peverly's wedding, a twenty-seven-year-old unmarried commercial traveller with big ears and sorrowful eyes. Instead of sitting, he advanced straight into the steaming cauldron of the kitchen with his sack of beetroot.

"You know what he's doing," said Peverly, shaking his head. "He's in there bribing Mrs. Billings with a dozen beetroots."

No one seemed particularly scandalized by this, and the three men resumed their assault on dinner.

The thick chatter of customers resounded through the room. Lips moved; the etched, silver faces of mostly men and some women floated all around, as if lifted up on the steaming vapours of the food they were eating: *"What they done is they brought in a good grist of bawbees for the buyin' of books, see?"* The words emanated from the moist mouth of a man who looked to be a hundred years old. He wore an eye patch to conceal some old injury and was now positioned over a cup of tea. *"Only they give up the readin' room on account of the craze for athletics. The young people have the craze, see?"*

Joe Harper caught these fragments of words, and looked up to investigate. He saw a man he took to be a quarryman by trade, and a Methodist by religion. The other he could not make out; he would be a timber fellow of some kind. Both of them looked old enough to be stinking drunk at the Ballyghiblen Riots. Harper wondered if it was true what they said about the water. He had heard it said by a half dozen different people that the water at Killaloe Station kept you alive for over one hundred years easy.

He re-focused on the meal in front of him, his arms pistoning up and down like a machine designed for eating food. It was a machine operating harmoniously in the dining room of the Balmoral Hotel, and it seemed likely to Joe Harper that himself, Peverly, Imlach, and Bothwell were the best parts of it, at least the best greased and smoothest working. It was a pleasant sensation, of being exactly where he should be, at exactly the right time. It still kindled in him when Bothwell returned from the kitchen, dispossessed of his beetroot.

Scotty Bothwell pulled up a chair and sat down next to Imlach, who nodded and went back to his food, which was all but cleared away except for a small bale of cabbage.

The talking did not resume until Gordon Peverly pushed his plate away, and started up a lament for the old days, "the good old days," he called them, when he'd hawked dog coats and buffalo robes to rivermen up the Bonnechere.

"Did I ever tell you the time I sold my first walking plow?" he asked of no one in particular.

"You did," Imlach said promptly.

"You did," agreed Bothwell.

"My first mower?"

"You told that, too."

"What about my first binder?"

"You told about the binder."

"How about the down comforters?"

"You told that."

"The fancy flannelettes?"

"You told about the flannelettes, the cream separator, the haying rakes, the cashmere hose, and all forms of sundry implements," said Joe Harper. Having put Peverly in his place, he gazed contentedly about the room. On the walls he saw the faded floral print of the wallpaper. In front of one wall stood a hutch made of maple. The cups and saucers inside it had not been brought out in living memory. It was presumed that Mrs. Billings kept them safe in there for when Royalty showed — and ordered ham. The tables were broad and coarse, like groaning boards, rimmed with rough people claiming room for themselves with their elbows. Across the room someone had spread the pages of the *Renfrew Mercury* in front of him, to demonstrate the likelihood that he knew how to read. Harper made out the dark columns of ink, the stern, moustached face of a military fellow staring out at him, calling him to his duty. WHERE THE CATS GO, began a scarifying piece at the top of the page: *Domestic Ontario cat skins sold extensively in London Market.* He would not tell Nellie about that one, he thought. She wouldn't appreciate the idea of her cat being wrapped around the neck of a British girl, or any other cat either. She was soft for cats.

Harper saw that a big broad fellow about the same age as him now occupied the doorway. He recognized the blue navy coat, the round, black hat circling nervously in a set of enormous hands. The hat had been worn for so long that a depressed shadow had established itself in a band around the man's hair. It was the same fellow he'd seen outside in charge of the coffin box. Harper felt a surge of discomfort for him. The man gave off the distinct sense that he'd hauled his cargo a very great distance, all by himself like an ox, overland, from the West. He stood forlornly and somewhat abashed in the doorway of the Billings's place, as if preparing at any moment to be snubbed in the Chateau Laurier by a black-vested *maître d'hôtel*, who was speaking fluent French at him. Harper wished he'd step inside, quickly, and sit down.

"Someone better plant that hayseed before he gets blown off the field." John Imlach nodded at the fellow, and inserted a sliver of wood between his teeth.

"That Brown fellow you mentioned?" Harper leaned in to his companions, and spoke lowly. "That's the farmer who brought him here. He's the fellow looking after the coffin outside. A sod buster, I bet. He's a genuine sod buster."

Scotty Bothwell, settled firmly in his chair now, flexed his shoulders, and kept appraised of the conversation around him only marginally. He was just six years out from Aberdeen, Scotland, and had already established himself in eastern Canada as a champion and trophy-winning swimmer. He surveyed the ham-eating clientele of the Balmoral Hotel and saw that it included a farm dealer with Massey-Harris. Bothwell secretly acknowledged him as the Grand Master of the First Grand Lodge of the Pembroke Masonic Temple. He then realized he was enormously hungry.

"I'm favouring the ham," he offered gravely.

"The ham is good," said Gordon Peverly.

"You can't go wrong with the ham." John Imlach had acquired a pedigree in the rolling of wood slivers between his teeth. Privately, he believed it made him blend in among the local people. He now had it spinning like one of Booth's rivermen rolling logs on a spring run.

The three men peered over at Joe Harper, expecting him to conclude this old, practised jocularity with a remark of his own. But instead Harper was watching the stranger as he stepped nervously into the heat of Mrs. Billings's dining room. Almost immediately the Polish girl jostled him as she dashed by loaded down with a kitchen-full of dirty plates. The stranger nodded to excuse himself and sat down at an empty table. Relieved for the man, Joe Harper returned his attention to his companions.

"If I were you," he said, "I'd go with the ham."

14

If there was a moon it was eclipsed by a grey sheen of clouds, strung like laundry across the village. Nothing seeped through its layers but the noise of two ravens, set up in different pine trees and loudly hectoring at each other. Beneath them four commercial travellers emerged from the front entrance of the Balmoral Hotel. They exhibited no degree of intoxication beyond an evident fondness for the lyrics of the old country and a careful lolling gait as they negotiated the frozen, mud-wracked road. The warbling notes of "Green Mountain Smilin' Anne" were heard once more on the pitch-black streets of Barry's Bay.

Gordon Peverly led the way as he typically did, followed closely by Scotty Bothwell. They were trailed a distance off by the tall figure of Joe Harper and then John Imlach, who casually lifted the red coal of an incessant cigarette to his lips. All four of them toted the heavy black cases of their trade. They did not trust to hand them over to the help at the livery, or to anyone else on earth.

The men tramped down the line like four schoolboys up to no good. The only items missing were a few calico kerchiefs with bread and jelly inside them, and four bamboo fishing poles. Each of them was excited by the age-old thrill of boats, of leaving the solid world behind and floating like ducks on a great pond. Not far off, in the dark regions of the bay, they heard the repeated low shrills of a steam whistle, a low haunting blast, deeper than a train's; the distinct and mournful signature of John Hudson's paddle steamer, the *Mayflower*. "You could set your watch to that whistle," people said. "Of course, your watch'd be wrong."

Gordon Peverly cut forcibly into the cold night. He regretted now not secreting on his person a half flask of Hudson's Bay Co. whiskey to tug on while he sat up next to the glowing boiler. He imagined that boiler squatting in the belly of an old boat, like a cozy hearth. He was getting older, that was the reason. Suddenly he was panicked by the almost visible notion of a creeping sobriety, squirming across the country from one Temperance Hall to another, and which had now attached itself to his own leg, like a slug. An unmarried and younger Gordon Peverly would have had a flask, for sure.

Bothwell who *had* secreted a half flask on his person, walked happily enough, a step behind, singing, *sotto voce*, songs to the dead men drowned in the Bonnechere, and the Petawawa, and the hundred other rivers that drained into the Ottawa; *Turn out brave boys with hearts devoid of fear.*

Joe Harper had in mind a peculiar arrangement of his wife's hair, claimed by certain magazines to be fashionable, although he could not imagine any arrangement of a young woman's hair that was not entirely fashionable. From the hair he descended to a brown mole the size of his baby finger located beneath his wife's right shoulder blade.

John Imlach was not married, and possessed no interest at all in the old timber songs. Instead, he thought about being rich, how he would parlay his way behind one of the dark mahogany desks of the General Supply Company, mounted by an enormous telephone, cased in ivory.

The four men panted up the bluff to Stafford Street, using the lamp in the sawmill office as a beacon. Muffled behind a clapboard enclosure came the endless drone of the saws. The office itself overlooked the embankment before the lake. A single kerosene lamp lit the interior and showed the silhouette of a man behind the windows, staring at the far, piney woods. It seemed the fellow was intent on staying there until every one of those trees was gone. The drone of saws faded, became suddenly louder, faded again, and the sweet smell of fresh-hewed timber drifted through the air, like perfume.

Two hundred yards away, supported by the cold water of Lake Kaminiskeg, the *Mayflower* banged her way forward. A wreath of golden light streamed from the cabin, casting a fiery zigzagging path in front of her. Out of the dark a dog barked at an unseen intruder.

Coming up behind the men, and pressed regally among the cushions of a buggy operated by the Vankoughnet Brothers Livery & Stage, was Mrs. McWhirter, kept warm, if not completely crushed, by a buffalo robe. She was making it abundantly clear to the young drayman sitting beside her that she preferred land to water and the train best of all. After all, Ethel Prince had sent her daughter, who was seven, mind, only seven, straight from Madawaska to Killaloe Station all by herself to buy the stores. Just a girl, seven years old, and for ten cents, she went forty miles to do that. Of course she was told plain: you get off at the third stop. Not the second one. That second stop is Wilno, and you do not get off there but you wait for the third stop — Killaloe. Mr. MacDonald was the conductor, so you had no worry on that account. Mind you Ethel Prince's girls — you never had to worry with them anyway. They were sensible. You could not find six more sensible girls than what Ethel had brought up. Not like today, she said. Not like the brats they were sprouting up today.

A distance behind her, bringing up the rear of the procession, a flat, four-wheeled wagon pounded the frozen road. An old Belgian mare, who made a dull clopping noise as she walked, tugged it forward. She had pulled that same wagon or one just like it for thirty years, and moved now with a tired, practiced gait, as though sleepwalking.

On the back of the wagon lay the coffin box slicked with a stain of melted snow. Inside it, Herman Brown rested stiff against the gouged road, his arms crossed and palms lying flat, where J. W. Christie had last placed them. He lay beneath an airtight lid that Mr. J. W. himself had constructed at some extra cost. It now proved moderately effective in keeping out the cold November night of eastern Ontario.

Though you would not know it to look at him, Herman Brown had never cared much about appearances. But now, his moustache was clipped neatly above the lip, and his hair parted on the left. He wore his finest store-bought clothes and over top of them a blue waistcoat cut by his uncle, William Boehme of Combermere. Five days ago his life had ended — the longest rest from labour he'd ever known, and he celebrated it in the only means left to him, by lying stone still on his back as the wagon clattered on the hard earth.

Herman Brown's rewards were to be few; several square feet of Madawaska valley earth that still needed to be dug up for him. This meant that old Billy Wapous might have to drag himself out from the timber shed and soak the earth with coal oil, set it on fire and soften it up for digging. It was November 12, though, and Billy might just as soon decide to stash his body in the charnel house, stacked there with the rest of them for the winter.

The dead man was almost there now, a short boat ride remained, then a few miles by wagon to the alpine hills of Schutt, Ontario, where the hawks circled, behind the Baptist church looking out across the hills at the same homestead he was born in. That was where he was headed, at last, where he belonged, among the berries that grew in summer; raspberries, blueberries, blackberries both high- and low-bush, and later the red, translucent choke cherries, raked off the branches by the handful, wrapped in cheesecloth by his sisters and drained two days for making jam.

Finally he was going home. He was going home to the hills, and the valleys that lay ankle deep in pine loam. He was about to travel once more across the yielding surface of Lake Kaminiskeg where he'd taken the trout with nothing more than a piece of red cloth attached to a hook. He was returning to the Conroy Marsh where he'd brought down mallards with Leonard Marquardt, in season and out, fished pickerel, pike, and black bass, where he'd come upon bears, and had seen wolves poisoned — their frozen carcasses stood upright in the deep snow by surveyors who had themselves photographed standing next to them, fearless, brazen as hell.

He was coming back to the sacred land of his birth and his memory, to the valleys in which he'd seen the last white-pine timber raft drifting down into oblivion and history. This was where he'd shot deer, tamed foxes, poured maple syrup into emptied eggshells and nestled them in the snow to set. Here he had piled stones year after year into long fences begun by his father before him; stones that were brought to the surface by the clash of lightning. Each year there was lightning and each year the rocks heaved out the earth and lay white upon it like gnarled, granite teeth knocked out by a mighty punch from an assailant.

Herman Brown rested in a woollen suit with a silk handkerchief protruding from his breast pocket. His eyes were closed tight and did not show how the right one was more piercing than the left. He had the Brown forehead, wide, high, with a lot of room for thinking. Too much room, some said. But they did not say that to his face. He had endured the great engine of the Grand Trunk Northern as it clattered out of Oba, Ontario, toward Gogama, and further to Capreol. These places had no meaning to him, and did not link anyone to anything. He was born in a Schutt farmhouse, close by Palmer Rapids, a short hitch from Combermere, three hours by steamer from Barry's Bay, providing the steamer was not sunk or run aground on a shoal. *Oba, Gogama, Capreol.* These towns were unknown to him, like the capitals of Europe, and had he known them he would have felt only contempt.

All the events and circumstances of his life were locked inside him now with no possibility ever again to get told. They would not expand into grandiose adventures over a bottle of whiskey at the Balmoral Hotel. They would never again contract into curt monosyllables uttered like swear words while felling trees in the winter bush. They were closed up inside him, and would never get out. With each mile, with each span of railway track, and every revolution of the wagon's wheel, he was disappearing into the blank forgetfulness of time. The countless, stray memories of his life, packed so tight in him, were gone. They vanished like those pigeons his papa had witnessed, blacking the sky for eight hours at a time; dark storm clouds made of pigeons, eclipsing the sun. A man threw a stick into the air and dozens came down dead — good-eating birds, more plentiful than flies. That's how thick a man's memories got; so thick he could not hold them in his own head anymore, and it became necessary to bore a hole above his eye and let them fly away, like pigeons. They were all gone now, a fellow out in Penetanguishene saw the last of them ten years ago.

Herman Brown rattled on the back of a wagon with the cold night sky frowning down on him. He had lived his short life among people who knew the proper way to do things; how to extract bear fat and make axle grease out of it, how to use raspberry leaves to cure the mysterious ailments of women. He had stood alongside his mother and gathered the tall, yellowing mullein stalks that she boiled and strained for the curing of earaches. He drank tea and turpentine for the alleviation of a chest cold, and even though he had not got into a moving picture house, nor ridden in an automobile, nor seen the skyline of the city from the platform at Union Station, he *had* eaten fried black bass with new potatoes, green beans, and low-bush blackberries covered with muscovado sugar, which was as fine a meal as any man had a right to eat, especially when folks were said to have starved around these places. In the bush near Dacre, leaning on a snakeboard fence, staring at a line of dark trees, and starving. He had milked Jerseys and hauled lake trout from under the ice, and he had hunted with the contentedness of a hunter who brings home fresh meat to a family of thirteen.

Of course, he had also gone into the bush and become a timberman. He'd slept in a camboose with fifty-one other snoring and farting men and ate pork and beans seasoned with wood ash, and sea pie on Sunday. He had done that, but best of all he had knelt in a field of raspberries at twilight while Rebecca Chiles had undressed herself from the waist up, for no other reason than to be seen naked by him.

Then finally he took the Grand Trunk Pacific for three days to Yorkton, Saskatchewan, and found that things were hard there, too. He farmed, and when he wasn't farming, he worked for a millionaire named Levi Beck. He played billiards in the Balmoral Hotel. He hunted prairie chickens. He drank some.

Now he rested. He remained fixed to the land. All that remained was for the passing bell to din against the sky, while his tired body was folded into the earth.

The wagon on which Herman Brown rested was not so much being directed anywhere as it was moving on instinct alone. Robert Pachal, walking alongside the horse, no longer pretended to be in charge. He had already tied the reins in a loose knot to shorten them, so as not to tangle up in the animal's forelegs. On the drayman's seat was flung his battered luggage box; he wanted to walk instead. He preferred the solid earth under his feet now, for he was dull with fatigue. Even the prospect of getting on a boat seemed a matter of course to him, as though it were something he did every day. He'd rattled across a country on three different trains, and should a man in uniform step out from behind a tree to explain to him he was now to board a dirigible, he would have climbed into that, too, without paying any regard.

He plodded on, flushed, almost stupefied, by the onslaught of food that had packed itself into his body: ham, beets, waxy rutabagas, and a great heap of potatoes, mashed up and crowned with butter. The ham he had relished a great deal, too. There was nothing he appreciated more than a thick slice of ham, and the one he had just eaten was done up the proper way, put in the dripping pan fat-side up, and seasoned with a handful of timothy hay. It was a good size too, for twenty-five cents. You could not complain for that amount of money, given the size of the portion.

The wind was still cutting into the darkness, and the cold had mounted somewhat. Nonetheless Pachal was glad to be out of that crowded dining room with all that shaking and rolling as each new timber train clamoured into town. In his mind he could still hear the baleful crying of the blind piggers going on across the way in the tap room; in particular a tired, drunken voice that pressed to the ceiling and stayed there as though it had no intention of ever ceasing. He had sat by himself in the corner across from a small, ancient woman collapsed in a gathering of linen folds, her two walking sticks resting against the chair. He tried forcibly to sear that dining room into his memory for it was only the second time in his life that he had ever eaten in one; the smells of a hundred meals cooked every night for thirty years wafting from the faded wallpaper. The wallpaper itself bubbled up in places, as if the ancient odours of food had packed themselves in behind. He remembered the raucous laughter of women working side by side in the kitchen.

It seemed to Pachal, now that he had the solid earth under his feet, that they'd all been decent people, easterners or not. Even those four commercial travellers gathered at one table with their sample cases stacked around them. Decent enough men. Pachal was flushed with a sudden goodwill. It was based on being tired and well fed. In truth, he was giddy with exhaustion. Fatigue coursed through him like syrup, lolling him closer to the soft underworld of sleep. He fought an urge to shout out loud to the sky, "I am Robert

Pachal of Yorkton, Saskatchewan, uncle by marriage to William Boehme of Combermere, husband of Elizabeth Anne Brown of Schutt, Raglan County." Or was it that other place, Renfrew County? He said nothing of course, only whistled in the dark, to prove to himself that he was actually there, and to entice the northern lights from the dark places they slept in.

Pachal closed his eyes and saw the endless journey meld into one enormous spar of anthracite. He was working quite actively on the composition of a letter, piecing it together slowly in his head, laying out each word as if building a fence. *"Dear Elizabeth Anne, I have spoken already by the telephone to your uncle William. The food is the tastiest, and I consider myself lucky to arrive on a day when ham is getting served. You know how I like it, and it is cooked in your way, too, although this one has been rolled in crackers and not bread crumbs."* It occurred to him that the current issue of the Yorkton Enterprise was off the press and already circulating through the townships back home. His name was in it. His wife could be reading it this very moment. The thought of his own name preserved in ink caused Pachal to intensify his letter writing intentions. He had never written a letter to Elizabeth Anne before, and was not writing one now. But he was practicing for it. He'd get on that tomorrow morning, first thing, from the house she was born in. *"Dear Elizabeth Anne, I am writing to you from the same room that you were born in —"*

The dark pressed against the treetops and vaguely alarmed him. Absently he checked his pockets as if he had forgotten something; the lock of his daughter's hair braided into a flower by that Métis woman at the fairground. No, he had that, he intended to present it to his wife's mother when he got there. It was something else. Pachal cast about in his mind for any other task he might have failed to perform. He had come a million miles from home and there was nothing about him that showed his achievements except the size of his portmanteau, which he did not have. Just a tattered box of a suitcase. He was a simple man; he assumed simplicity was the same as goodness. How could it not be? He felt a sudden, naive urge to share that goodness out here among strangers. He had brought one of them back home, after all. He had done his best.

Pachal was interrupted by two shocking whistles that blew out from the steamboat, closing on the wharf down the road. He slowed as the horse did, mounting the crest at Stafford Street, and saw a thick smudge of smoke merging into the dark. The boat was box-like and inelegant, a black silhouette a hundred yards from the shore yet.

Pachal stopped for a moment and cast a look behind him. Out of the darkness of the land a few lamps glowed from windows, carrying the warmth of bedsheets, of children dressed in flannel. From the village lights he saw the dark line of sawn boards stacked ten feet high, and curling off like an enormous wall. "That is a mighty big pile of boards they got there," he said out loud, and headed down the hill.

15

THE STEAMBOAT CAME IN HARD WITH A NORTH WIND pushing on her side.

"Let her out! You slake that boiler now," John Hudson hollered throatily down the hatch. Young Tommy Delaney sweated from the forehead and armpits, shut the canopy tight, and let the steam escape — screaming in two high whistles up the pipe. It was a sound that never failed to shock him. He felt the power of being a grown man reverberate through his skinny arms.

"Hard now!" Hudson bobbed like a mother hen between the pilot house and the lower deck, grabbing to the crude ladder that ran below, and pummelling himself up and down a few rungs. With each frantic manoeuvre he stood, head poking through the hatch, positioned at the heel of Aaron Parcher's boot. Aaron commanded the view from the pilot house, a square wooden box mounted on the front of the boat. From there he saw the federal wharf at Barry's Bay coming up fast, too fast. They were being buffeted forward by the wind.

Beneath him, he saw his boss's black beaver hat sticking fussily through the hatch; he considered briefly the virtues of kicking him in the head. It was not the Christian way of doing things, but it was sorely tempting. He knew instinctively, with the wharf end already blocked by the screw steamer, the *Ruby*, he'd have to throw a curve on the wheel and bring her in tight to avoid a knock-up. That was tricky enough without John Hudson climbing up and down the hatch, shouting blasphemies at Tommy, and scaring the daylights out of the one paying customer they had on board. The man, his name was either Leach, or Peach, the pilot couldn't remember, crouched on a box by the boiler and kept his eyes grimly on William Boehme, who sat impassive before a game of forty-five going on between John Murphy and Paddy O'Brien. Those fellows were used to this sort of thing. Spades were trump, and O'Brien, in less than three hours, had managed to get up six pennies.

A good kick to John Hudson's head would have brought Aaron Parcher a great deal of satisfaction, but it wouldn't help him avoid slamming into the *Ruby*. For that he needed the intervention of God Almighty, or at least Dougal Gates, the *Ruby* captain who at that moment providentially heaved a stout timber over the stern and played the *Mayflower* like a billiard ball. Parcher felt the hull ricochet by the moored boat, and then crack coldly against the dock, sending a loud rifle shot through the night. John Hudson was not going to like that. The idea satisfied him in some malicious way.

"Jesus Christ Almighty!" roared Hudson who was prone to take it personally every time his boat slammed the dock at Barry's Bay. It seemed he only had to nudge the thing and people presumed him to be on a proper drunken rip, when in fact, on this night at least, he was flagrantly sober. In his mind it was the height of injustice to be slandered as a drunk, without the benefits of having drunk anything. "Tommy! You banged up that damn wharf!" Hudson shouted down into the gloom of the boiler area, then leapt from the opening amidships onto the wharf, and started wrapping the hemp line to the stanchions.

Aaron Parcher ran a coat sleeve across his face and chopped a salute to the captain of the *Ruby*. Aaron was a short man with a smooth face. His moustache and eyebrows showed a distinctly fainter colour than his hair, most of which was covered up by what he considered to be an extremely dashing hat. He climbed down out of the pilot house and started to throw off the hawsers. The paying passenger came up — Leach, or Peach — struggling with a black valise that he flung out on the dock with a mighty groan.

"Hudson, that is the worst ride I ever been on. You are leakin' amidships. You got no goddam doors on her. You got a boy stokin' her. You got a pig farmer at the helm. And you have the gall to charge one dollar and a half. One dollar and a half? For what? So that a man can have the privilege of drowning?"

Hudson feigned deafness and gave off the cool appearance of a man who did not give a damn about anything. His hands kept working on a knot.

"Maybe you would prefer that *Titanic* there?" he said evenly, doubling up two half hitches into something he assumed was a proper marine knot.

"I ain't no pig farmer," shouted down Aaron Parcher. "I'm a wheat and dairy man." He lit a pipe. "Besides, if that *Titanic* had some farmers running her she might be on top the water instead of at the bottom, where she is now."

But Leach-or-Peach would have none of it. "I have rid this boat before and this is it. You are not such a big man as you think, Hudson. I don't care what you're the reeve of, I can write a good letter, you understand? And I will, too. You'll not see me on this boat again."

The aggrieved fellow tugged at his valise, which he managed to swing up from the wharf. It gave off the loud and unmistakable clink of bottles.

"What you got in there," hollered Hudson. "Sandwiches?"

Leach-or-Peach wrapped two hands on the grip. "It's lucky for you I'm catching a train shortly, or I would disabuse you of a few of your ideas. I do not like your attitude!" He glanced up at Aaron Parcher. "Yours either." Then he lilted off down the wharf with his vast luggage tilting him to the side like a one-legged man. "One dollar fifty," he shouted back into the wind.

Hudson battled an urge to get up and fling the man into Lake Kaminiskeg. It seemed there was no shortage of porridge in need of cooling these days, not with so many little men blowing off their fat mouths in some other place where it was not needed. He returned, grumbling, to his knots.

Aaron Parcher stepped to the wharf. He looked up, hoping to see stars, but all he saw was the hard, dark canopy of night. Sometimes in November the stars cascaded like water over pitch black rocks, but tonight he would not see any stars — just an indiscriminate mist swirling under a night, dark as creosote. The sky would not open tonight.

He watched his boss tying off the last remaining knot. For the first time he saw the crooks of age beginning to disfigure the man, the rifts of worry and consternation had suddenly combined with passing years to rearrange his shoulders and his long back. Hudson stood up suddenly.

"Well then?"

"Well," Parcher fired back. He was sharp-eyed and from where he stood he saw the passengers starting to come down the bluff by the lumber offices.

"I guess we should do it." Hudson was not so much asking Parcher as much as he was telling him, daring his pilot to say different. Aaron Parcher knew the answer as well as him.

"We will not get her through with that lifeboat on," he said. "Not tonight. Not through the Narrows."

"Not in the wind," said Hudson.

"No. Not in the wind."

Hudson furled his top lip around the corner of the bottom one. The lifeboat was an old pointer. Typically it trailed out to the stern of the *Mayflower* on a ten-foot length of rope. She'd run timbermen up the headwaters for twelve years, held fifteen people, and drew only six inches of water fully loaded, but she weighed close on a half ton, and with her dragging in the wind he'd never get his boat through the Narrows.

"Tommy!"

The youngster emerged from the side of the *Mayflower*, where he'd gone in to get warm and successfully insinuate a cigarette off Paddy O'Brien. "Tommy, take that pointer off and lash her to the wharf." Tommy Delaney walked obediently halfway down the wharf, slid the knot off quickly, and began to line the old pointer back to shore.

"I suppose it's against regulations."

Parcher looked over to see if Hudson was making a joke at him. But there was no indication of it. It was then he understood that John Hudson was on his way to being an old man; he had moved over a threshold right there in front of his eyes. A moment had passed and he was now moved over onto the other side of being young. It happened right there on the sagging federal wharf. Parcher wondered if it would happen the same way to him.

"I suppose it is." He spoke curtly. He did not possess any great respect for John Hudson. As far as he was concerned the man still owed him twenty-seven dollars for pushing three barges of corundum down river to Havergal, which he had done as requested. It was only because in five days, Aaron, with his family in tow, would be gone up north to Kirkland Lake for good, that he was able to tolerate the man so easily. It felt as if half of himself was up there already, and that allowed him to look down on John Hudson with some sort of amused detachment. He was a cheap, worried fellow who saved his only good words for voting day, and Aaron was glad to be putting some distance between them. But in fairness, he knew they would not get the *Mayflower* through with that pointer dragging at her, that was a fact.

Tommy Delaney tied the pointer off and came shuffling back. The wind was up, the air had the stiff smell of snow in it, unfallen yet, sewed like seed in the clouds, and waiting there to bloom.

The two remained standing together; Hudson towered above the younger man, but Aaron, the stronger one, was built like a barrel, and took up a stout column of space. Where he stood the planking of the wharf sagged under him.

They waited in that position for the passengers who came forward, hitting the dock like a platoon of soldiers. A voice boomed across the pell-mell clatter of feet.

"Captain Hudson? John Hudson?" A strong hand snaked through the dark, looking to be shaken. "Scotty Bothwell. F. S. Castle Co., Ottawa. You know Imlach here, Harper." An entourage of thick hands crossed in a klatch of hand shaking. The young pilot was intimidated by all the socializing, and just nodded shyly.

"Parcher," he kept saying, "Aaron Parcher."

"Gordon Peverly. Corticelli Silk Co. Drapes, ties, bedding, ladies' corsetry. My pleasure, mister."

"He has not been onboard before," informed Joe Harper.

Peverly let his sample case down gently on the dock. "How are the accommodations, first class?"

"Things are the same as what they were," Hudson uttered profoundly.

"He wants his own milk jug for sitting on," warned Harper.

The pilot laughed. He was about the same age as Joe Harper, but Harper's moustache was scrubbed off, his face hairless in the prescribed city fashion for young men. Harper's appraisal of the pilot confirmed that he possessed eyes the colour of cold lake water, and looked to be a competent man. His downfall was the collapsed straw boater of a hat that gave him the distinct flavour of a country bumpkin.

Gordon Peverly marched decisively down the wharf, scissored his legs over the board that blocked the bottom half of the doorway, and plunged head first into the hold of the *Mayflower*. He found himself in the dark, smelling the thick fumes of coal oil, tar, pipe tobacco, and something else, unpleasant, that he could not discern. A lantern hung from a nail. Beams of yellow light leaked across the walls and deck.

It took several moments for Peverly's eyes to re-size themselves to the gloom, and when they did he saw he was standing in the guts of what looked like a dilapidated tool shed: bolts of iron littered the floor and binder twine snaked everywhere, like a growth of thistle. As far as he could tell the boat was a complete disappointment — nothing but a frame box flipped over on a flat pine deck. A doorless opening split the boat on each side. One window boasted glass, the others had nothing to boast about. In the very back jutted the grotesque machinery of a Fitzgibbon boiler. It looked unfathomable and vaguely mediaeval, more like a device for torturing people than powering up a paddle wheel.

It was here that Gordon Peverly saw three men, frozen in a painting, rendered in the Italian style, or at least *Italianate*. It was a word his wife had pilfered from some fancy magazine or another and was suddenly fond of using. It seemed the sun could not go down without it looking *Italianate*. Peverly saw that two of the men sat motionless, peering trepidatiously at a hand of cards. The one fellow standing, swivelled his head and appraised him, calmly.

"Robert Pachal?"

The card playing ceased a moment.

"Not me, mister. Gordon Peverly. Corticelli Silk — "

The players turned resolutely back to the game, leaving Peverly with the odd sensation that he did not exist. He heard a scraping from behind the boiler. A youngster stood in the rear, crimson with sweat, as he shovelled slabs into the open mouth of the firebox.

Peverly nodded and opened up bluffly to him. "What sort of ship you got here, son?"

The boy looked at him in a squinting manner, as if deciding whether he was friend or foe. Finally he blurted, "She's a sternwheeler, that's what. Seventy-seven foot long. She's fifteen foot at the beam." Beam was a nautical term that he had learned from Mr. Hudson, and he was constantly on the lookout to use it.

Peverly was suitably impressed. He fired up a cigarette

and gave one to the boy, who was positively waiting for such an occurrence.

"Yes, sir," he rested his shovel on a bulwark. "That is a mighty good cigarette." He seemed to be expert on what was and wasn't a good cigarette, and blew on the coal in a very professional manner. "I was on her when she went down last year." He paused for another puff and was made even more loquacious by it. "We rammed a sandbank," he said proudly.

After several more deep and meaningful inhalations, the youngster walked Peverly through a labyrinth of pipes to the paddle wheel at the open stern of the boat. A heap of fragrant pine slabs lay there. "She takes a mighty pile a fuel, that's what I do see, every six minutes, load her up with them pine slabs. I'm the fireman. That's what I am."

He led Peverly over a thick, snaky device laying on deck making a sucking, gasping noise like a shored fish. "That's the siphon. You don't want no water in that hull when she's got a load. Twenty-six tons. Twenty-six tons fully loaded. A course she's empty now. We had twelve tons a corundum crystals in her last month, right here for the rail yard. But now she's empty see? But for that dead fellow who's coming." The boy hitched his trousers in a studied way. "Herman Brown is the dead fellow, that's who. The sportsman. He's from down the way." He actually made a gesture with his thumb, signifying to Peverly exactly where "down the way" was situated. "I'm the fireman. But when Aaron there takes his family to Kirkland Lake — first we're going huntin', me and Aaron. Then he's heading up. Once he done that I could end up being pilot, just like Aaron." He showed the proud, uplifted face of a fifteen-year-old unwanted Home Child from Cork County, Ireland, who was about to become, at least in his own mind, the acting pilot of a Canadian steamboat.

At that moment John Hudson stuck his head through a glassless window. "William . . . your charge is here."

Two hands of cards slapped face down on a butter barrel. Peverly watched the men rise up as one and clamber out the side of the boat.

The first horse pulled up clattering on the old wharf and pawed with one hoof at the boards. Hudson and his pilot moved to the sides of the buggy, attempting to assist the old woman over the side.

"Hold her," shouted Hudson. But Aaron did not know if he meant the horse or the old woman. Finally, one of the commercial travellers stepped forward and put two steadying hands on the bridle.

"Don't you go dropping me." The woman threw back the buffalo robe in an irritated fashion. She did not approve of getting fussed over like this, and allowed herself only reluctantly to be lifted over the side. "My travelling bag, you have forgot my travelling bag," she groused.

"No, we've got that, don't you worry. Tommy! Tommy! Where's —" Hudson bit into his tongue. He would not go on cursing like a timberman while he was holding an old woman two feet in the air.

"I suppose I can paddle my own canoe. I suppose I've paddled it enough places, haven't I?" She spoke these words defiantly into the face of Aaron Parcher who held her up at the other side.

"You have, ma'am," said Aaron. He turned as Hudson did, and the two men carried her carefully along the wharf. Mrs. McWhirter's legs dangled down weightlessly. She had a sour look on her face, but otherwise she appeared entirely comfortable, as if being carried about by two men was her usual means of getting places.

Gordon Peverly emerged from the boat in time to pull off his hat.

"Evenin', ma'am," he said, bowed stiffly, theatrically, and stepped aside.

"Don't let them forget my bag," she shouted at him, her voice muffled in the enclosure of the boat as the men swung her inside.

On the flattened turf before the wharf Robert Pachal finished shaking hands with his uncle-in-law. He saw that William Boehme possessed a modified version of his wife's angular face, was a grave, skinny man who looked like a youngster, though he was on to sixty years old, and wore a short-brimmed hat jammed to an extremely studious forehead. A moustache brushed his bottom lip, his eyes were dark, his brows were as thick as beards and did not so much arch as jut straight across his skull.

"This is Patrick O'Brien here. You had words on the telephone machine this afternoon." The man named Patrick O'Brien stepped forward showing a pink, mottled face and a mane of silver hair in full retreat from his head. A pair of round spectacles, thicker than the sole of a man's boot, festooned from his face and his body seemed to be locked together at all the wrong places.

"My name is Paddy. You call me Paddy. You'll be staying at my hotel tonight. We'll look after you, Tilly and me." The man was stopped short by a violent cough, spat raspingly into the lake, then added, "This here is Bill Murphy."

Pachal took up the hand of the man named Murphy. He felt it slouch from him, as if shyness ran in the man's blood. Bill Murphy nodded, and gave a step back. He was an indeterminate man of forty-five, with long grey sideboards. His chest stuck out thick and round. "I am sorry for your troubles," he said. Pachal was not entirely sure, at first, what the stranger meant, but he nodded appreciatively.

"We'll take him up front, where the horses go," said William Boehme quietly. He made it a habit to speak softly, even softer in the presence of the dead. It seemed to Pachal that it was the sort of voice that men listened to, the sort of voice he wanted to take back with him to the West. The quiet man, the one named Murphy, went to the rear of the wagon to give a hand. Paddy O'Brien excused himself on account of his back being a useless sack of bones.

"I snapped it fellin' trees," he explained, ruefully.

Pachal moved to the back of the box as well. He was grateful finally to have something to do, some simple instructions to respond to. He had a part to play now in a family that was somehow his own, even though it existed out here among trees and lakes.

"You show me what to do," he pleaded, bracing against the coffin box. He felt the grain of the pine boards pressing against his beard. Up close the steamboat knocked softly on the wharf.

The pilot came up and made the fourth. There were no slats or handles for grabbing on so it was necessary to slide the box off sideways, first onto the shoulders of William Boehme and the pilot. The two see-sawed it for a moment, which allowed Murphy and Pachal to get a grip underneath.

"Steady . . . Steady!" Paddy O'Brien took up the point position and led the way. The box tottered a moment like an empty throne.

"Steady boys." O'Brien uttered his instructions with a flourish. Despite the advanced and well-known feeble condition of his eyes, he waved the procession forward with the full confidence of a trained scout. "On to there," he said, and pointed out the flat, open bow of the *Mayflower*. The deck was bare but for a heap of crusted horse dung, a rake, a pitchfork with three tines missing, and the brace of a hardwood bumper.

"How are we?" William Boehme reached blindly with his foot.

"Fine, fine. Slide her." There was some tricky manoeuvring so as not to drop the thing, then it was done. The pine box lay flat on the bow of the *Mayflower*. A cold wind shivered across the water.

"Let's get him home," instructed William Boehme. Pachal saw that his uncle-in-law did not appear such a young man any more, but more like a willow leaf with the living matter dried out of it. A tired man, helping with a task, wanting it to be over. He looked like a man in need of sleep.

Up in the pilot house Captain Hudson peered down nervously and stabbed another hand-rolled cigarette between his lips.

16

John Hudson let go a lungful of tobacco smoke and watched it billow cloudily up the windows of the pilot house. His mind had wandered deep into the nature, and cost, of illuminating marine lights, like the one the *Ruby* had on her. His heart was set on one of those chrome-plated carbide lamps, but he doomfully prophesied that it would arrive in pieces up from Chicago or another damn place, and cost a fortune whether it was broken or not.

For now, as the boat thumped from the harbour of Barry's Bay, he would have to make do with the light spilling out from the lamps of Murray's sawmill office. He found it vaguely irritating that someone stood in that office, right now, counting money, which is what he presumed was going on. Counting money. That's all anyone did anymore. There were not enough tall pines left to make a decent tent peg, but somehow fellows were still hunched over in offices, counting money. More than ever, in fact, fellows were hunched over in offices, counting money.

Along the south shore, lamplight spilled from a few scattered houses and threw gold, shimmying spikes across the water. The village of Barry's Bay glowed behind them like a dying fire. He would be counting on those occasional lamps to act as beacons until Blackfish Bay, at which point the lights got blown out, and nothing was left but a few farmhouses with miles of vacant black between them. At that point Aaron would be running her straight down a tube of darkness with only the shushing of pine boughs to tell him where the shore was.

"Running lights," Hudson postulated. That's what she needed. A good pair of running lights for when the stars went black on him.

Next to him, the pilot kept his large hands loose on the wheel and swung the boat closer to the black, invisible presence of Mask Island. He concentrated on a series of dark forms as they merged and gave way to other dark forms. For the most part he was content to pay no attention to John Hudson. His attention was situated on four hundred and twenty acres of farm and bushlot in a far northern place called Kirkland Lake. Somewhere, in a *Dominion School Reader*, Aaron Parcher had come across the remarkable fact that the whole of England could be fitted into the Great Lakes. He took a personal pride in this fact and now imagined those four hundred and twenty acres of his to be a great lake made of soil, into which various countries were getting fitted. First he put Switzerland in. Switzerland fit pretty well. Then Italy. And France. Maybe not France. The exact dimensions of France eluded him. Scotland, though. You could put Scotland in there and have room left over. The pilot let Scotland drop like a clump of sod into his new property, and was pleased to see there was still room left over to section off to his boys.

"Running lights is what she needs," repeated Hudson.

Aaron Parcher was a devoted eater of carrots, both stewed and raw. It followed an old maxim of his father's, *"You never seen no rabbit wearing spectacles have you? Eat your damn carrots."* Aaron did, and as a consequence prided himself on possessing the eyes of a nighthawk. It seemed to him if you looked close enough out there, it was possible to see the horizontal black of water merge in a seam, like pastry, with the ragged shore. Also, if you listened carefully you heard the swishing of wind on tree boughs, except if the wind got way up, and then you couldn't hear a thing.

"Why's that?" he asked finally, about the running lights.

"For goddam seeing. That's why," Hudson spat vigorously at a squashed tobacco tin and peered up close through the glass to demonstrate the crux of his argument. The panes had not been cast properly and made a man feel liquored up just looking through them. Below him stretched the familiar section of cabin roof, and beneath that the flat bow of the boat where the horse teams usually went. It was empty now except for the pine coffin-box placed on it, like a compass needle pointing through the dark. He tried to remember what that dead fellow in there looked like; one of big John Brown's boys, which meant he would have the big Brown forehead, and would shoot you dead in the woods on suspicion of being a partridge. Herman Brown. It was Herman Brown who'd cracked that bear on the nose with an axe handle the morning it tried to make off with the Waddel's little girl. Or was that Chester Brown? Hudson did not remember, and did not care. They made young men soft now, that was the problem. Not like before, not like Big Joe Mufferaw who lived up the Ottawa, or even old Jake Dennison who died off the tip of Lake Opeongo after going hand to hand with a bear. Eighty years old and he went hand-to-hand with that damn bear right up to the last.

John Hudson's lean body bristled in the piercing cold of the pilot house, and he clucked disapprovingly at the encroaching flabbiness of young men. There'd be a war any minute and then what? They'd be sending out office boys to fight proper soldiers. He regarded young men in much the same way he regarded finding a hair in his butter. They all grew toad-like in city offices, making gossip on the telephone, that was the problem.

"The world is going to shit," he said finally.

Aaron Parcher was a farmer for the most part, and did not share his boss's worldly outlook on things. He looked over at him, expecting a rant, but did not get one. Instead, Hudson grabbed toothily on to a chunk of his lower lip and began to chew on it.

Running lights were a botheration, and they would be considerably more of one once Aaron took off on him and went up north. He'd not get a better pilot than Aaron Parcher. Not for that money. Not for any money. He would not get a man who was as steady and who'd work as cheap, either. Even to find a fellow who could see as good as him in the dark would be a challenge. Hudson did not doubt that the man must eat a peck of stewed and raw carrots just to keep his vision up; it was sharp as a nighthawk's. His own vision was more instinctive than anything. He looked out and saw the black water of Kaminiskeg slap over the bow and roll erratically to the coffin box. A rim of suds, like beer, foamed up stickily before getting obliterated by the wave behind it.

The vessel steamed past Mask Island, clattering against the water in a rhythmic two-beat; the ancient muffled song of a Fitzgibbon boiler as it churned a paddle wheel. Hudson watched a lone, blazing window drift behind him on shore, replaced by a black canopy up front. He had thumped that steamer up there for nine years now and there was nothing different about this run except the lateness in the year, the cold, and maybe the darkness. Despite assuring himself this way, a furrow remained dug into his forehead deep enough to plant seeds in. Hudson spat out a half inch of cigarette before converting over to a pipe.

"How is it?"

The pilot nodded.

Hudson nodded back. Fourteen years on steamboats all told, and tonight, for some reason, he felt the queasy distaste of being on water, on cold water, more than he ever did. Should have had that drink, he told himself. There was a bottle hidden beneath a plank behind the boiler. There was another bottle hidden beneath a rope stuffed into a butter barrel up front, and, if he remembered correctly, there was another bottle hidden in the — Hudson resolutely put the notion out of his mind. He was not about to let the absence of few drinks ruin a good seven dollar and fifty cent run. He had allowed that western fellow to ride free, since it was him who was bringing big Herman's son back. The queasiness still squatted on his insides, though. It plagued him like original sin, coming out of the dark to wrap itself around his chest the way that bear had done to Raymond Taskerton when he came home drunk down the Opeongo Line.

"I got no Certificate of Registry," he confessed. "I got no Certificate of British Registry either." Hudson nodded abjectly to his own smeared reflection on the glass, satisfied he had taken the first step toward absolution or at least forgiveness. But it was only a half step and he knew it. He was also without a qualified mate, did not have a proper acting captain, his inspection certificate was two years expired and lay folded somewhere, probably in a tobacco tin. He carried no water pails or fire appliances, did not own a license to carry passengers, and had sworn biblically into the eyes of Mike Davis, Inspector of Hulls, not to carry passengers. There was also the matter of having left the lifeboat attached to the federal wharf at Barry's Bay.

"You put that pointer on her and she's not getting through the Narrows," Hudson reiterated.

"Yep," Aaron Parcher said. His mind was fixed elsewhere, mostly on oats and barley. Barley first. That's how he would lay out those new acres, seed them with barley the first year.

Hudson waved his head gloomily. "They'll send some Ot-terwa fellow down, you watch. He won't know his horsefly from a deerfly, and he'll want a certificate of goddam who knows what." The Captain put his bottom lip into his mouth again and let it fall right back out. "We chop the place out from the bush while those flies come down on us, we haul out rocks, shoot the damn bears, and they send down a city boy wanting a piece a paper in goddam triplicate." The triplicate part of the business infected his craw the most. "It snowed yet?"

"It ain't snowed yet but it's coming." Aaron gave out this information as though pleased by the prospect of it. All prospects were pleasing to him now. Four hundred and twenty acres did that to a man. Especially if they were out of range of Captain John Hudson and the irritating issue of those twenty-seven dollars still owed to him. "It's starting to blow some," he added. This, too, appeared to be another unforeseen complexity he would have to unravel for the man, for no charge either.

"Well, that's why I left the damn boat back there, ain't it?"

"I guess that's why."

"You are damn right that's why. That's exactly the reason why I done it." Hudson splayed his long fingers on the ledge and then shoved them back in his pockets. It was cold. Even if you scooped the wind off the night it was still cold. He stared unpleased into the thick dark and rehearsed the pouring out of a glass of Goodman's. The sturdy, stiff neck of a green bottle fitted into his hand like a useful tool; he heard the glug of liquor washing out the bottle like a trout stream, and splashing around in a piece of crystal. He saw no particular reason why tonight should not be a night for bringing down the good crystal, a seven dollar and fifty cent, out-of-season, final-run night. He'd have a few satisfactory mouthfuls of Goodman's — four, or perhaps three hundred — and in the morning put the *Mayflower* back up for the winter. After that, he'd concentrate on getting customers back into the hotel the way it should be. Maybe he'd even sell off a tract of timbering rights. Of course, there were his political obligations also. It was clear to John Hudson that the world was going down into a great puddle of shit, and that he, as the democratically elected reeve of Radcliffe Township — actually he'd won by acclamation after Ruddy Rakosky chopped his foot off with a broad axe — still, it was clear he had to do something. At least to stand up as a bulwark against the future. For there was something awful coming down the pipe, he knew that for sure.

The man stood cold and lanky in the pilot house

watching the toes of his left boot push the loose washers on the planks beneath him. The lake was a frenzied chopping surface, and the paddle wheel thrummed hard against it. She made a different sound now that he had shortened the buckets on the paddle. The theory was that being shorter they wouldn't grind themselves to a stop on a sandbank, like last year. Of course it meant they didn't get as much purchase on the water either. Hudson was not a true mariner; he did not understand the brutal, unpredictable physics of water. But he knew the wheel spun faster now and that's why the boat sounded different. A higher pitched noise, more like a whine. He did not give a damn what it sounded like providing it was not stuck on a sandbank. He was still indignant at the memory of his *Mayflower* stuck like a piece of meat within sight of that road that never had a soul on it except for when his boat ran aground. Of course, at that point, it got immediately filled with farmers who stood with hay stuck between their jaws, shaking their heads like they'd spent their whole lives in the marine academy. It had turned into a scandal with those ladies on board, too, and Hudson burned under the memory of ferrying everyone over in the pointer and refunding fares in the hot sun.

She had not sounded the same since those buckets got shortened; a high, faster thunking noise as a result of the engine cranking harder. Made sense, thought Hudson. He looked up from the pile of rusted washers beneath his boot.

"Maybe I'll go on down below," he speculated. He was hopeful Murphy or O'Brien would have a jar open; he'd go down and sneak a necessary jiggerful. His resolve, which had stood up in front of him as solid as the rock at Tatty Hill, had faded like the song of a bird after a gun goes off in the forest. His own face looked back at him from the window-panes, squirrel-like and fearful. No. He would not do it. He would not sneak a jiggerful. There was more pleasure in waiting for it.

Steeled in his new resolve, Hudson smacked his pipe on the window-ledge and sent down a smudge of burning ash to the floorboards.

17

Mrs. McWhirter sat as close up as she could to the old boiler without catching herself on fire. It was an enduring, sodden cold, like it was before the big snow in sixty-nine when the roofs caved in. She sat cushioned by five Purity Flour sacks, folded over and positioned on top of a milk jug. Behind her, heat wafted out from a pot-bellied stove in dire need of blacking.

The dark and dirt of the old boat pressed gloomily from the corners, revealing to her how desperately a woman was needed about the place. Lamp chimneys gleamed black as fry pans, and had clearly given up all earthly hope of ever getting polished again. What light came out fell nearby, casting some soft fleshiness on the faces of the passengers, and illuminating a short circle of decking at their feet. Everything else remained dark and mysterious, as if the night sky itself had crowded into the boat, too. All she saw out there were the secret things of men stashed away in the dark and hidden for good. Various articles of metal lay at her feet: busted pulleys, threaded pipes, chain links, rope, the broken teeth of a harrow still stuffed with dried clover. A coil of binder twine snaked treacherously about, size seven, she figured. She knew her gauges pretty well. Above her head a few dozen lifebelts bulged down from a grid of strapping. Up front, it fell dark again, and everywhere clung the sweet odours of coal oil and anthracite.

The woman contemplated her feet. Currently, they were wrapped up in thick black boots and hung beneath her like oven mitts. The feet were good, it was the legs that had gone rotten. They barely scraped the floor enough to make a tapping on the deckboards.

"I am against the playing of cards for money," she announced, her voice was unequivocal, her round face bobbed slightly as though she found herself in constant agreement with everything.

Paddy O'Brien shifted his large, fused back to the woman and put a spade down on Murphy's nine.

"I am against that too, ma'am. Against all forms of gambling."

The act of O'Brien turning his back on the cards and eclipsing them from her view was apparently enough for the woman, for she beamed with all the enthusiasm of a Salvation Army worker who has just shed light into the perfidious backrooms of a Bytown tavern.

Despite the cold, the boiler and the pot-bellied stove behind her kept up a good heat. Mrs. McWhirter felt herself soggy with warmth. Just like tea in a teapot with the cozy on, she thought. It was not such a bad situation being on a boat after all. Of course, it was a pigsty of a boat, and she preferred the train. She preferred to be fastened down hard on land, with no chance of drifting off with every wind. Clean too, that's what a train was; that Arnprior express had a flushing water closet on it. It also had that young McDonald lad who wore a blue serge uniform with buttons down the middle. She had an eye for young men, fellows with a drop of shadow between the shoulder blades.

The old woman wobbled her head about the hold and

appraised the four commercial travellers. They were trim-looking fellows, and dressed in store-boughts, but they were hairless to a man. She could not make out even the trace of a whisker on their faces, which glowed in front of her like the chapped skins of naked babies. She knew about naked babies for she had given birth to nine of them; two had lived. She had also caught several dozen more midwifing up in the hills of Renfrew Country.

"What has become of your faces?" she shouted.

Paddy O'Brien, who nursed a secret, precious vanity about his silver hair in particular, looked back alarmed. A stout sixty-two year old, he suffered from the nagging fear that his good looks might drop away at any moment, leaving his face to give out on him suddenly. He glanced across his shoulder and realized with some relief that his face was not the object of scrutiny.

Gordon Peverly, who had recently disobliged himself of a burgeoning moustache on account of his wife, opened his hands enthusiastically to the heat from the boiler. All of his attentions were shifted to the old woman.

"Madam. You have cottoned on to a fact. You'd think with faces like these boys have, they'd be growing out their beards as fast as possible." He reached for Scotty Bothwell's chin, and tweaked it. "You take Mister Bothwell here. Well, of course, no amount of beard is going to fix a face like this. This is just plain beyond hope of fixing." Apparently Peverly's theatrics were wasted on the woman, for she continued to glare at them suspiciously. Peverly in particular.

"You got no hair!" she insisted. "None a you do. You all got your boughten clothes, but have no hair on your faces!"

The four commercial travellers sat glumly on pine boards and were silenced by the charge made against them. Gordon Peverly, who seemed to consider himself excluded from the indictment, shook his head morosely at his companions. Obviously they had let him down in a shameful manner. Harper and Imlach hunched guiltily over their cigarettes on the far side of the boiler.

"The truth is they do it for the ladies," started Peverly.

"The whole procedure is for the attracting of females. These boys have studied all the science of it up and down." Peverly braked himself and gave a nod across the way, daring his companions to state otherwise. There were no immediate takers.

"I been a few places, now," warned Mrs. McWhirter. "I been up to Renfrew for the nursing."

"I'm telling you the truth, ma'am." Peverly was now thoroughly warm to the task and opened and shut his hands to demonstrate that no falsehoods were hidden in them. "These girls today, city girls. I'm talking about city girls now; they want men looking the same way they do. They peek in the mirror there, and they see those pretty faces they've got," Peverly gave a fair rendering of what he thought a pretty girl looked like when she looked at herself in a mirror. "They want men looking the same way they do, see? It's a quirk they've picked up from Paris-France."

"Hah! Paris-France." Mrs. McWhirter emitted the contemptuous snort of Upper Canada. It was a sound that followed immediately upon mention of fancy cooking, poodle dogs, votes for women, and Paris-France. Even the card players, and William Boehme, protected in the dark by their mute, straightforward masculinity, turned their bearded faces to have a look. The mere mention of such a place as Paris-France elicited the eternal and disconcerting image of fops and fornicators, weird foods that were not fit for eating, and a language spoken so fast it was somehow unhygienic. It was a term that rang with the guaranteed stupidity of all strangers, foreigners, and things that were not Canadian.

"You take Joe Harper here, ma'am, recently married. A fine, big-hearted woman she is, too. She said to him 'Mr. Harper, you are a sorry enough specimen without looking like a walrus on top of everything else.' So he has not let a smudge of beard dark his face. Isn't that right?" Harper could only allow his head to hang down in shame before the facts. "And John Imlach, over there, ma'am. He can shave himself so close, it ain't safe for him to leave the house. He won't step out the door without a stick for fending off the ladies who chase him about. The poor man can hardly stay a bachelor. Isn't that right, John?"

"I do my best," uttered John Imlach.

The woman had followed this patter with growing suspicion.

"There are women about who do not know their Shorter Catechism," she threatened.

This likelihood hung somberly in the hold of the *Mayflower*. The four commercials made various rueful gestures of their faces to acknowledge the growing state of rot that now infested the Dominion.

Paddy O'Brien and William Murphy sat away from this and fixed familiar looks at one another, unified by the worthlessness of city people. William Boehme delivered a smile at young Robert Pachal, and thereby included him in the solidarity of blood, the safety of farmers, and the brotherhood of all men who work with their hands.

Gordon Peverly had not finished yet. "I'm afraid it gets worse than that, ma'am," he resumed gravely. "There are women in the city who now smoke cigarettes in plain view!"

Mrs. McWhirter would only allow herself to be taken so far. "Oh, go on," she came back, contemptuously.

"No, ma'am. I'm afraid it's the truth. It's in all the newspapers. City girls, puffing away. Mister Imlach knows all about it, isn't that right sir?"

John Imlach leaned back on the rough walls of the *Mayflower* and tossed the remains of his cigarette out the open side. He was a private and uncommunicative man, but did not object to being held up as an authority on the habits of good-looking society girls.

"They are lighting up in the Palm Room of the Chateau Laurier, plain as day." There was an irrefutable, even biblical finality in this pronouncement, followed by a grievous nod. It appeared that Imlach had made a brave, single-handed effort to stop the phenomenon, but had unfortunately failed.

"Well, good Lord. Those girls ought to be given a licking."

Mrs. McWhirter shook her head. "It's the city does that to them." She sat limp-legged, struck dumb by the ruination of womankind. She did not understand things anymore. It used to be a fellow unwrapped his fiddle from a sack of Purity flour and you danced to it, in winter usually. You did butchering in late fall, in spring you stone-boated rocks from the field, and otherwise you milked, you cooked, and most of all you paddled your own canoe. Those were the commandments a woman lived by; it pained her to find matters would be left in such a mess once she was gone. It was because of the city, and the battering that the flesh took there. All it ever did was ruin a woman. And once the women were ruined who'd be left to look after the men? They'd all be drunk as pigs in no time.

Mrs. McWhirter sat in the heat pelting from the boiler and felt herself drift off under the folded snow of many years ago when the world had not gone spinning so crazily.

The beating of the paddle-wheel droned into the boards and set up a dull, rhythmic knocking. An hour of it had rendered Scotty Bothwell almost insensate. He felt the engine throb under him, even through him, and experienced a sudden cold premonition of loneliness. For some reason it took the shape of a fine crystal goblet on a table. The goblet was empty and the table had no one sitting around it. Bothwell stood up and stretched. He was thinking like an orphan again and determined not to. He called up the faces of living relatives on the other side of the ocean, and grinned at his best friend, Gordon Peverly, who was practically pressed against him.

The man took three steps to the side door of the boat and rested his palms on the board. It looked to him as though it was inserted there for the sole reason of stopping people like himself from tumbling out the side. He was struck by the crazy fancy that the *Mayflower* was not a steamboat at all, but an airship — with one wrong step he could tumble down forever through the dark. That dark, he saw, came down like a stage curtain, straight to the water that cupped up grey waves in the wind. It would snow soon, he thought. Within the hour.

"I suppose it will snow soon enough," said a voice. It was the voice of Robert Pachal, a stranger, a man from the West who farmed wheat and Holsteins, who was on a boat in the darkness of another world, and wanted very much to talk with confidence about what he knew. He wanted to talk, period, to prove he could do it. He wanted to include himself in the intimate and universal comfort of talking about the weather.

Scotty Bothwell turned to face him. He saw a man peering outside in an intrigued manner as though there were something to see, and he was determined to see it. Bothwell introduced himself, and noticed that a mess of stains had distributed themselves fairly evenly about the man's coat. Their hands met, guardedly, in a manner that demonstrated that Bothwell was a member of a masonic lodge, and that Pachal wasn't.

"Pachal," answered the man. "I've farmlands in Saskatchewan."

"Well, me, I started out selling Hunyadi Janos Water to cure constipation. But am middling high up in selected groceries for F. S. Castle Company. You are a wheat farmer?"

Pachal nodded.

"I've sold some oats around here. The seed, I mean."

Pachal nodded again. They were shifting on to familiar ground now. He felt his confidence growing. "Victory Oats," he offered. "Victory Oats is very good oats. The stem is soft and good for cattle feed. The crop may lodge on you, but it's there."

"What's it bring?"

"Seventy-seven cents is the best I've ever done."

"I guess what you need then is a good little European war to bring you up to one dollar a bushel?"

Robert Pachal looked out stammeringly at the night, and flushed uncomfortably. One dollar a bushel is precisely what Neibrandt had said the price would get to when the war started.

"It's coming," said Bothwell, "the war, I mean." He peered out into the sky, as if armies were already massing there in the night. "He is a relative, that fellow out there?" He indicated the bow of the boat. "You brought him a long way?"

"Yorkton, Saskatchewan. My wife's brother. He had a misfire of his hunting rifle."

Scotty Bothwell thrust up his bottom lip in an ambivalent manner.

"Well," he offered consolingly, "I grew up owning a .22 bore and it's a wonder to me that I managed not to shoot my own brains out." He wanted to go on, but there seemed nothing more to say about it so he fell silent.

Pachal reached in his pocket for his pipe and squeezed in a wedge of pouch tobacco. He dragged a match against a beam, but the winds swirled in and sucked it away. This was signal enough to the two men and they picked their way back to the others who were still gathered about the heat from the firebox.

There the young fireman stood in his glory, heaving in enormous shovelfuls of wood slabs. Periodically he rubbed hard at a swath of soot running down the side of his face; the effort did not so much remove the mark as relocate it.

"Every six minutes, or eight," he shouted, "depending on how high the wind is up." He did not see how people got their money's worth unless he explained the finer details of shovelling slabs into a firebox.

Gordon Peverly sat in the warmth, but he was bored now. He was easily bored. The absence of talk had become stifling to him and he was eager to get it back going. He saw Bothwell approaching and ambushed him.

"Mi-ster Bothwell," he exclaimed.

"Mi-ster Peverly."

The two men fell into the easy, swapping banter that came of numerous long days fuming bad cigars on slow trains. George Bothwell got the show started.

"Tell me, Mister Peverly, how are things proceeding at Spot-Cash and Company?"

Peverly leapt in loudly. "Now, Mister Bothwell, it is a funny thing you should ask me that."

"Is it?"

"It is. You see I'm no longer travelling for that particular company."

Bothwell was scandalized. "You're not?"

"No sir, I'm not."

"And why not?"

"Why not?"

"That's right. Why not?"

"Well, you might say we had a disagreement."

"Disagreement?"

"That's right. We had a disagreement. You might say that."

"I said that," said Bothwell.

"I know you did," said Peverly. "I heard you say it."

Mrs. McWhirter bobbed unrestrainedly. Even though she was prone to a sporadic and indiscriminate deafness, she still enjoyed the entertainments. All efforts at humourosity met with her approval, and she sat as content as she had been when Master Jack, the Child Dancer and Bird Warbler, clapped his feet at the church hall in Palmer Rapids and whistled the exact, erratic song of the bobolink.

Robert Pachal leaned against a beam and grinned in spite of himself. He wondered if there was something in the water out this way. You drank the water and before you knew it you could not shut up.

"What sort of disagreement?" demanded Bothwell.

"Well, sir, it was some little disagreement about my worth to the company."

"Your worth?"

"Yessir. To the company. You see, I told them I was worth twenty thousand dollars a year to that company — "

"Twenty thousand?"

"That's right, twenty thousand!"

William Boehme and Paddy O'Brien disengaged their faculties from the cards and leaned forward, away from the chunking clatter of the paddle-wheel. They sensed the familiar acceleration that takes place before the delivering up of a good one, and would not have it drowned out by the noise of any machine. Tommy Delaney held a shovelful of pine slabs in mid air, transfixed. Only Bill Murphy of Rockingham stayed aloof. He'd attended the premier performance of *Floradora* at O'Riley's Opera House and Temperance Hall up at Renfrew in 1909 and considered it beneath his dignity to show interest in a travelling rube show being put on by a band of commercial fellows.

"So what happened?" Bothwell had reached the stage of positive exasperation.

"That's what I'm getting to. I'm getting to that part. I said to them, 'Sirs, I am worth twenty thousand dollars to this company — '"

"Yes?"

"And they said to me — "

"Yes?"

"They said to me . . ." Peverly milked the moment.

"Yes?"

"They said to me I was not worth *twenty cents!*"

Paddy O'Brien led off with a satisfied *guhhah*. William Boehme brought his hands down, approvingly. Mrs. McWhirter cackled like a schoolteacher performing the witches in *Macbeth*. Tommy Delaney shouted, "Hoe-lee," and bounced the shovel blade off the deck. "Twenty thousand, hoe-lee, yes sir! Twenty thousand." He looked around at the passengers with a contented boyish face, as though he had personally thought the entire thing up himself.

Robert Pachal began a sage-like chuckle into the back of his hand. He was fearful of emitting an hysterical laughter that had somehow co-mingled with his fatigue and was wanting to burst out of him. He tried to etch everything onto the shifting blackboard of his memory. He wanted to get this all down, for his wife, for his daughter, for what he vaguely thought of as the future, and for the fifty-eight other relatives who had strewn themselves up and down Saskatchewan. He would take every detail of it back home to them, like a gift from some exotic place.

The boat erupted into such a festive outbreak that even Bill Murphy moved his face in a way he presumed was amiable. He had just put down a six to make forty-five, and consented inwardly to a type of theosophistic and universal harmony among all living things.

Joe Harper stretched his long legs, and spied the red-haired fellow, the sod buster, striking yet another futile match against the ribs of the boat, and bringing it to a pipe, where it flared and vanished for good in the wind.

"Here, let me do that for you," offered Harper. He couldn't resist, and groped about in his vest pocket where he kept the mechanism; a Northern Ready Automatic Cigar and Pipe Lighter. He had been in possession of two of the astonishing devices, one sold for eighty-five cents to a disbelieving one-armed man in Dacre, the other he now raised up, having already struck the flint stone, so an inch of flame sprang up as though flaring from his own flesh.

Robert Pachal stared wide-eyed at the flaming tongue.

Harper opened his palm quickly. He meant only to impress the fellow, not to bamboozle him.

"The Northern Ready, is what it's called. Can be carried in your vest pocket. The world's first automatic cigar and pipe lighter." Harper brought the instrument within inches of Pachal's face, poised it between thumb and forefinger. "That's fuel, there, coal oil, it's coal oil they use." He drew his finger obligingly down the length of the tube. "Flint-wheel for sparking the wick. Got to keep it dry though, it's no good to you if the wick is wet."

"No . . .," Pachal sounded unsure. "It's a lamp then?"

"Well, it's a lamp in miniature. It operates on the same principle, though." The two of them fell into the instant fraternity that descends on men when they discuss mechanical devices, and especially the principles of their operation.

Bill Murphy stared up the boat, and made out the ladder that went up top to the pilot house. He felt a sudden inclination to be home, to be curled up with a pamphlet containing Gray's *Elegy*, which he was attempting to memorize. His thoughts were of his sister, who had died twenty-seven years ago of influenza at the age of seventeen. She was his twin and Murphy had chosen the inscription on her headstone: *Be Ye Also Ready.* For twenty-seven years Murphy had been ready. Each time a raven flew over his head he was ready. The man folded his arms across his knees, and waited patiently for the cards to be dealt to him.

At an angle, away from him, Mrs. McWhirter had set up an agitated moving of her head. She was ready for the next entertainments and tapped her boots on the deckboards, as if threatening to dance.

William Boehme sat erect on a crate, twirling the hairs of his moustache without knowing it. His fingers throbbed, even though his palms sweated. The burning presence of rheumatism was in his bones. It was the tailoring, he thought. A lifetime of being who he was.

Young Tommy Delaney, the fireman, felt the wind come up and push substantially against the flat sides of the *Mayflower*. Whistling a vague air of his own composition, he stuffed his slabs more vigorously into the mouth of the firebox.

"What time we getting to Combermere?" demanded Gordon Peverly, who was impatient.

The youngster put down the shovel and straightened the upper parts of his jacket with some formality.

"What time would it be now then?"

Peverly drew out his watch. A film of vapour had clouded the face of it, and it was necessary for him to buff the glass on his coat sleeve.

"Around nine o'clock."

"Git there by ten," prophesied the boy, as the steampipes rattled on both sides of him; a near sound, like pads of snow falling from the pines.

In fact snow *was* falling. In the darkness beyond the boat, a curtain of snow waved in the wind, stopped, started, and stopped again. The *Mayflower* plodded through it. Her tin stack creaked at the wires, and beneath it a blaze of yellow lanterns burned a flickering stain on the water. The whole operation moved through the darkness like a lit-up birthday cake, driven by a fevered paddle-wheel slapping blindly against a freezing, wind-whipped lake.

From inside the old boat came the sound of voices, the eternal snapping down of cards, the odd, broken fragment of a song sung throatily and devoid of embarrassment: *"When Sandy was living before he was dead, he gave us good grillades to eat with our bread."* This was followed by clapping and the warm sounds of laughter.

18

THE WIND RACED THREE THOUSAND MILES, GUIDED BY THE moon and the polar tug of icefields. It crashed stiffly against the glistening rocks of Fort Severn, split there, half of it hurtling west; the same legendary wind that bent a man like a nail at the corner of Portage and Main. The eastern arm of it met the churning funnel of itself rolling cold off the Ungava, gave way to it, was forced down the horn of James Bay. There it swept the lonely rocks of Akiminski, shouted its ineffable language to the Cree at Fort Albany, flared like buckshot down the waterways of the Moose River, the Mattagami, the Nottaway, soughed in the black branches of boreal firs, and left them clattering like snooker balls.

Scraping the stone harvest of the Shield, it swung east through Kirkland Lake, Temiskaming, and Temiskaming Station. It turned over black ravens in mid-flight, swirled in the headwaters of the Ottawa, massed in rough formations, and proceeded in an almost orderly fashion down the twisting chute of the river. Caged by the walls of the valley, it shushed the supplicating arms of the great pines, proceeded south east, cargoed with cold, uncurled through Sturgeon and North Bay where it turned into the hard, domestic wind of eastern Ontario. It whistled through the caulking of the farmhouses, smoked the lanterns on the table, then flattened in a cold, stabbing formation across the water.

"It's up," said Aaron Parcher, staring out through the glass of the pilot house. The wind had blustered hard on the east side of the Narrows, the way he'd expected. Even inside the channel it only butted them, forcing the paddle-wheel to grind harder against the black face of Kaminiskeg. Now that he had turned the corner on the inlet and faced the open waters of the lake, the gale was suddenly furious, vibrating the window-panes of the pilot house, and whistling through the seams.

"You keep your nose half into it," instructed Hudson, as though Aaron did not have the sense to do this on his own. There was nothing he could do except stand and watch as the young pilot expertly played the wheel, cradling it with a gentle motion, his fingers splayed over the varnished wood.

It was always treacherous there in the wind between the river and the lake. The water opened suddenly and the wind flung itself straight out between the hills, leaving a boat to spin round like a dropped bonnet, thought Hudson. You'd be spinning like a lady's bonnet if you were not careful.

The captain scanned the distance in the west where the hills of the Madawaska Valley should have heaved up magnificently to the sky. Now there was nothing but darkness, a dark fur with silver veins showing in it, like pork fat. For a moment he either saw or imagined the glimmer of lamplight way ahead in some trapper's cabin. That's all he would see tonight, a surly bushman with a shotgun, signalling out into the dark the one way he knew; with the lonely flicker of burning oil. But there was nothing to it. Just an amphitheatre of darkness. The one light he saw for sure winked from Aaron's place, the farm at Parcher's Point, just off shore, a hundred yards away, if that. The point split the lake from the river and was overrun by three generations of Parchers.

"You not going to yank the whistle?"

The pilot shook his head. It was his custom on trips home to pull the greasy rope for his family, and make the steam whistle scream its airy greetings from the pilot house. The pitch went out unmistakably lower than a train whistle and brought a troop of Parcher children running to the shore.

"Not tonight," he said. "It's too late. They'll be down sleeping."

"Like hell they will." Hudson was forever skeptical about the willingness of children to go to sleep. He braced his palms against the ledge, pushing at it, trying to hurry his boat down the last quarter mile of open water to the river. Once they were inside the estuary by the trees there, they were home safe.

"It don't sound the same, does it?"

"What?" said Hudson.

"It don't sound the same since you had them paddles shifted."

"She's turning faster."

"She don't like the wind, that's all."

"No, she don't. She never did." Hudson folded his arms around himself. He did not like the wind either; not having it blown full blast onto the side of her. That was the problem with being a steamboat magnate; when your steamboat was essentially just a floating shoebox with no lines for turning aside the wind. Shoebox or not, Hudson did not want his flagship pitching up sideways on shore and rotting into history like one of those tumbledown shacks in the woods. He felt the burden of these responsibilities build up in him, promoting a strong urge to go downstairs and stop worrying. He would pull O'Brien aside on official business and pat him down for an official whiskey.

"I'm going below," he declared, implying that urgent nautical matters had suddenly arisen. But Hudson did not move. He steeled himself with considerable dignity against that familiar burning pitchfork that was forever getting jabbed in his ribs. The urge to drink, that's all it was. He felt the delicious triumph of holding out against it, and surveyed instead the vast estate of himself. John Hudson, most recent member of the Court of Revision, and reeve of Radcliffe Township. He surveyed his triumphs, recent and old, recalled with a visible grin how it all started seventeen years ago. He was a whippersnapper, thirty years old, staggering drunk out the Balmoral Hotel. He was crossing the footbridge at Byers Creek when the Monsignor himself, Monsignor Biernacki, came across from the other side, showing the stark disapproval of the Lord Almighty. The Monsignor had stopped a moment and said loudly, "Drunk again, John?" To which Hudson instantly and famously answered, "Me too, father, me too." The remark flew across twelve townships and guaranteed John C. Hudson's reputation as the greatest political orator to ever cross the Burns and Hagarty county line. According to Judge Fairbanks, who was retired and lived in rooms at the Balmoral, it was a comment worthy of Aeschylus.

"Goddam Aeschylus," said John Hudson aloud to no one but the handsome fellow with the ornate moustache, grinning back at him from the glass panes of the pilot house. He was briefly lost in the rewarding subject of himself.

He found himself again in a sudden blast of wind. He heard the close, vibrating hum and felt a general queasiness of his stomach, of the pilot house, of wind and water. All around the dark furled and unfurled like smoke, allowing nothing through but the rasp of hard-breathing wind. The sensation briefly sickened him, and then he understood why.

"We ain't moving! For Christ sakes, Aaron, we ain't moving!" It was the worst thing he knew of, to hear the boiler up full, to hear the axle of the paddle-wheel grinding on its pivots, and to know that stupid boy was still heaving pine slabs in the box. And not to be moving. *They were not moving!* Hudson looked out frantically into the night for something to gauge by, something stationary. But all he saw was the dark indivisible night. "Damn it," he spat.

The wind was screaming at him.

He looked around for something, anything to get a bearing. Right then a sound cracked out from the back end of the *Mayflower* and echoed up front through the pilot house. A chunking, heavy sound, like a crate dropping on a wagon. Hudson spun back, hissing.

"What's that?" He stared stupidly at the pilot. "What the hell was that?"

Hudson knew every sound that old boat had ever made and would ever be capable of making. He knew a snapping rivet from a wood split, and the high rattling sound of the firebox when maple got burned instead of pine. Probably he had imagined the whole thing. He looked over at Aaron Parcher for reassurance, proof that he'd imagined that cracking noise, like a barn roof giving out beneath the snow. But Aaron looked only scared and pallid, and then it came again, a distinct crack, this time like ice breaking across a lake.

"Something gived," gasped the pilot.

Hudson threw himself at the ladder and caught his coat on a nail head, ripping it straight up the length of his back, as he hurtled below to the deck. Parcher swung over, keeping his left hand on the wheel, and saw his boss, Captain John Hudson, on his knees, staring up at him, his face obliterated into a white hollowness.

"Christ Almighty! She's cracked in two, you hear? She's broke wide friggin' open!"

19

For the last time Paddy O'Brien dealt the withered cards face down and turned over a black, turnip-shaped spade. His opponent, Murphy, snapped down trump, instantly, in a practised, irritating fashion. O'Brien poked about in his own hand for a corresponding black card.

"Spades, hay?" He found one hiding beside a jewelled queen. "Have your damn spade." O'Brien flung it down with what he trusted was an equally irritating flourish of the wrist.

The tailor, William Boehme, sat next to them contemplating his own fiery knuckles. A deep burn raced through them and had for years. He turned his attention from his knuckles to young Robert Pachal, who stood erect, as if waiting for "Rule Britannia" to come to an end. Boehme nodded at him. She had done all right, Elizabeth Anne had. She could've done worse than this one. Boehme approved of him, at least for now. He approved of his silence, his hands, farmer's hands, the size of shovel blades at least. He'd never seen hands so big. The tailor looked again at his own immaculate fingers, felt the nagging heat in them, and glanced back in time to see O'Brien finesse a spade down on Murphy's spade.

The card showed face-up — the nine of spades.

It was then that the *Mayflower* lurched for the first time. She gave out the low sound of snapping boards, wood rending open, groaning, followed by no sound at all.

Bill Murphy pitched from his barrel to the floor and gazed up at Paddy O'Brien, astonished. He seemed to be wondering why his friend had suddenly punched him in the face. The man pressed rigid and breathless to the deck, assuming, like a child, that if he remained still, no harm could come to him. He held his own palpitating heart frozen. Rigid, unbreathing, every vein in his body tied tight in the effort to squeeze the hull together. By sheer force of will he would keep that crack from sounding again. He did not want to hear that sound again. The elemental sound of something gone wrong, something gone extremely wrong on water.

"Hey!" Young Tommy Delaney staggered out shouting from behind the boiler, a shovel pinned to his chest. "Hey, there's water!" He did not seem the same bluff fireman anymore; the bluster had peeled off and now he was just a boy, yelling for assurance from grown men, seeking explanations as to why the ice-cold surface of Kaminiskeg oozed through the eyelets of his boots, instead of staying out there on the other side of the boat where it belonged. He saw Bill Murphy sprawled on the deck, and Paddy O'Brien pressed down to a crate with a balled fist shoved to his chin. They both looked more like frightened children than grown men. "Hey," the boy shouted, "Hey," as though yelling at cattle. Then she lurched again.

With the second shudder William Boehme cracked against a beam and saw water breaking in from both sides at the back.

"God Almighty," he breathed. Then he was on his feet, smashing into the chest of Robert Pachal, who had stepped across to grab on to him. "Get up front!" he ordered, and pushed strenuously at him. Boehme remained planted firm, scrutinizing the dark end of the boat. Her back was broken; he saw that. He saw the lake surge in unresisted, stabbing at his legs. It startled him to find young Pachal still pressed close to him. He thought, wildly, that somehow he'd managed to heave the man back out to the prairies where he belonged. He pushed him hard again toward the gaping doorway.

"I'm not able to swim," sobbed Pachal. "I'm not able — "

Bill Murphy slid down the deck, like a sack. A shape, black, crow-like, swooped by, knocking Boehme sideways against the hull. The tailor staggered upright, saw that it was Hudson who had gone by.

"John," he shouted, his voice lost in a collapsing of wind and water. Already the captain stood nearly waist deep in water, fixing his hands against the boiler.

"Help me." Robert Pachal reached his arms, imploringly to his uncle-in-law, heard the defenceless mewl to his voice and was violently ashamed of it. "What is it you want me to do?" he pleaded. What was there to do? Where was the place that a man crossed over that made it all go away? You walked out across a prairie slough after ducks, the ice gave, the water, the water — . The water was at his knees now, cold, crippling him. He felt Boehme grab on and push him up.

"Out the side, son!" The tailor yanked at a jutting fixture and used it to propel them both forward. They lurched, like sticks, angling up to the doorway.

The *Mayflower* tilted back severely from the weight of the boiler, swooped two feet and then further as the water folded in from the back end, leaking between the boards of the hull. Then she lunged. The lake rushed in wildly, as though searching for something. It sluiced thickly over the boards and pummelled into William Boehme's midsection, driving him down.

"Help me! Here!"

It was Robert Pachal, somewhere close to him, bleating like an animal. Boehme summoned the fury of his life, grabbed fast on the doorframe, and felt the soaked mass of his coat tugging at him.

"Get outta here!" he screamed.

Overhead, a dented oil lamp heaved from the nail and fell, slapping the water. It rolled and gave off a soft, terrifying *pfft*.

Everything went dark.

Tommy Delaney had just righted himself from being flung against the piping of the boiler. He saw Hudson stride grim, giant-like, the tails of his coat floating out behind him.

"Mister Hudson — the water . . ." Delaney did not bother to finish. The boat lurched hard and then the lake stove in from both sides. The youngster watched it rise up his boots, faster, faster. Then he was detached from his knees. A frozen scythe had made a swift pass though his legs. He bolted forward and barely escaped colliding into Hudson, who bore back a few steps from the boiler.

"Get out!" Hudson roared at him. He was in a cold rage. A sudden, furious hatred of all things, water in particular, flared in him. He hated the fresh, freezing lake water of Kaminiskeg, and he hated the old Fitzgibbon boiler. He tipped down, face full against it, reaching for the valves. His hands felt a burning razor shredding them from inside. It was the valves that worried him. He needed those valves. She'd blow apart unless he got the valves open, and without a boiler he'd have no steamboat operation at all, just a wrecked hull. He'd be the sole owner of a ruined, rusted heap of rotting, useless iron.

It did not seem possible to him that there was anything more annoying than the press of ice water on a man's groin. Some sort of commotion was taking place up front, screaming and crashing and that annoyed him, too. Too much carrying-on nowadays, that was what annoyed him about things. He remembered a different time, when a man canted logs for Gilles, or Booth, and smoked tobacco from Pontiac County, when such a man waited for a fiddle to get pulled out from a flour sack and then danced like hell in the barns at Dacre and Tatty Hill. When he was done dancing, he worked, and when he was done working, he put his money on a coal black stallion at Costello's track, and if he lost his money that was just tough beans. When he was done everything else he shut his mouth and went to sleep. Not now though, not these days. Hudson let go a convulsive gasp and had no further opinion about these days. The water was at his chest, between his ribs, flaying his heart.

He was struck by the fantastical idea that this was it. *This was exactly how a man died.* Amid hostile actions and the back stabbing of enemies. Just like this. The lamp snuffed out. No women at the bedside, hunched, draped in dark clothes, wailing for him as though he were some biblical king. His arms drifted weakly in the cold, like threads that had got loose. Already they did not belong to him. He thought of Edward, his son. The child's nose ran, he held his head bowed, the way he did when his father was about to put a licking on him. Of course Hudson would not hurt the child. He was a man, that's all. He'd never intended to hurt anyone. All he wanted was what men wanted, desperately; to right the situation, whatever that situation was that happened between a father and his boy, between the epochs of the world, to get out from under the mess that a man gets in, to stroke the boy's head. Of course, it was far too cold for doing that. His hands remained underwater, like stationary fish. Occasionally they scraped against the hard belly of a Fitzgibbon boiler. But they did not rub against the fine, sand-coloured hair of a boy's head.

It irked him that he would never again see the warm splay of lamplight. He would not look up and see stars hanging thick as sponges on a June midnight. Nor would he feel the lick of Gillman's brandy on his tongue, or the hot juice that came in dirty bottles from the stills up Dohlan's Mountain. He would not see the blue sides of trout flashing to the surface on a line. He would not see anything except the starless nights of Lake Kaminiskeg, which circled like fingers of ice, drumming on his throat.

"You son of a bitch!" Hudson roared at the dark and crow-like appearance of death. Death had come stomping across the surface of a lake and now had climbed into the pitch black hold of the *Mayflower*. This was it; the same rotten son of a bitch with the pitchfork that was waiting up the turnpike, waiting his turn to wrestle him. He drove his clenched paws into it. He heard it laugh at him. He watched it rise to cleanse his mouth, lapping up his nostrils until the water co-existed with the dark.

And then there was nothing left for John C. Hudson to punch at anymore.

Joe Harper was closest and got to the old woman first. She had a coarse wrap folded around her that slipped halfway down and loosed up her elbows so she could jab them freely into his face. Harper reached up top of him and yanked down a lifebelt from the ceiling, which he endeavoured to wrap around her flimsy body.

"Let me do this," he pleaded. He was acutely conscious of time, of things having to be done now.

"Oh, get off me. Get away!" Mrs. McWhirter did not want these fellows fussing with her at this very moment. She had settled herself in the cushions of a calm spot. Up in front of her was a wall of terror, but behind it was a calmness, and that's where she was, in that calmness. It was there that her memories settled about her like stuffed dolls. Some of them had turned bleeding red, though, like the raspberries she had picked off the earth. She had picked a mountain of raspberries, and she had walked seventeen miles to church and thought nothing of it. She had allowed herself to get kissed by an unknown man behind the rockpile in Klotskie's field in Brudenell on the day of the church supper, and had been troubled her whole life by that simple act. It was an act that changed the course of history. A man, a stranger, his beard, her soft skin, the rich, abrupt smell of pipe tobacco up close, engulfing her. A stranger had kissed her, and shortly after that she had seen the glory of God in the endless flaming rings of the Fatima apparitions that appeared in the sky over Fort Stewart, Ontario. That was sixty-three years ago. Hardly two or three breaths away. She saw now how crucial it was to arrange all of these things and to tidy them up. That is what she presumed would happen; a certain final neatness to all things, not to be tugged at by men who wore their faces shaved smooth with vanity, and went about selling items they'd not even built with their own hands.

She attempted to express this somehow, but the words did not come anymore and she could not summon them up either, beyond a clenching of her frail arms. She had seen that young boy, the fireman, step out from behind the boiler, his mouth wide-open with fear, his teeth gaped, missing, or otherwise black from the premature indulgence in shag tobacco. Then the water spilled up to her like washing suds flung across a floor, and the world was gone even crazier than it ever was before. It was on its way to being sideways now.

"Ohh," she cried, "Ohh, you . . ." She kept flailing at the man who had converged on her. At another time it might have offended her to no end; this presumption that she was in need of some special fussing over. Of course she wasn't. She was a cripple, that's all. Her legs had hung down twenty-five years, useless as ornaments, with a sporadic pain that wracked her when it rained and sometimes when it didn't. At the moment she did not feel a thing; the pain had stopped. Nothing wracked at her legs anymore, and she was grateful for it. She had entered the region of no pain. Her legs had calmed entirely and were no longer a botheration to her. In fact, she was fine as a fiddle, really. She realized it was dark now. Someone had the good sense to damp down the lamp so it wouldn't burn its white, irritating light into her eyes, and keep her from getting a good sleep. She had that coming to her, she did. A good sleep. She realized with a short cry that her world was over. There was no train to Combermere, and never would be.

Joe Harper could not see a thing, but he felt the woman vanish from his hands like smoke. Somewhere, weirdly, he heard his name getting called.

"I'm here," he shouted. He was in the folds of being frozen to death. A hot ripping pain seared through his flesh. He heard Bothwell's name yelled out, but no answer.

It was Gordon Peverly doing the shouting, he knew that much. His voice had shafted through the momentary presence of light, that brief moment before the storm lantern rasped down the length of a nail and nose-dived to the water. The old woman was gone. She'd been flung back, in front of him, flailing at his face.

Harper still had the lifebelt pressed in his hands, she could be in it for all he knew, except that of course she wasn't. She wasn't on the other side either. She wasn't anywhere. No one was anywhere anymore. Not him, not even his own hands. He tried to see his hands but couldn't. They were empty; he'd wrapped the belt around his skinny waist, instinctively, the moment the old lady went under. Bothwell. Where the hell was Scotty? He'd seen a look of wonderment on the man's face, beatific almost, as though he had made some remarkable discovery. He'd been staring down at his own groin as the ice water cleaved into him, then looked up with pure wonderment in his eyes. It was dark after that. The captain, Hudson, had come and gone, disappeared in that same dark. He'd dropped down the stern of the boat, and not come up.

"Out the side!" The voice presumably came from the throat of Gordon Peverly. Usually it was Peverly who took charge. Presumably it was Peverly who slapped against him like a tree bough. Something did. Something smashed into Joe Harper from underneath and reminded him to look upward. Always upward, to where heaven was, at least where it used to be the last time he checked on it. But the truth was that Harper did not so much believe in heaven; he believed in the future instead. He saw a rectangle of shimmering darkness, a less dark surface of silver fur showing from the side. He dove for it, twisting his long body through the roaring water.

Joe Harper was under again, like in the Carp River four years ago; the same panic was on him of life pressed flat against death. There was barely a way to tell one from the other, he thought. The water dropped into his mouth like a stone, and choked him. He could not swim, but the belt and the frantic waving of his limbs buoyed him until he broke the surface of the lake. He was outside now, outside of the big black box. I can die here, he thought. Here's where I can do it more properly.

He floated outside the steamboat into the open lake. Somewhere out there Peverly was shouting for Bothwell, like a lost dog. Harper saw the sky, black as a gun barrel. The boat was mostly sunk now, and coughed up rude gargles of foam as she slid down further. Only the pilot house remained above water. A lamp still glowed from the inside, and cast a gold shimmer into the night.

Gordon Peverly clung to the top of the pilot house like a barnacle. Grabbing on to him was the pilot, Aaron Parcher. Peverly banged his ringed fingers against the windows. He felt the other man's sturdy shoulders clench beneath him.

"Listen!" In that moment the wind broke and seemed to be sucking back to reload. He heard the sound of things gone wrong. Even more wrong than freezing to death. What he heard was the sound of a terrible injustice being perpetrated as if on a child. A person was screaming out there and it struck Gordon Peverly that a person should never scream like that. He cocked his head but heard only the violence of wind. The boat fired a quick shotgun sound and pitched down a foot.

Aaron Parcher managed to loose himself from Peverly's shoulders and shimmy his way to the roof of the pilot house. He'd got a lifebelt wrapped on him, and was gasping.

"I live right opposite here, that's my father's landing." He pointed his arm straight into darkness. "I can make shore!" Aaron looked down intently at Peverly, who attempted to nod through the shaking of his chin. "I can bring out a boat! You hear me?"

"I'll be frozen up," shouted Peverly. "I'll be a goner by then." He felt right now as though to be dead was a startling defect of his character; one that would make it impossible for his wife to walk the streets without people pointing at her. He heard it once more, closer, the blue shrieking pain of men who were hardly men anymore. Soldiers sound like that on the battlefield, he thought lucidly, though beyond a punch-up in Bytown tavern he had no way of knowing.

"You hang on, mister. I'll bring us a boat, see?"

Peverly fully intended to nod at the man, but was not capable.

The young pilot released himself and began pumping for the shore with fast, powerful strokes. A glimmer of light showed there — at least it had — maybe a hundred yards away. Then a white bubble hiccoughed to the top behind him. He did not see it, but the *Mayflower* groaned and slid beneath the surface. She vanished in less than twenty-five feet of water.

The sounds had settled down some, and Aaron Parcher was grateful for it. He could not think straight with screaming going on. The sound of it lit up the dark like wolf wailings, as though a wolf pack were swimming alongside him. It wasn't a wolf though, it was the cry of a man, and Aaron pitied him for it.

At least now he was able to put these thoughts from his mind and concentrate on what he was doing. He was swimming, straight toward an orange light that showed about the size of a thumbnail. He kept it positioned in the slanting V of the waves as if he were looking through the notched sights of a .300 Savage hunting rifle. That's what it looked like. No sooner had the thought entered his mind when he remembered promising Tommy a hunting trip on Saturday. He'd take Tommy out for whitetails and partridge then. He was not to forget that, and afterwards he'd transport his entire life in crates and wagons to the Barry's Bay train station. For he was getting the hell out of Renfrew County and going somewhere else. Aside from the intimidating business of manifests, bills of lading, and the safe storage of a woman's precious things, he was looking forward to it. He imagined his two boys, their eyes big as dollars, pressed to the window of a train, while his wife sat beside him concealing her own excitement in a quiet pretence of being shy.

Aaron pummelled himself forward to the orange light that seeped like toffee from the attic window of his farm. He felt an affectionate intimacy with that lamp. He knew even the length of wick left curling in the oil, the womanish curve of the glass chimney, and how it left a small circle of light wavering on the ceiling when the wind came in. The glare from it illuminated a crosscut saw hanging from a hook, ten pounds of rusted nails in a slim churning barrel, twine, a broken hoe, and all the other battered bits of metal, rope, and wood wounded in the war that Aaron waged every day against the earth.

His arms slapped the surface of Kaminiskeg. The lake rose and fell, folded into sections created by the wind and pushed him back again, so the lamplight showed the same distance off as before. This was a frustrating business and it was just the beginning. Aaron's mind raced over the impending necessities of getting to shore, of rounding up his father, his brother, skidding the rowboat down to the water, rowing out, unpeeling Tommy from the flagpole, lifting half-dead people from the water, rowing back, and getting warm again by drinking tea. Hot tea would be the trick to the thing. He imagined it fighting back a cold tide of pneumonia that rode up his lungs like bilge water.

He would plant the tea first, or was it barley? He couldn't remember anymore what he had in mind, and tried instead to forget about it. What mattered was getting the work done in order. Get there first, proceed to the next matter. It was bloody cold, though. He couldn't pretend it wasn't cold. He was vexed with himself for not stripping off his coat before fastening the lifebelt on. The coat tugged him now like a loaded wagon, and wanted to draw him down to a place he didn't want to go. Get the thing done, that's what counted. To that end, he sought out the light spilling from his attic window. But it was not there. It had shifted to the left and peeked only sporadically over the triangular tops of the waves.

Aaron Parcher directed himself hard left to compensate and slid like an otter over surging water. It was cold. Ten minutes maybe is what he had. A young man could last twenty, twenty-five minutes if he was mule-ish. He estimated ten minutes more till he closed the gap between himself and that light. It hadn't moved any and still stayed maddeningly on his left.

Aaron could not escape the sudden, appalling suspicion that everything now related back to those twenty-seven dollars that John Hudson owed him. It was obvious to him that if those dollars had been paid up properly, he'd be on the Madawaska by now, tying the *Mayflower* up to the stanchions at the Hudson House and getting on his way home to eat. For he was hungry in a way he never had been before. It was a hunger that churned in his stomach and seized at him. Probably it was the cold that did that to him, he thought. The bloody cold.

He looked again for the glaring lantern but couldn't find it. Possibly his wife had walked up the stairs and cupped her palm behind the chimney to blow it out. Wouldn't that be something, he thought. *What time was it?* No. It wasn't the time he was after. It wasn't time for blowing out lanterns. Not yet. He did not see how that mattered. What mattered was how hungry he was. The pilot felt the cork belt slide up a bit, to where it was not so useful to him.

Of course, he would have to wait some before he got his wife's cooking into him, he knew that. First he'd have to make shore, round up his father and Howard, skid the boat to the — Something extremely hot ripped through Aaron Parcher's stomach. He went under the surface, and when he came up he tasted the sweet warm flavour of blood. The good thing was his wife's cooking. She did a ham as good as Mrs. Billings and her whitefish was not bad either. Whatever it was she did up he'd shove it so fast into his stomach that —

He sought the light again and couldn't find it. This left him with the bewildering, helpless sensation that it was now *behind* him. That was discouraging, that and being so hungry his stomach felt torn open. The only place left for him to look was the sky and when he looked there he saw it was snowing. Snowing hard. In fact it was snowing as thick as bedsheets. The strange thing was that it was snowing underwater, too. But when he looked close that second time, he saw it wasn't snow either. He had a good long look and saw it wasn't snow at all.

It was fireflies!

Aaron Parcher saw the green phosphorescent trails of a million fireflies, blazing through the summer nights of his life.

20

Lake Kaminiskeg came in under the coffin box and lifted it softly like a pillow, separating it from the flat bow of the *Mayflower*, and freeing it from the sinking boat. It rose, then dropped hard with a crash, the way a man wakes from sleep on a cold morning when the stove's gone out, and the barn animals are baying for their food. Waves crashed the side of the box, and skidded across the lid.

Within the plush interior the body of Herman Brown slid with a slight rocking motion, head first under the surface of the lake. He was wrenched left and right on the pitching water, lunged down as the icy rivulets came sluicing in the seams of the pine box, then stabilized, the water repulsed by the workmanship of J. W. Christie which had preserved Herman Brown from putrefaction, and now kept him bone dry. The coffin box heaved upward to the surface where it angled slowly, like a raven's wing.

Several yards away a man popped like a cork from the chopping water, his mouth half open. He was crying and chattering in the cold, and immediately draped a heavy, sodden arm around the neck of Joe Harper. Harper felt himself in a panic, drowning, sinking down like an anchor.

"I can't swim," gasped Imlach. It was John Imlach who had burst up from the waves. His jaw fell slack beneath the surface and he came back up again, choking, as Joe Harper tried to float free from the strangulating weight of his friend's arm.

"Hold my coat, I got a belt on."

But Imlach heard only the crashing walls of death as they trumpeted into his ears and through his blood. He slammed a free arm in Harper's direction, as if he meant to kill him. His left hand cocked like pliers on his friend's coat front.

"Let go, let go of me!" Harper was screaming in fury at his best friend, but Imlach paid no attention to him.

Harper went under again. A seizing rip of cold convulsed his chest. Water slid like rough glass over his eyes. He was down, and he stayed down. Two feet from his head he saw his own life assembling together. He saw a boy spit over a bridge into the Rideau River. An older boy on a trolley, carrying a fishing pole, got off at Bank Street to fish the canal, pockets stuffed with grasshoppers. These scenes played in front of him like images in a moving picture show, close enough for him to reach out and touch. Harper reached for it, he tried to grab on to the life that was pulling itself away from him. As he did, the top side of Herman Brown's coffin box collided with his jaw. Harper flung both arms over the top of it. He was carried up, breaking the surface inches away from Imlach's head.

The head itself bobbed there as though chopped off now, and somehow asleep. But in fact the body was still attached to the head, and the man was not asleep, either. The two clung to the box, weighting it at one end so the water sloshed in while the other end lifted like a spar. Waves broke in two on the boards and slid down into Harper's face.

"You alive?" He saw Imlach's head slap hard on the lid of the box, not moving.

Finally the man let go a spasmodic choke. "What?"

"You alive?" Harper heard a distant screaming, whipped by wind, and wondered if it was himself.

"I'm alive." Imlach spat up some water.

It wasn't Harper screaming after all. He was crying. It was someone else.

"Christ, you hear that?"

Imlach sobbed.

Ten yards away a glow shone from the pilot house, which barely showed above the water. Harper saw men clinging to it, arms smashing at the darkness, a tableau of shadows and fear. He wanted to scream. He did scream. He knew that by screaming he could stave off the cold that was killing him, as though putting a bung into a barrel. He screamed and then did not make a sound.

Three feet away the lake broke open, a white, bearded face pierced the black surface and came up gasping through a spout hole in the water.

"Here, get here," Harper yelled. But the fellow just hung there gasping. His face showed the red, blotched colour of rhubarb and he looked at Harper without seeing him. Suddenly he surged close up tight against the coffin box, coughing, crying as Harper got a grip on him and jammed him to the side.

Paddy O'Brien's spectacles had come off and his eyes were bewildered and fish-like without them.

"Oh Lord. I'm not up to this," he shivered, and hung down limply.

"Kick your feet!" Harper instructed.

But the man could not kick; his boots clamped to him like horseshoes. Instead he shook his head in a petulant way.

"No, I'm bust," he managed.

The screaming came on again, closer this time, as though stalking him. Harper heard the anguish blowing in it. It didn't seem possible that a man could bear that much anguish, not for long anyway. He coiled his own body inwardly as tight as he could, like a fist, closing it tight against the pain, clenching it so he could not hear that scream anymore. From somewhere he heard the hissing of a gas lamp, which was not possible, then the frantic hollering of a name. It was Gordon Peverly shouting for Bothwell. His own named was getting called, too, and he was strangely reassured by it. Then John Imlach started in and Harper joined him. They both kept shouting for Gordon Peverly, who appeared as summoned, plowing through the water. He had released himself from the roof of the pilot house, and flailed toward the voices.

"John?" he cried.

"I'm here! Me and Joe."

"Where's Scotty?"

"He a-he . . . he got huh-yanked down." Harper's breathing had turned hysterical.

Paddy O'Brien shook his raw face. He could no longer tolerate men going on about such stupid things anymore.

"Tilly, she's at the hotel there! You hear?" He reached over the width of the box and tried to implant this knowledge with his hands on John Imlach's coat.

"Careful, mister."

O'Brien broke out into a long, swooning cry.

Gordon Peverly jockeyed himself opposite Harper and jerked his head back to where the steamer had been. He hollered out Bothwell's name, one more time over the rattling wind, and then saw him.

But it was not Scotty Bothwell who broke the surface of the lake. It was the tailor; he came up head first, finishing off a terrible choking that began when he was still under. William Boehme saw a group of men clung to a long box. Herman Brown was inside that box; they shared the same blood. Four men gathered around it now, conducting a card game or something. Paddy was there, he was sure it was Paddy. But his beard had gone limp and dangled from his face like knots of seaweed. They were shouting, to him perhaps, waving to him, but he could do nothing about that. There was nothing left in him. He couldn't summon the fury that a man needs to fight with, and to stay alive. His legs were long and pulled him down. They had gone to sleep on him. He could barely kick anymore. He couldn't stop that chill from stabbing him. All he could imagine was being asleep. But it wasn't a real sleep — the kind that folded warm into his body. It was the sleep of dying, and he knew it. He was not afraid of it, even though he knew it meant doing without the touch of wool, or seeing Louisa come in from the garden with a clutch of yarrow to put in a jar by the window.

"Jesus Christ!" Boehme hollered out the name of his Lord over the pitching water. But the wind stole his words and blew them far from the shores of Combermere, Ontario. He felt a cold that few men knew; colder than slipping a boot deep into the Madawaska River when the ice came off in May, a shuddering cold that jangled like a toothache. His boots were getting yanked down, urging him to struggle more or to cease trying to struggle altogether. He couldn't decide. I have made a mess of this, he thought. But it was never one man's fault entirely, he knew that. The blame was spread out amongst all men, some more than others. Herman Brown had got himself shot dead in a prairie town, his sister had married a man named Pachal, a man with red hair and big hands. Boehme could tolerate death, his own death, but the possibility of that young fellow dying this way, out here, after coming so far. He felt an upsurge of pity for him; he was innocent. How was it that some men were innocent, and some men —

William Boehme experienced a great tunnelling within himself. It made sense now, the sand was leaving the waist of an hourglass. Each of those grains of sand was a memory, and in the passing of those memories was remorse. For every memory . . . for every hair on his wife's head . . . There, pinned to her collar, he saw the mother-of-pearl broach she wore on special days. As the water climbed over him, that too passed away.

Gordon Peverly kicked and managed to surge the box a foot closer to the drowning man. The fellow came up again flashing eyes, black and wide as a Clydesdale's, then went under and did not resurface. Water closed over his face, like a curtain.

"He's dead," muttered Peverly.

Paddy O'Brien had gone off his head and began to scream, "Do not swear. You hear me? Swear by yea or nea, that's all!" He seemed to think this of great importance for John Imlach, but Imlach only groaned. His thin lips were entirely blue. He was dead from the shoulders down. It was not a painless death either. The lake tore into him like a bear trap.

"There, over there!" Peverly lifted an arm off the box and pointed.

The white flagpole of the *Mayflower* emerged from the water at a steep angle.

Tommy Delaney hugged himself to it like a porcupine on a thin bough. Under him clung Bill Murphy of Rockingham. There was barely anything of him remaining above the water.

"Get over here!" pleaded Harper. "Make your way here."

The boy gasped hard and blinked.

"Swim to us," hollered Peverly.

"I never swum!" shouted the boy, fiercely.

"Come on, mister!"

Imlach angled off the box and slapped water, but Bill Murphy did not hear. He was beyond the flailings and the loud vexations of men. He was sat already in a comfortable chair; his sister six feet away at the melodeon — *Some heart once pregnant with celestial fire*. Either she was singing this, or it was being sung by the wind. Murphy didn't care. It seemed suddenly important that he climb the hill to St. Leonard's church and wash her gravestone with a small sponge before taking up a spot in the earth next to her, where he belonged. There was no one else for him anymore, just the terrified, vain shouting of men that clattered in his ear, and a cold that was never in the Bible. *I have not sinned excessively, though*. Murphy's mind leapt to the white pine that waved like a fan over the roof of St. Leonard's, then to Eliza Murphy. Dead from diphtheria. He spoke in a formal manner, directing his words to the men who waved at him from six feet away.

"I cannot hold on," he stated, and then was gone.

The boy clung fast to the pole and didn't know if he was crying, or just chattering from the cold. He knew he was holding fast to the flagpole of the *Mayflower*, the last few feet of it that stuck out from the water. It was the same pole he'd painted milk white, just as Mr. Hudson told him to do, and from which he'd hung Chas Murray's baseball jersey the day Mickey Dohlan knocked a ball over the bluff into Lake Kaminiskeg in the fifteenth frame. That was some time ago. Four months maybe, and him and Aaron were going hunting on Saturday. It was Tuesday now.

Tommy Delaney heard fellows shouting at him to let go, but he would not let go, no sir. He was just a starving Irish boy, a Home Child, landed at Halifax, shipped west to slave for a drunk man and righteous woman who beat him with a board for dropping milk. The smashing of stars inside your brain, that's what it felt like when a fellow cuffed you with a board on your own head. No sir, he'd not let go again, ever. He was a stupid bastard, is what Mr. Hudson said. Those rich fellows would ship him right off to stop bullets in a war. But he was fireman, too, no one else but him was fireman, and Hudson did not let him go hungry either, but kept a chit for him at the Balmoral at Barry's Bay and it all was writ down in ink there in that ledger under the glass counter. His name was writ there, too, for Mrs. Hudson had taught him to write his own name, and he had took to it, so that now he could write his own name down on any piece of paper he felt like. He could even carve it with a buck knife into the trunk of a birch tree if he wanted.

His name was writ right there in that book, and Mrs. Billings made sure he got served up the good portions of potatoes and spring ham. There was pie too, raspberry was his favourite, but there was blueberry and apple, and he'd never been hungry again. Nor had Mr. Hudson ever struck him, either, but gave him five dollars instead for being fireman. He did not sleep in that damn barn anymore with the cattle either, but on the *Mayflower*. No sir, he would not let go. His hands were locked around that pole, and he would not let go of it.

"I ain't never swum," he shouted. "It's too cold!"

And he squeezed the pole with two fists, the way Mick Dohlan squeezed a baseball bat when he knocked the game-winning ball so hard that it bounced off the federal wharf and splashed into Lake Kaminiskeg.

21

THE MAN'S CRIES ARCED BENEATH THE NIGHT AND WERE forced down across the water by a thick roof of clouds. Each scream sang the chorus of terror, though strangely he was not particularly terrified. The truth was he was afraid of water more than anything, the unfixedness of it, the way it yielded on a whim like the sinewy threads of temptation. He had little experience with water, with anything that was not rigid, and did not stay the way it was.

All Robert Pachal knew about water was that it fell down on him from up top, or lay like clear glass marbles on the leaves of alfalfa, and damped the wheat stooks into a dark shade of tan. It did not come up from underneath him, like blood oozing out from a wound.

Sometimes it runnelled down the side of a train window, like a series of clear tongues, or lay in deep black pools in the rock holes of north Ontario. He'd seen that himself, on his travels. Sometimes it wound shimmering with silver, like the Qu'Appelle River as it glinted through the valley of his homeland. But it did not heave up at a man and swallow sections of a boat in front of his very eyes.

Pachal knew nothing of boats, either. He knew, years ago, an old ferry that ran aground on the Saskatchewan River. Folks tore it apart for the timber, almost before the passengers had got off.

He knew nothing of boats and very little of water. He was afraid of water. He was terrified by the way it could separate a man and wife. And child for that matter. A girl child; the soft, unbelievably soft nape of her neck. For all of this he screamed continuously like a train whistle, jettisoned by cold, fueled by the culmination of unfairness and the silk impossibility of a young girl's hair. His own daughter. Not two years. She was not two years. This struck him as the most unfair of all — *Two boys dead by drowning*. It was a good thing it was not her, not her who was fighting in the water.

This realization came to him, shocking and lucid. It was not her. It was not Elizabeth Anne either. It was him. The way it should be. It was better if it was the man. The Lord Himself wanted it to be the man. He was a man, age twenty-five, born on Christmas day. He thought that a man, born on Christ's day, and having come halfway across the country, should have something else in store for him than this. It was a mistake, the wrong destiny, inflicted on the wrong man. He was Robert Pachal, the farmer, he had seen the giant spokes of sunlight wheel on the stacked wheat stooks of Ebenezer, Saskatchewan, in the great Dominion of Canada. For some reason he saw the letters embossed in gold on an immigration poster. "Dominion of Canada. The Most Fertile Country in the World." He remembered fields of alfalfa, and Durum Red, waving in the gun-coloured water. A fat partridge splayed over top of it, just waiting to be cooked. Probably already *was* cooked. They'd have you believe it, too. They'd have you believe the partridges of western Canada flew around already plucked and cooked. He heard Kasper Neibrandt saying that. He heard his wife call from the room upstairs, *Come to bed Robert, come on up here, to bed* —

The lake water seized him from underneath. Even the wind seemed to come up from there. The sky could not be seen, but it pressed down tight, like something mechanical. His arms and torso flailed as wildly as before. The world had given way, broken in two. He had a leg on each side of the broken world. The same two strong legs that had carried him across a continent, but proved now to be useless in the water. His legs had nothing to fix against. There was water, ice cold and vicious, attempting to destroy him, the way the soil back home had tried to destroy him; the soil, the matted sod, the cold, the dust, the heat, the coyotes, and the lack of rain. Everything had tried to destroy him, but had not.

Robert Pachal considered it essential now to grab on to Mr. William Boehme, whom he'd tangled with in the doorframe of the *Mayflower*. But the man was not there. He offered no guidance; his voice did not proceed calmly through the telephonic machine. Where was he? Where was anyone now? They were gone behind the whipping surface of waves, and a curtain of black.

Suddenly the curtain opened.

Pachal heard the murmur of voices. In front of him four men clung to a box. He saw the rough pine coffin box that Christie's men had hammered together in a few moments in the cold of the warehouse on Haultain Avenue. It was black now. It had been amber once, he was sure of it. *Mister, we're here. Come here!* That's what he heard. *We're here, come on, mister!*

He saw men hanging on Herman Brown's coffin box. He was just moments away from it, a few arm lengths. Pachal fired his arms up hard. The Devil's tail had wrapped around his boots again and was tugging him. He threw his arms up and cleared the water, briefly, from his throat.

He heard words mottled in wind. They made no sense to him. Pachal stretched his arm out. He saw his finger touch the flesh of another man's hand; one of those eastern travellers. But it did not touch for good. For a moment he scraped the tips of his fingers on the coffin box, then the water turned him entirely, like a corkscrew, and he was facing the other way, at nothing.

His screams leapt toward the hills of a strange place, to Schweig Hill, Moonshine Marsh, and the ponds and lakes that bore the name of the first man to die in them. Some had no name yet, or were known locally by a half dozen different ones. Pachal knew nothing of these names. He knew that the gifts God gave to a man were being taken away. His wife, his child — he exhaled his longing into the wind so that it might be carried to them. His boots and the soaked cloth of his trousers pulled at him. His belt, the buckle on his belt, the braid of his daughter's hair, wrapped in paper stuffed beneath a flannel undershirt, a Hamilton watch, Herman Brown's watch, stopped at 7:28, the coins of Levi Beck in his pockets, the weight of his memory, all of it was dead weight. Even his beard tugged him down.

Robert Pachal flexed his feet, searching for the bottom, but there was no earth to settle on.

And this was the most terrifying of all.

22

A WOLF HOWL CIRCLED INTO THE GALING WIND AND disappeared. All that remained was the chafe of wind scratching on the face of the waves.

"You heard it?" called Peverly.

Joe Harper moved his head up and tried to suck air into his lungs. "The fellow drowned."

"Who drowned?"

"All of them. They all drowned!"

Peverly looked away from him and screamed out loud for his friend, Scotty Bothwell. He hollered again, louder, as though trying to float the man to the surface on the volume of his voice.

"Scotty went down . . . it was too cold," insisted Harper.

Gordon Peverly pointed an indignant look at him. He'd sat too many times in that sofa chair in Bothwell's apartment, with the gaslight shining on the bellies of his aquatic trophies, to believe that his friend was dead. He'd seen him leave a heat of swimmers behind on Meech Lake, so the fellows coming up had to make room for him coming back. He could outswim a fish, that man.

"He's too strong a swimmer!"

"He's dead." Harper felt strangely emphatic about it.

"Jesus Christ!" John Imlach pursed his thin lips. He'd had enough of this. "We're dying, for God's sake."

Peverly stretched across the coffin box and grabbed his coatsleeves to soothe him.

"That pilot, he swum to shore. You hear? He's getting help, he's bringing a boat out." He swivelled his head through the dark, indicating that in a matter of minutes the place would be swarming with rescue boats. All he saw were the waves coming like infantry, heaving up and laying down on the other side. Every second set hurled in broken and sharp as teeth. Nothing was visible beyond them. "That fellow's bringing a boat back," he repeated. "You hear me?" He was unsure if he spoke it out loud, or shouted it in his own head. Exactly where that fellow was bringing a boat to, and how the hell he'd ever get it there, was not clear.

For the first time in his life Gordon Peverly considered being dead. It would happen with a convulsive choke among the ice shavings that knitted themselves together on the water. The wind would gale into his sockets and he would no longer possess the adoration of his wife. She would not even distantly tolerate him. Numbing death, slow up to a point. After that he would go out fast, like a lamp. Or like a bug stranded on a pond. He would put up all that buzzing for nothing, just to be dead in the end.

He yawned uncontrollably. What they needed was a systematic plan for staying alive. That was how things operated at Corticelli Silk Co., every move planned, coordinated, carried out.

"John, you can swim?"

A terrible ringing had started up in John Imlach's ears, like hornets planting stingers into his brain.

"Can't swim," he fired back.

Peverly stared at him.

"You said you could." He saw his plan cracking up already,

betrayed by the falsehoods of men.

"I was lying, alright? Jesus Christ, where you gonna swim to?"

It appeared Imlach was in one of his moods again. Peverly looked across the box at Joe Harper, who shook his head weakly.

"What about you, mister, you swim?"

Paddy O'Brien looked at him with ringed, uncomprehending eyes. He remembered being a boy and getting kicked in the spine by a shoed piebald.

"It was Tilly that bought that old Muskoka chair for settin' in, son, on account a my back. She done it for me!"

"Okay, mister." Peverly swallowed and looked up at the bruised heaven, wanting to catch the eye of an angel of mercy. All he saw was the snow, already on its way down to meet them.

Paddy O'Brien had been howling for some time, loud and steadfastly, into a slanting snowstorm. Finally Peverly couldn't take it anymore.

"I'm sorry, mister, but you're getting on my nerves."

The man paid no attention to him.

"Punch him," commanded Peverly, "punch his face, John, punch him!"

John Imlach was reticent; not because of any overwhelming human kindness, but because his arms had gone to mush and had no bone left in them.

"He's gone off his head. Strike him!"

It was true; the fellow had gone off his head altogether and was garbling up his talk with what sounded like a choking version of a song.

The stranger began to prophesize at them.

"You swear yea or nea fellows and not around her you hear? Not a them what can kill your body but of Him . . . it's Him you be adread of. That's right! A Him!"

"Alright, mister." Imlach wished the fellow would shut up, and tried to jostle some sense back into him. He held

Paddy O'Brien with two fists stretched across the box. O'Brien clung back to him at the coatsleeves. His mouth bolted open again and he started crying like a banshee.

"Mister!" Imlach loosed his right hand and punched him square in the face. It was a good blow, in tight. The man's head snapped back but gave off only a wet thud, like slapping a fish on the ground.

The man made a gargling sound and John Imlach cracked him again, harder. O'Brien blinked his swollen eyes and made a careful straightening out gesture.

"I'm no good boys," he sobbed. "I'm done in, I'm too old." He let out a short moan then and craned his head around to some place he thought the shore might be. "Tilly's at the house, I'm tellin' ya, my Tilly!"

Imlach prepared to crack him again, but the man suddenly lay his head down on the coffin box as though having a nap.

An hour passed and they did not say a word. Around them a vague slush of ice assembled milkily on the water. Occasionally a moan loosed itself from the trembling lips of Paddy O'Brien. The wind had not given in and made a constant shriek. Snow swarmed them, slanted in, hurtling through the gullies in the waves.

They clung two men to a side; Imlach clenched across the coffin box onto O'Brien, Gordon Peverly and Joe Harper cinched in the same way. Harper's hands were visible and naked against Peverly's coat. He couldn't feel them at all. Nor did they hurt in any particular way. They just didn't exist, except as two white claws grappled to a coat, extending like bones into his own sleeves, where they disappeared. He doubted if they were attached any longer to his body.

"Joe?" Gordon Peverly's teeth now vibrated like a tea cup when a train came in close by. He heard them clacking but could not put a stop to it. "Joe! Come on now."

Harper nodded and tried to smile. A wincing agony showed on his lips. "I got no hands," he uttered, and at that moment they slid from Peverly's coat and bounced against the surface of the box.

Harper attempted to squeeze his fingers on the rim, where the boards met, and managed to drape his arms once more across the lid. It suddenly intrigued him that within the wooden box he was clinging to was another box, this one made of mahogany and shining with varnish. In it was the body of a man, and in that man had been a soul. Harper thought now that he did not believe in the soul. The soul to him was a candle that burned where his brain was, and his heart. Of course, he would not say that.

"My hands," he moaned. He sounded infant-like and was ashamed for it. Harper did not believe in ingratitude. He would not have a perfectly good life soured. And it *was* perfectly good. He was a good part of it, too, as was Peverly and Imlach and Bothwell. Somehow Bothwell had been disqualified, heaved out into the water and wiped from the face of the earth, as though he didn't matter. It puzzled Harper that a damn lake should have the ability to kill Scotty Bothwell. It was as if superstition had taken precedence in the twentieth century. He felt a sudden urge for vengeance; to stab the wind in the stomach, and pacify the cold with the steaming stacks of foundries and the red-hot engines of automobiles.

"Damn," spat Harper. "Gordon, I've got no hands."

Gordon Peverly had no hands either. Nor did he have any other parts of his body except for what bobbed on the water, and even that had gone on him.

"I'm not dying," threatened Peverly, and began to undress himself. After considerable shaking and scraping, the first boot came off. He worked at the other, rubbing what he assumed was his unshod foot against the shod one. A queer splitting sensation shot out from his feet, of toes cracking off one by one.

His boots off, he started in on his neckwear. He removed the necktie laboriously with one hand, and flung an end to Harper.

"Hold on to that, Joe."

Joe Harper lashed the tie around his right wrist and heaved up as much as he could on top of the box. He lay his arms on top and hung there, lashed to another man, panting from his own drowning weight.

"Take that coat off." Peverly spoke with confidence now. He had a plan hatching. He saw no start to it yet, and no end, just the middle part that resembled the gnashing of gears in the innards of an oiled turbine. Those gears were *him*, his human body comprised the cogs and pulleys of a great machine that obeyed the touch of men, and the ideas of men, too. "It's dragging you down. Take it off!"

Joe Harper hung exhausted in the dead weight of a buffalo coat. He recalled years ago watching farmers rake the white powdered bones of buffalo on the Kanata fields for fertilizing. Boxcars filled with bones, coming in from the West, one after another for years, then they stopped.

"It's from Nell," he pleaded. "I've a belt on, I'm staying up." He heaved his shoulders to demonstrate there were still parts of him that were not yet fully submerged. If he took the coat off, his skin would go with it and he would die. He was sure of it.

Peverly moved on systematically to the next stage of the plan.

"John? You hear me?"

John Imlach had the yawns. A deep cold was into him and he yawned like a boy awakened at sunrise to go fishing.

"Stay awake John, come on now, you stay alert!" Peverly's command was undercut by a shuddering yawn that snaked out of his own chest. Joe Harper also had his mouth open wide and for some moments the three men hung on the coffin box, yawning strenuously. The fourth man appeared asleep already. He lifted up his head to groan, looked about, and realized he wasn't alone.

"I'm no good to you boys, I'm all done in."

John Imlach jostled the fellow across the top of the coffin crate. He could barely see him for the snow slanting in his eyes.

"Stay awake, mister." He felt a certain proprietorship

over the man, having landed two good punches on his face. Imlach saw the snow all around him, not so much falling as hanging at an angle. Water raked his face, smelling of cold and mildew, like piles of mouldy leaves. This is a damn pickle, he thought.

"Hang on, John!" The voice came from the gloom at the other end of the box.

"I'm hanging on," returned Imlach testily. He was hanging on like a drowning animal to the sleeves of a stranger. He was glad for it, too. He did not want to die alone, at twenty-seven, with prospects of advancement getting discussed behind the oak doors of the General Supply Company.

The wind pushed in a steady surging direction from shore, which showed, tauntingly, the golden light of a lantern from a lone farmhouse. The snow clung like a mantle, was rinsed off by terrifying tilts of the coffin box that laid itself down beneath the water. Ice formed in front of them in the shape of countless, slushy dumplings. O'Brien moaned, Imlach clung to him in rigid, cold fear. They floated on the hard pine shell, lashed together by a necktie, their bodies chewed by the November cold, hair turned brittle by the wind that screeched like a chorus of owls. A gull wheeled around them, curious about this macabre flotilla, then, its curiosity satisfied, was gone.

John Imlach, maddened by the ferocity of cold, turned his neck and hollered, "Jesus Christ, Gordon. Do sumthun!"

It was only right that Gordon Peverly was in charge of doing something. He was the senior man, if only by months, and he could swim. If Imlach could swim, it would have been him doing something. Only he couldn't. Gordon could swim. Not like Scotty Bothwell, of course. He was no trophy winner.

Gordon Peverly roused himself in a panic from a cat nap. He'd reached that place where sleep and being dead were the same thing. He'd missed the train, forgotten his wife's birthday, his life had fallen to pieces during one short moment of rest. It was essential he get back to the plan. Everything depended on his plan and the following of that plan.

In its purest form, the plan was not to be dead. He couldn't recall any further details except that one. Fortunately his boots were off and the dead anchoring weight of them was free from his body.

"Okay, I'm swimming out of here." Peverly winced as a set of waves slithered over his neck. He looked at Joe Harper who nodded back dumbly, then glanced down at the blue lips of John Imlach who seemed to be holding some grudge against him. He kept the necktie wrapped to his left hand, and detached himself from the coffin box.

Peverly floated in the frigid water of Lake Kaminiskeg. He was frightened and sensed his own secret worthlessness, like an odour no one else could smell. It had clung to him beneath his skin, and was not cured by racking up profits for the Corticelli Silk Co., or two stiff drinks, or the beseeching elasticity of his own bluff words. Now that he was mostly dead he felt that somehow the smell was ready to get off of him. He even felt it float away, like a slick of oil on the black water.

The necktie bit into his wrist as he lugged it hard behind him. I am pulling my weight, he thought, I am pulling my own weight. So far it seemed the plan was working out. He was not dead, he was in motion, his legs kicked, his one arm flapped against the waves like an injured gull. All he needed now was a place to get to. Suddenly he found it. His left foot slammed on a rock and sent a coil of agony up into his groin. *Damn, I have broke my foot.* Peverly got the other socked foot up on it, and stood momentarily with his shoulders above the waves.

It seemed to him that standing on a slippery rock, chest high in freezing water, was the same as being saved.

"Boys!" He could not hear himself and was swept immediately into the churning grey sludge below the surface. Peverly got his face back up over top. A few yards off a black comb parted the night. *That is a damn tree branch.* His feet twisted on the stones and staggered him. He cracked his cold kneecaps on a rock, regained himself and hauled Harper in toward him. The coffin box surged forward. Paddy O'Brien drifted off the side, back first, and floated limply into his arms.

"Come on, mister. We're here."

Peverly stood on a rock. Behind him a clutch of scrub cedars shot up from the cracks between more rocks. He saw the bleeding white stains of gull shit and snow. They had washed up on rocks not much bigger than two snooker tables set side by side. He shoved his hands under the man's armpits and staggered backward, collapsing offshore in two feet of water.

Paddy O'Brien lolled his head and felt his eyes open. He knew that right now they must be soapy-looking from a lifetime of wearing spectacles.

"Son — " he started. He was calm. It was essential he say a great deal now. An entire bookshelf of encyclopaedias, crammed with everything he knew, all needed saying; the sky, the hoarfrost, the caravan of smoking forest when they burned the grant land to clear it. "I can't read," he gasped. He wanted to tell about signing the original deed to the fourth concession with an X, forty years ago. It seemed essential the young man know this, that someone know. He spoke very rapidly now, or thought he did. He was telling how he'd branched out into the telephonic business, not having the ability to read or write, and assuming it wouldn't prove a hindrance there. He was not talking so much as having his lips move, up and down. He made a gesture, but his arm felt no longer connected to the rest of him. "My Tilly . . . you . . . you . . . you tell her . . ." Her face radiated through the hollyhocks.

A rivulet of water rolled from his nostrils. He turned away. He did not want to be seen at this moment, not at this precise moment, not by a stranger. "Mister — "

A long, droning gurgle came out from his throat.

Peverly held him until it was finished. Then he dragged the body up to the rocks.

23

THE THREE MEN FELL TO THE ROCKS AND LAY THERE heaving. Gordon Peverly bit his lip in order to keep his mouth shut. It was important to him that he keep his jaw in order. Under no circumstances did he want that rattling sound to come out of him, not after what had come out of that other fellow. Prostrate, shivering in his stockinged feet, he watched the snow come down, waiting, breathing, feeling the bare flicker of his own life. He waited two minutes. Or five. Or an hour and five. He waited as long as was humanly possible.

"I'm taking his boots," he said defensively. He anticipated opposition from some quarter, but none came. He got up painfully, and limped to the dead man.

O'Brien was laid out on his back. The snow grew on him now like a layer of bulrush seeds. Around his throat the skin had turned the blue luminescent colour of a sunfish.

Peverly unlaced a boot from the man and yanked it off.

"Sorry, mister." He spoke intimately, sensing that the rituals of death needed to be observed strictly. Only by such formalities could he remain alive. Peverly pushed his foot into the boot, noting with almost childish glee that it fit. He did the same with the other. Instantly his feet began to throb. A layer of pain burned from the ground.

"Joe," he shouted. "You all right?"

Joe Harper lay contorted on the ground, coughing. He convulsed violently.

"I'm all right," he said.

John Imlach's high voice shot out from a hole in the dark. "Come on here, I found us a place." He was inside it, kicking at the snow. "Get up against this rock."

Peverly and Harper huddled in and felt a small, gracious relief. It was not warmer, but the relentless buffeting of the wind was broken off. They squatted together, numbed, laid low by the chattering idiocy of exhaustion. Imlach tucked his back against the rock and eyed enviously the brown buffalo garment that had Joe Harper swaddled like a baby. John Imlach would not wear such a coat. He'd worn buffalo back when a man wore buffalo. He wore nice pony now, and cowhide. You did not travel for General Supply Co. and go about like a bushman in a buffalo robe, at least not in the Palm Room you didn't. Still, frozen up on rocks in the middle of a lake, with snow landing on you — under those circumstances he considered buffalo was acceptable.

"Joe?" he chided. "You shoot that buffalo yourself?"

Harper sat with his head down between his legs.

"It's from Nell, he gasped. "Nell gave it to me." It had come in a large box with a blue ribbon laced around it. Mostly he wore it to please her. He found it suffocatingly hot for the train and hard to carry along. Now it felt like a baked loaf of bread, with himself plunked into the middle of it. Water soaked the woolly hairs and already a sheen of ice, like cake icing, shimmered on the exterior. He saw that Imlach did not have a proper coat on and was sat shaking like an aspen. "Put it on John. You got no coat."

John Imlach threw up his arms in an abject gesture of refusal.

"No, no. That's not what I meant." He had meant to make a joke, but he had come off sounding like a crying boy. "I was just fooling with you, Joe. You wear it. Keep it on."

Harper had already pulled the thing half off. "That's not right; tell him, Gordon."

Gordon Peverly shivered in the confines of his own pitiful jacket. Already it had rigidified and clacked like boards against his ribs.

"Put the damn coat on, John."

"That's right. Put it on. We'll share it up."

Imlach made a reluctant move for the coat. It shamed him to take a man's coat off his back in the freezing cold. It was two to one though and you could not go against the majority.

"All right. I'll wear it for a minute and I'll give it back to you."

"Give it to Gordon," shuddered Harper.

They huddled beneath a granite shelf and passed Joe Harper's coat around like a whiskey bottle. Peverly took his turn and gave the thing back over. He stared out at the black surface of the lake, out to the brink where the world ended in a different hue of black. It seemed likely that his best friend had died out there, died with the same rattle as that fellow who was lying on the rocks. Peverly put his mind to it but could not imagine Scotty Bothwell drowned and floating somewhere, not thinking or saying or giving a damn about a thing anymore.

John Imlach slapped Harper on the face. He was careful about it this time; he'd cracked that other man a good one and now he was laid out like a pine board.

Harper jerked apologetically.

"I was thinking of Nell," he said, and tried to comport himself into some sort of normal fashion, sitting up stiffly like a man waiting on a bench for a train. He had no feeling except a sporadic cough that racked his chest.

John Imlach fell back speechless. He did not believe that

a commercial traveller like himself who lugged the modern world with him in a sample case and had smoked cigarettes in plain view with a woman, could get washed up on frozen stones in the middle of a goddam lake to die of exposure.

"This won't do, Gordon. We're freezing."

"We're freezing up pretty solid," agreed Peverly.

"We don't get a fire going we're finished."

Gordon Peverly required a few moments to think. His first plan had worked out to general satisfaction. They had been drowning and now they were not. Unfortunately they were still dying, dying of cold this time. It was a coin toss. On one side you were dead, on the other side you weren't. Peverly put his mind to the essence of cold. What was it? What was the essence of cold? He considered cold; the hues, the different shadings of the hues, the suitability of using a tablespoon of bromo chloralum dissolved in water to purify a sickroom, and how a lady wore her hair piled up with pins and when those pins dissolved the hair came down like —

He felt a hot stinging rawness on his face.

"Gordon, wake up! You fell off."

Peverly recomported himself. Cold. The problem was cold. Heads or tails — cold or warm. Then suddenly he had it.

"Fellows, what we need is a good fire!"

Imlach could not resist glaring at him.

"What about some jellied veal, for Christ's sake?"

Joe Harper roused himself and fumbled in his vest for the world's first automatic cigarette lighter. It took time to maneuver the cylinder from the pocket. He tried a desultory snapping of the stone. There was no feeling in his hand. Nothing flickered from the device at all.

"It's soaked through, it's no good."

Peverly felt that he had more skill in operating such a machine than Joe Harper and snatched it from him. It was not easy to hold. Clearly it had not been designed for when a man was frozen. It trembled, wedged far away in his fingers. He pressed the black stone and heard it click like a trigger on an empty chamber.

"It's no good. You need dry wick," groaned Harper.

"You'd need a fire to dry up that wick," agreed Imlach.

"What good is it then?" demanded Peverly. He ground the stone again. "What good's a device for starting fires if you need a goddam fire to get it going?" He kept snapping but the instrument slipped deeper into his palm and then dropped to the ground. "Shit. It's no good, the damn thing."

"It's soaked through," shot back Harper. He was nursing a secret plan to become automatic gas lighter king of the Madawaska valley, and did not appreciate having the merchandise slandered. "You can't make fire out of water, can you?"

Peverly looked around for something dry to start a fire with. He did not see much of anything dry. Except rocks. He put his mind to the scientific nature of dryness. Then it came to him: a man's breath. A man's breath was dry.

"Try blowing on it!" Peverly picked up Harper's machine from the snow and began to puff. He blew raspingly, and with each breath pictured water evaporating off the wick like snow pulling back from a spring field. His lungs fanned rhythmically, stretching and folding like a pair of worn leather valves, ventilating the night.

The instrument was passed from one man to the other in turns, and in turn they fired their breath on to it. Harper's buffalo coat moved in the other direction. They huddled on rocks, trying to spark life into Joe Harper's automatic gas lighter. They pressed insensate fingers to it; Harper's thumb grew cloven and dented from flicking at the stone. Peverly flicked for so long that a growth of powder, like a black sickle moon, showed under his thumbnail. He held the instrument in his hand and glared. It irritated him that such an efficient-looking device could not keep men from dying.

Using his left hand Peverly attached his right thumb to the flintwheel and blew his last rasping breath out before flicking again. For three hours they had been blowing on the machine. Peverly felt a faint resistance against his thumb, the flintwheel, for the first time, fighting back. He heard the scratching of sandpaper. Then a short, gold flame leapt from the pit of his fingers.

"Jesus Christ," he blasphemed. "It's shooting out stars, look!"

From the top of his thumb an entire constellation spewed into the night.

For the most part John Imlach had lost his father's specialized skills in the making of fire. He had grown into manhood beneath the hissing of gas lamps, and the comforting heat that bucked from a basement boiler. But like all J. S. Castle men, he was an instinctive scrounger. He'd find snow to burn if he had to, and sell it on commission. He was not against dirty work if there was profit in it, and for that reason he got to his knees against the base of a rock, and began to dig. His fingers stabbed the crust of snow until they broke it. Beneath he found a few handfuls of packed loam which he lay down in a growing heap beside him.

Gordon Peverly pressed to his knees applying the living lick of flame to the loam, egging it forward into a spume of scarlet fur. The pile cackled and blew apart in the wind.

Imlach watched the glowing fury of embers. He rained down his handfuls of fuel, reaching and jabbing for more. He unearthed a layer of matted humus and yelled as though he'd discovered gold.

Peverly oversaw the operation. He blew delicate and strategic breaths, as though he were God, starting the whole thing up many years ago in the first garden. The image appealed to him. He cupped his frozen fingers against the sudden upsurge of wind, waved his hands like a sorcerer, and laid on the magic ingredients supplied by his assistants. He swung easily from the Christian faith to a heathen one; he would sit cross-legged, drink the blood of sacrificial animals, pray three times daily to Mohammed. He was adaptable. Through his hands passed one cake of ancient gull shit, the cone of a hemlock, the crisp, tannin-filled leaves of the stunted pines. He swayed, gesticulated, and uttered the age-old incantations of fire-making. He invoked the name of Jesus Christ many times, as though the Son of God was not so much his saviour as an old drinking companion from his bachelor days.

It seemed to him that men of his generation were godlike in their abilities. They could make fire out of nothing.

Joe Harper, a long bent figure in a buffalo robe, scoured the perimeters of their miniature island. He threw his fist blindly into the air and hit something. He hit the black, icicle-like branches of a pine tree and cut himself. I am bleeding, he thought. The realization was fitting, even profound somehow. He grabbed the branch, throttled it down until it snapped, and stumbled back to the fire, waving it like a regimental flag.

"I got us a branch," he boasted.

The gnarled stick went into the flame. It smoked, a licking orange fire raced up the ribs of it and fanned across the branchlets, curling, singeing like the spatter of bacon.

The thing was going. They had a bona fide stick on fire.

Gordon Peverly sat before the fire and gazed at his pocketwatch, which struck him now to be a miracle of engineering. He'd been three hours in that freezing water with it, a few terrifying hours on the rocks, and here it was in his hand, ticking ferociously. It seemed to him that a man's heart ticked like that, in the final hour before he died of tuberculosis. Peverly angled it into the fireglow and saw the time; 3:22 of a Wednesday morning, November 13, 1912. There was something comforting about placing himself so exactly in time. There was even something heartening about the elaborate curlicues of the Roman numerals circling the face of his watch. You couldn't beat a good Elgin, he thought. You could pay more, but for the keeping of time, an Elgin was best.

"It never stopped. Never stopped once." Reverentially he returned the watch to his pocket.

John Imlach lay close to the fire and trembled. He was

attempting sleep. The trick was falling only nine-tenths asleep. That final tenth would kill you. Imlach lay neither asleep or awake. Mostly he twitched uncontrollably.

Eventually Harper spoke.

"What time is it?"

Several hours had passed but Peverly did not bother to haul out the watch this time. It was a fine watch, but he'd lost his enthusiasm for it. He stared into the fire, which hissed a hole through the fresh snow.

"That boat comes through here soon," resumed Harper. He tried to pump some hope into his voice, but did not achieve it. It was demoralizing to see Gordon Peverly in a funk. He had always imputed to Peverly the characteristics of a life that lunged unstoppably forward, like a train. At this moment without Peverly, he was just a shadow. "She'll come through in the morning. You saw that boat Gordon, the *Ruby*, at the dock there in Barry's Bay?"

"What time?" asked Peverly.

"Ten o'clock, ten this morning. Before noon, anyway. Noon at the latest." Harper was being cautious. It was not the sort of thing he wanted to go out on a limb about. "She runs down to Craigmount in the morning, and comes back through in the afternoon. She'll pick us up coming through. It's Bart Schnall's boat, the Craigmount Company. You know Bart."

Apparently Peverly couldn't recollect making the acquaintance of anyone named Bart Schnall, and continued his morose survey of the fire.

"Joe . . .That fellow . . . he . . . he gave it up, Joe, I had him." Peverly looked down into his arms as if he still had the man nestled there. "I had him and then he threw his head back, straight back. The gurgle came out — it just kept coming, and after that he was gone."

Harper nodded, but he felt it to be a useless gesture. "Scotty's dead." He did not know why he said this.

"He's dead," repeated Peverly. But he meant the stranger who lay flat out on the rocks twenty feet off. Peverly struggled half upright and slid closer. "Joe," he glanced over at Imlach, shamefully, to make sure that he'd not be heard. "Joe, I need a smoke awful bad. I won't make it without a smoke, I can't, Joe."

Harper nodded and checked himself. Three loose Sweet Caporels had turned to muck in his coat pocket.

"I understand you, Gordon, but we don't have anything to give you."

Peverly assented to this with a nodding, grievous dignity, and fell back.

"We're getting off in the morning, though. We'll have a good smoke then. We'll enjoy the best damn smoke ever." Joe Harper heard a vapid hucksterism in his voice and was sick of it. There was a certain honesty in giving up. Either a boat was coming or it wasn't. Either they were dead or they weren't. What they did didn't matter. It was a realization that ran counter to everything he knew. It blasphemed the religion of Timothy Eaton and Thomas Edison. It undermined the first principle of the modern world: that with action a man could shape the universe. He could make steel bend, and reverse the course of rivers. Harper realized that such a philosophy did not apply here, not out of eyesight of the lecture platform and city newspapers. He was just a man here and even the wind was capable of killing him. Harper changed gears drastically.

"You know what, Gordon?"

There was no answer, but Harper went on anyway. "I wish I were in that Market flophouse with a whore. Just like that judge was. I'd rather be dead drunk with a whore. In a flophouse."

Something in the conversation seemed to awaken Gordon Peverly's interest.

"With a whore?" he inquired timidly.

"That's right." Harper rammed his chin defiantly to his own chest, and left it there. A wind whipped the fire. "A big fat one."

"A big fat whore?"

"That's right, a big fat whore. A great big fat whore."

There was a pause, dark and dramatic. Peverly whispered urgently, "Joe?"

Harper struggled forward. He was convinced a dreadful secret was about to fall out of Gordon Peverly's mouth.

Peverly got a finger into the cuff of Harper's coat and pulled him down to him.

"Joe?"

"What's that, Gordon?"

"I'm telling Nell what you said."

Harper looked square into his friend's face.

"Gordon. You're not saying anything. You know why? Because you're dying here on this rock. Like an animal."

Peverly shook his head sadly.

"I'm telling her you said what you said."

"And while you're dying like an animal, me and John'll be having a good smoke."

Peverly would have none of it.

"Joe Harper," he sighed. "Barely married a year either. How could you, Joe?"

Peverly waited for a come-back, but all that came back was a wind that clanged off his face.

Harper was asleep. A strangulating snore came out of his mouth.

It was John Imlach's idea to burn the lifebelt. The canvas wrap smouldered for a while and then the cork caught. The fire smoked. A mound of bullet-sized cedar chips guttered in the wind and drummed red fingers on the dark ceiling.

"Five and twenty to nine," announced Peverly, hurling down the laws of time as though it somehow made things better.

Imlach had no interest in the eternal laws of time. "I don't give a damn what time it is."

"It don't matter whether you give a damn or no," trumped Peverly. "It's still five and twenty to nine."

"I'm starving," finessed Imlach. "I'd rather be drowned than starved to death."

Peverly gave the matter some thought.

"I don't know, I'd rather freeze than drown."

"Starving's worse."

"Freezing's not so bad." Peverly was not sure. Drowning was the worst, probably — choked up in the dark with lungs pounding against the lake, closing on you like a lid.

"Whatever." Imlach cut the thing short. "When's that damn steamer coming through?"

Peverly thought ten o'clock, or eleven. No later than noon. "That's what Joe said, anyway."

"It's not going to see us," stated Imlach, flatly.

"They'll see us. They'll be looking for us."

"Why's that?"

"Cause we're missing."

"So?"

"So they'll be out looking out for us."

"Who?"

"Everyone. Those fellows on the *Ruby*."

"Those fellows on the *Ruby* are pie-eyed. They won't see a thing." Imlach knew that even cold sober in full daylight all anyone would see was a flat surface stretched tight as a fishing line between sky and water, and that would be the shoreline.

"Come on, John, you're only saying it because cause you're starving and you're froze to death."

"They won't see us." Imlach would not let go of it and they sat off from each other, estranged and bitter.

They remained that way until Joe Harper began to scream.

Harper slept with his legs crooked across the stones, up close to the fire. He didn't know if he lay on a mat of snow or the splatter of herring gulls, and it didn't matter. What mattered were his feet. They were small feet for a man his height; quick, agile, forward-going feet, and they were cold. They had improved somewhat with the fire going; he had reached across with both hands, lifted his legs and plopped them one by one close to the flames. He was now snuggled up with a warm, dark-haired woman he presumed to be his wife, and found himself rolling his fingers absently on the flecked mole that floated on her shoulders. He felt a familiar stiffening at his groin. It intrigued him how there was always that. No matter what, there was always that. It was remarkable really just how much heat emanated from a woman, even a small woman. Best of all was the way it circulated down his legs into the frozen buckets his feet had turned into.

He felt her warmth melting back the icefields, the way it did when the spring sun glared on them. And it must have been glaring, for his feet were on the warm side now. Hot even. In fact they were hotter than toeing bare feet in the sand in late July. For that matter an old bucket of sand stood next to the stove in case of mishap; he was up on that stove, a brand new Beach Monarch ornamented with chrome. For some reason he was dancing on top of it like a performing monkey — without his shoes on either.

Joe Harper woke up screaming. Down the long funnels of his legs he saw shoots of flame sprouting up like crocuses where his toes should be.

Gordon Peverly lurched to him, bucked up Harper's knees, and doused his boots in the snow.

"Hold it, Joe, you're on fire!"

Harper arched his back, yelping as a sheet of vapour hissed through the dark.

"I'm done for," he moaned. "I'm crippled."

"You're alright, Joe, they didn't melt right off or anything."

Harper would not be consoled. He was frozen and half dead and now he was a cripple, like that old woman who drowned in front of him. Even if he got thawed out, he'd limp about for the rest of his life, and be an object of smirking pity. He was a cripple and had burdened his wife with it, too. People would look at her and say, "Oh, there's Mrs. Joseph Harper, she's married to a cripple."

Harper let out the emphatic, outraged sob of a child. The sky had opened like a chest and every one of its rotten contents had landed on him and no one else.

"Fuck," he said, for perhaps the third time in his life.

Then, "Shit." There was nothing he could do about it, and he broke down and wept.

John Imlach had little tolerance for weeping of any kind, especially by men. He crawled over and hastily piled a heap of snow about his friend's feet to make sure they did not ignite again.

"Hold still, you just melted up a bit, that's all."

A searing pain jangled up Harper's leg and took his breath from him. He twitched from the hips down and waited for the hurt to drain out, which it did slowly with the heaping on of more snow. He looked and saw a dense grey, the colour of a steaming Dreadnought cargoed with the urge to kill people. The rest of the world lay flat as a fry pan. A few low shadows from the cedar boughs hung beside him and quivered on the rocks. Harper saw that a desultory sun had risen. It had risen several hours ago; a wash of grey filtered through the dark, quelling the wind. He turned to the wilted heap of clothing that contained Gordon Peverly.

"What time is it, Gordon?"

Gordon Peverly hunched around his own knees, trying to suck in heat from the fire. It was getting on to noon, Wednesday. Peverly shivered and returned the watch to his pocket as if inserting it into a hole in his body.

Noon.

That was something, thought Harper. It was better than nothing.

"Where's John?" He cast about the smothered amphitheatre of stone, took in the brittle junipers freighted with snow. He saw his own shadow fluctuating on the rocks.

At that moment John Imlach stomped in from the shore. He pressed a ragged bale of kindling under his arm and staggered forward flourishing a green bottle.

"Look here, I got something." The bottle was encrusted with dirt and petrified cocoons. "I bet you some shanty man heaved it in the lake." There was a pronounced, hysterical tone to his voice. "It's cleaned up some, here; I filled it with water for you." He handed the bottle to Peverly, who guzzled hard on it.

Harper struggled up eagerly, took the bottle from Peverly, and felt the hard line of cold bite into his stomach like a drill bit.

"Oh, my God, that's good."

"Isn't it though? Good water alright." A glazed, tubercular-looking radiance shone from Imlach's face. "I guess some timberman was having a snootful and he hears the foreman coming up so he flung the bottle in the lake. That's how it ended up here." John Imlach concluded this narrative with a raging intensity, and then collapsed to the ground.

"I burnt my feet off," complained Harper.

Imlach was still conscious and hauled himself up near the fire, where he gave Harper's feet another close inspection. He saw a boot tongue fused into a matted loam of wool socks, resembling the pink slush of a gutted fish.

"They're not burnt right off, Joe."

Harper shuddered and would not be consoled by kind words from John Imlach. What the hell did Imlach know about anything but removing money out of people's mattresses and stuffing it into his own?

The long blare of a wolf stretched through the morning. It started up like a steam whistle, then ground into some savage mechanical noise, slashing through the cold. Harper quivered, then moaned. Scotty Bothwell was dead, his own feet were fried up, and he was sucking lake water from a dirty bottle of high wine. He took another gasping pull and visualized the last forkful of food that had entered his mouth sixteen hours earlier. The water was good, he thought, but it could go into your mouth and drown you, and if it didn't go into your mouth it killed you some other way. It seemed there was no amount of water a man could drink or not drink without getting killed.

"Listen!" Gordon Peverly pulled himself up from the earth.

"That's a wolf," declared Harper.

"No, listen! You hear it?"

The three men engaged in the contorted, neck-twisting business of listening hard, angling their heads against the wind.

The sound came out of the fog; a rattling, subduing into a light rhythmic thump.

"The *Ruby*. It's the *Ruby!*" Peverly gained his feet and hurried to shore. Evasively he stepped around the dead man and mounted, without shame, the beached coffin box to get a better look. "It's out there! Hey, hey we're here! Save our souls!"

He turned back to Imlach, who assisted Joe Harper and brought him limping to the rocks. The three men stood waving and hollering. Finally they saw it; the angular nose of a steamboat punched through the fog, a hundred yards off. It steamed, insensate, like a small iceberg skimming the grey. Peverly waved the urgent semaphoric language of desperate men. He screamed his throat raw in the wind.

Imlach fled back to the fire and returned with a smoking cedar bough that he swung wildly in the air, scattering a few glaring ashes that died indignantly in the water.

The steamboat drifted in front of them and then evaporated. A small, fleshy wound opened in the cold of the day and the *Ruby* dove head first into it, pulling a cloak around itself before it disappeared. For a few moments the slapping of paddle-wheels muffled back at them, then expired, flattened by a curtain of wind. A stain of black soot remained pasted on the sky.

Imlach strode back to the fire, threw himself down, and began to quiver disgustedly.

"They don't know we're even missing," he moaned.

"They know," Harper insisted.

"How do they know?" Imlach's angular face drew itself into a rigid triangle of fury. "They don't know nothing. They don't know how to run a goddam steamboat without sinking it. They can't even *read*, for Chrissakes."

Harper heaped a few black frozen sticks on the fire.

"They know!" he repeated. "She'll get us on the way back. She'll drop a load off in Combermere, and head back to Barry's Bay." He wanted to elucidate more on the matter but was overcome by a blinding urge for tobacco, and for warmth.

John Imlach made an inarticulate noise and attempted to hurl himself into sleep.

Harper said nothing. He kept his eyes to the flicking hands of the fire and tried to shut himself down entirely. His plan was to hibernate, like a bear. He would wake up groggy with dreams and amorous for a mate. He would lick the red ants off the stones of the Ottawa Valley until he was fat and flush.

For several hours Gordon Peverly lay prostrate on the earth, awake or sleeping. Finally he realized he was awake and lying in considerable pain on his side. The tick of his heart reverberated through his cheekbones. At eye level he saw the edge of the lake cup to him in a ring of black rollers. Beyond stretched the shore; the grey metal bush.

His heart ticked again and this time he knew what it was; the defiant machinations of a good two-dollar Elgin pocketwatch. Peverly could not stand it anymore. He yanked his back off the cold rock. It piqued him that a foreigner in a cap shade could put together a two-dollar watch that kept ticking while he, Gordon Peverly, who had the advantage of being handmade by God, should stop working altogether on this damn island. He was cringing under that injustice when the steamboat came down Kaminiskeg for the second time.

The *Ruby* slipped tranquilly from the grey wall, inverted this time, as if in a mirror, turned around, unballasted, and riding visibly higher. A smudge of black fumigated from the stack and mingled with the stratas of the sky.

"Hey, there!" Peverly shouted a quavering noise into the air, noticing the steamer lay further off than before and moving fast as a water beetle. "Joe, John!"

Imlach was up, waving the buffalo coat about his head in wide, lassoing circles. Joe Harper moved to his knees, hollering.

"Hey, mister!" Peverly screamed lamely. He could not think of the proper words at the moment. Neither could Imlach, who managed only to bubble incoherently.

The boat appeared to pause deliberately to taunt them, then plowed back into the thick curtain of early twilight and disappeared.

"That's it then." Joe Harper folded himself back into the big coat. They would not last another night. He was not convinced they had lived through the first one. Harper saw himself entering a dark cave from which he would never come out. A sob broke his throat and cleared the way for the others that crowded behind it. "When I'm dead," he managed, "you take the coat."

"We're in a pickle now." Imlach looked back to the fire and saw it was dying, like everything else. There was nothing left to burn, nothing to eat, nothing to live on. They had poured everything into the fire, like whiskey into a drunk's mouth; the tree bark, loam, pine needles, torn-off branches.

Gordon Peverly saw his two friends sag to the stones.

"We're still not dead," he insisted.

24

Twelve-year-old Howard Parcher raised his gun and crept through the darkening battlefield of the shoreline, keeping the lake to his right shoulder, and his eyes peeled for the clattering upsurge of a partridge. His strategy was to shoot a partridge and lay it down for dinner, just as his big brother Aaron did. While he was at it he'd kill every Prussian soldier lurking in the woods of Radcliffe Township. He understood that the one purpose those soldiers had in lurking about the woods was to commit unthinkable crimes on the persons of young girls, in particular Angelina Sorbetskie who lived in a farmhouse next to the piling yard at Combermere.

The exact nature of those crimes he did not know in any satisfactory detail, but they left him flushed and agitated, like he'd been last summer when the three Blakely girls went laughing and whooping into the lake, and came out with their dresses weighted down and dripping with water. It was something awful they did though, he knew that. So awful you could not talk about it. The one time he attempted to explain to his mother what it was those Prussian soldiers did to a girl, he got in worse trouble than when he set the cookhouse on fire.

Howard Parcher assumed for the most part they hid behind trees and waited to shoot you in the back. For that reason he pivoted dramatically every few moments while he tread the shore. Even though he was only twelve years old, he was an excellent soldier. Those Prussian swines hadn't figured on finding such an excellent soldier in the woods of Radcliffe, or one who was such a crack shot either. That's why they were all dead now. They died instantly and dramatically, the way soldiers die in a boy's mind, cleanly, without shedding a drop of blood, or screaming for their mothers, or ripping open tunics to find out if it's a gut wound. They lay scattered about the bush now, like split firewood.

Young Howard Parcher did not allow himself to be prideful about his accomplishments as a soldier. The Parchers were not the sort of people who did that. Although, in truth, he could see his chest swelling a little, especially when Angelina Sorbetskie found out how he'd saved her single-handed from the worst thing that can happen to a girl, saved her whole family and the horses, too.

The boy sat down on a blackened cheeko and chewed a wedge of cornbread his mother had packed for him in a leather wallet. He was half way into it when Dougal Gates's boat, the *Ruby*, slipped out of the grey and plied straight and swift as a bicycle for the Narrows. The boy waved his hand mightily, the way soldiers did, hoping Dougal would pull the whistle for him, but no one did and she steamed by silently, growing smaller until she was no bigger than a fly.

The *Ruby* was a better boat than the *Mayflower* anyway, even though his big brother was pilot. Howard Parcher knew the *Mayflower* was just an old wreck, and that Captain Hudson was a cheapskate who owed Aaron twenty-seven dollars. It did not surprise him that the weather was fit enough for the *Ruby* while the *Mayflower* had not budged from the wharf at Barry's Bay. Probably she took on a leak and was still up there getting patched. It was just as likely she had gone downriver to Craigmount.

Either way, he wanted Aaron back home. He'd got permission to go hunting on Saturday with him and Tommy. He'd kept asking and his father said alright providing it was alright with Aaron. He knew it was alright, because Aaron was moving up to Kirkland Lake with the family and he'd never see him again, except in a few years.

The boy pushed the last hunk of bread into his mouth and started back the shore way. He'd not got a partridge but that didn't matter so much anymore; he was going out with Aaron and Tommy on Saturday to do some real hunting. Buck hunting. Not with a .22, either, but with his brother's .300 Savage, or a .303. He'd get one, too. Not only would he shoot a buck but he'd have himself a smoke. He was of age for smoking now, at least in his own mind. He'd have his first smoke in the presence of grown men. The hard part was finding a way to get word out to Angelina Sorbetskie that he was now a smoking man. It didn't seem right that he should have his first smoke without her knowing about it.

The boy was immersed in this vexing problem when he saw the hat, gushing up and off shore with the waves. A heavy straw boater with a black band, like the one Aaron wore. Howard Parcher crouched carefully to pluck it from the water and when he did that he saw the man, floating twenty yards offshore. The fellow rested on his belly, wearing a coat like Aaron's coat, except it was stuffed up the back with a bladder or something, so he ended up looking like a fat man, all bloated. He was dead, too. He was dead as a board. Both his arms were flung out sideways, like boys did when they played in the lake and pretended they were drowned.

Howard Parcher felt a sudden fear that the dead man was about to lift himself up, head first out of the water, and speak to him. He fell on the slick stones, regained himself, and ran. The rifle stock slapped his thigh. The hat, which looked like Aaron's hat, hung in his hand like a dead bird, bent backward by the velocity of his running. Rocks yanked out from under him. He heard cannon to the right of him, to the left of him, and ran to the rhythm of the only verse he knew: *Half a league half a league half a league onward.*

Then he was in the hayfield. The red, rusted harrow sat unhitched in the hay, its curled spikes digging into the earth like the fingers of a man. He was running into the fearful existence of grown-ups, with all its lashings of fear and doubt. He knew once a boy had entered there was no going back to before. Everything was behind him now, like the barn door streaked black with creosote, closing so hard he'd never get it open again.

The boy ran up the hill and saw the chimney of his home; wood smoke spiralled from it as white and warm as what angels had their wings woven from. He made the stable. There was his father, standing inside, the way he always stood, grooming the sick roan.

"Paw, lookit!" Howard sucked some breath into him and held out the hat, hoping it would produce an explanation from his father.

The man took the hat and turned it over, but said nothing to him.

"There's a fellow drowned, I saw him, he's drowned in the lake."

The man scrutinized the boy carefully, even oddly, and scratched at himself.

"Where?"

"He's in the lake there, off the big rock."

Silas Parcher put the hat down on a hay bale and was confused. He did not look confused, he looked studious. He was thinking. Then he strode halfway out the stable, turned and said, "Hitch up Aaron's horse to the wagon and bring it down, quick."

The boy nodded meekly. He was torn by an indecision wringing through his chest.

"Paw — it's Aaron. It's Aaron out there." He uttered the words plainly. They felt like no other words that had come out of his mouth before, even tasted different. They elevated him to a plateau where he had never gone before.

His father glared at him. "What are you saying, son?"

Silas Parcher started down for the lake. He did not run. In recent memory he had run only twice; once because of a bear, the other time because a fork of lightning had started tracking him across the hayfield.

The rowboat lay in the dead grass with flakes of green paint curled up along the hull, like fish scales. It was in need of painting. That was something he'd meant to do and hadn't. Silas Parcher felt a flash of guilt shoot through his body. Sometimes it felt that life was getting away from him.

He flipped the boat and looked out past the big rock. A bundle of grey clothing, like laundry, heaved in the water, rising and falling gently, in different sections, exactly how a drowned man ought to look. He stepped into the lake and groaned, astonished by the knife-like cold. Without stopping he dragged the old boat off the land.

Silas Parcher strained his shoulders against the oars and saw the land fall away. He saw the stout triangle of the log farmhouse, newly roofed. The smoke of food and warmth meandered through the sky like a braid of woman's hair. He saw the barn, the outbuildings, also newly roofed. He saw Aaron's homestead showing through the black branches of the alders. All of it drifted away from him in the even, repetitive strokes required to propel a boat across chopping water. *Jesus Christ, You give me strength through this*, he instructed.

Silas Parcher directed the boat alongside the floating man, and turned the oars in. He reminded himself that just because a fellow had on the same coat as his son, and same coloured trousers, did not mean it was him. He took a handle at the man's shoulders and sank his fingers into the coat, bunched around the neck. Then he heaved the man part way over the gunwales, and saw the fellow had Aaron's face, too, staring up at heaven with an odd look. It was the look of a man who knew things needed to be done, but did not know precisely how to get them done. That same cast forged itself on the face of the father.

Silas Parcher heaved the body into the boat, and laid it out. Then he cried loudly in an unpracticed way for the death of a good man.

"Son," he cried. "Son."

In a few moments he scanned the water for the rest. If Aaron was dead, all were. He stared at the grey face of Kaminiskeg and knew now why Aaron had not come home last night, why the whistle had not sounded. He made out the north shore, peeking out under the dark that hurried down to it. In front floated Gull Island. There, on the dark rocks, he discerned the shifting motion of smoke, hardly distinguishable from sky. A black arm of soot waved at nothing.

That's where they were, then, the others, they were alive yet, washed up on the rocks.

Now, as before, things were in need of doing. There was a boat to get back to shore. There was driving the buggy six miles on hard road to Combermere, to O'Brien's House or Hudson's, for the use of the telephonic machine. There was giving out the news of death and drowning. He saw this being done like casting out a handful of terrible seed. There were words to shoot up the telephone wire to the Bay, to bring Dougal Gates back down on the *Ruby* to get those folks from the cold. There was six miles coming back, and unhitching a wagon. There was Aaron's wife, and Aaron's mother, and Aaron's children.

There was a burying that needed to be done.

Somewhere behind a rock fence that Silas Parcher had piled for forty years, was a life that had come to an end.

25

Gordon Peverly had known men to die in all manners of ways; asleep in bed, in the teeth of threshing machines, lying down in front of trains for their own reasons, struck by autos or lightning, gasping with smallpox, or keeled over with a boiled egg in hand. He had known people to die of swamp fever, lake fever, rheumatic fever, and scarlet fever. He had know a man to be electrocuted by the lines of a streetcar, and to walk three miles before falling down dead after being shot accidentally in the chest by a six-year-old boy. But in all these endless legions of death that now marched across the world, he had never once heard of a man dying while sitting down. At no time in his life could he recall picking up the newspaper, and seeing it written there: *Man Dies While Sitting Down.*

As long as he was sat down, he would be safe.

"Joe?" he hushed. "Sit up, Joe. Sit up, now."

He wanted to lift Joe Harper up forcibly, by the shoulders, and make him sit him up, but he did not have the strength left to do it. He'd been huddled in more or less the same position on a rock for nearly twenty-four hours, and could not begrudge Joe for being fast asleep on the ground. He hoped that's what he was; asleep, and not something else.

John Imlach was sat down sensibly for the time being but there was barely a piston left thumping in him. He'd gone back to the rocks and carried on cursing at the *Ruby* when she steamed by the second time, stood on his two feet waving and blaspheming, even after the silver wake had settled into a placid nothing. He'd come back with tears knocking down his face and sat up close to the fire, but the fire was not much to speak of; some little heat came from it as might come from a half-smoked cigar, but no lick of flame inhabited it any more. Nor was there anything left to burn except the box containing the dead man, which was nailed tight. Peverly did not have the strength to get up and search out a rock to smash through it. Even if he did there was not enough heat left to get it burning and even if there was he did not see how it made any difference whether he froze now or a few minutes from now, or whether he starved or expired from misery. The light had gone out when that *Ruby* steamed by for the second time.

Peverly remained seated despite his body pleading with him to lie down. Once, without looking at him, John Imlach called out his name.

"What is it, John?" Peverly answered, but nothing further came from his friend. A wind tossed in the tree crowns and he heard the distant staccato of an owl, or what he presumed was an owl. From an invisible place, in delirious moments, he heard the crazy, insistent ticking of an Elgin watch.

Mostly what he heard was the ear-splitting silence that prefaced death. It approached as a shadow creeping along the water. For a moment Peverly saw it coming, hanging on to the surface of the dark. He heard it banging too, grinding with the incoherent machinations of death.

From out of those machinations rose the cry of a steam whistle. It blasted through the dark and drove a long cylindrical hole through the side of the evening before it passed into Peverly's left ear and exited out his right.

John Imlach's head bolted from the crook of his own bony shoulders. He was up on his feet, wobbling like a foal, pulling at Joe Harper who roused grudgingly from his wife's arms. Gordon Peverly was up, too.

"Holy smoke! How do you like that?"

Peverly heard the sublime plunk of oars striking water, the groan of oar locks. He was up and covering ground. He lurched on top of slick rocks, side stepped the dead man, stumbled, and slammed himself flat-handed on the lid of the coffin box. He saw the dark meadow of water and, driving through it, a fleet of two boats squeezing out from the darkness, manned with living men.

Dougal Gates held up a storm lantern, radiant as the North Star. He was wrapped in a mackinaw and his bearded face aimed grimly at the goings-on in front of him. He saw the cruel huddle of rocks known to him as Gull Island, then a bootless dead man; Paddy O'Brien. His wife and Paddy O'Brien's wife had done the baking together for the Brudenell church picnic every July since 1896. The dead man lay rigid on the earth, half draped in snow. Nearby a rough coffin box was wedged on a stone. The waves slapped underneath it. Twenty-five yards away floated the corpse of Robert Pachal. His arms stretched straight forward toward the coffin box, as though reaching with all his might.

"Hallo, boys!" hollered Dougal Gates. "Where are you and *how* are you?" His voice lolled thickly over the cold. Then, in front of him appeared a man, his eyes wild and dark as plums.

Gordon Peverly staggered and raised an arm. He was in a position now to say something he'd wanted to say his whole life. "Boys," he choked. "Have you got a smoke for me? I'm dead for a smoke."

26

SAVED BY A CASKET
Patrick O'Brien Made Brave Fight For Life.
Survivors Tell Story
(By Staff Reporter)

Barry's Bay. Nov. 15 — In the cosy parlor of the very modern hotel in the old village of Combermere, back there in the hinterland of Renfrew County, the three fortunate young men, Messrs. Peverly, Imlach, and Harper, of Ottawa, told of their experiences from the time the boat gave her first list to stern on Tuesday night until they were rescued the next night. That first night they had kept from going to sleep by slapping one another's faces, and speaking words of encouragement to each other. They prayed for strength and for rescue.

AN AWFUL EXPERIENCE

"It was an awful experience," Mr. Peverly continued, with a tremor in his voice. "But here we are enjoying a smoke apparently little the worse for our experience. We have no words to tell you what we felt. There aren't words enough in any vocabulary to do so. All I can say is we have the highest praise for the way the captain and crew of the *Mayflower* behaved."

"I believe they will find the corpse of that old woman we tried to help in the cabin of the *Mayflower*," added Mr. Joseph Harper. "She was a cripple and could not make her escape." Mr. Harper appeared little the worse for his experiences, though he stated he had had his toes slightly burned and frostbitten. "Even if there had been a lifeboat in tow," surmised Mr. Harper, "she had gone down too quickly for it to have been any use."

The whereabouts of the body of the missing Bothwell seemed to be worrying the three more than a little. "I wish they would find him either dead or alive and end the suspense," said John Imlach. However, he does not think there is the slightest chance of his friend being alive.

A PATHETIC SCENE

A pathetic scene was witnessed when the men reached the hotel. Mrs. Hudson, the proprietress, mother of John C. Hudson, owner of the boat, and the owner's wife, hoped to see John Hudson amongst the rescued. When they were told it was believed he had been drowned the two women completely broke down with grief. At the wharf were the wives and families of Mr. O'Brien and William Boehme, two of the Combermere men who are dead. On hearing the worst they turned away to their homes . . .

KINDNESS OF RESCUERS

Mr. Imlach made it clear that he felt very thankful and appreciative of the kind courtesy extended to him and his friends while they were at Combermere. "At no place else in the world could we have been treated whiter," he said. "As for ourselves, strangely enough, not one of us even developed a cold, though the weather was bitter and we were chilled and soaking."

"What is more," added Peverly, "my watch did not stop working the whole time I was in the water."

The Ottawa Citizen

ROBERT PACHAL
DROWNED IN MADAWASKA RIVER
Leaves Widow and Young Daughter

Robt. Pachal, a well-known citizen of Yorkton, lost his life in the Madawaska River on the night of Tuesday, November 12, when the *Mayflower*, an old sternwheeler steamboat sprang a leak and went to the bottom of the river, carrying with it the twelve passengers on board, nine of whom were drowned.

Four bodies of victims of the disaster have been recovered, including that of Robt. Pachal, which has since been buried at Barry's Bay, Ont.

Robt. Pachal was a well-known and respected citizen of Yorkton, having been a resident of this district since infancy. He was born of German parents in Russia twenty-six years ago, and was brought to the Ebenezer district by his parents when an infant in arms. He was married three years ago to Miss Brown who, with a little daughter some two years of age, is left to mourn his loss.

His father, Mr. Fred Pachal, was almost prostrate when he learned the news. Uncles and cousins, to the number of sixty, were also greatly distressed.

Mrs. Pachal and her daughter will leave for her home at Barry's Bay, Ont., as soon as her affairs are arranged here, and will reside there in future.

The Yorkton Enterprise

27

THE WIND CAME NORTHEAST OUT OF OTTAWA AND TOSSED through a hedge of cedars, rattling the tarp on the old wagon as it clattered to a stop beneath the lee wall of the Baptist church.

A young man with stout shoulders decanted from the plank seat and braced himself in the cold. After suffering a moment of irresolution, he started across the tamped-down snow of the cemetery.

Before him the hill swooped dizzily into the village of Schutt, Ontario. A few bare patches of hillside showed, close-cropped by cattle and burnished with shining stones. Winter clouds heaped and scudded one on top of the other. It seemed to Leonard Marquardt that, even with the autumn bled from the trees and winter stabbing the place, it was still a sight.

Cold or not, he tugged the beaver cap from his head and held it ostentatiously in two hands in front of him. This was in case someone should be looking from behind the curtains across the road at the Nordholt place.

There was no doubt as to where he was headed. Marilyn Fluegal, who had succumbed to rheumatism, was the last person buried before the sinking, and her stone stood sharp and shiny in the clean air. Ten yards off was a wire fence. Nearby the earth lay quilted in two tawny rectangles. That is where he advanced to, his heart thick, and palpitating.

The headstone rose plain and black, two feet high into the air. *Herman John Brown*. He managed that part well enough. *Died Nov. 1912*. Herman would have liked that, he thought, said plain, carved in granite with nothing fancy to it. He looked away and saw the hills rolling in all directions. The earth was stunned, silent except for the incoherent and disrespectful speech of a raven.

A damn slaughter, thought Leonard Marquardt. A bloody slaughter as would happen in war. Here was Herman dead for no reason but hunting partridges. His best friend, back in the fields again, after making other men rich in order that he could stay poor. That's how he put it. That was the idea behind the whole thing. He'd seen through it, though, Herman had, a long time ago.

Leonard Marquardt shuddered. He was not like Herman. He would not propel the foreman into a bank of snow. He might slam a pickaxe into a vein of corundum crystals, wrap his hands about the teats of an ungiving cow, or clear windfall off old hunting trails. That was something he'd do.

Not Herman, though. Herman would do nothing anymore except lie here in the hills where he was born. He'd come home, no matter what, and Leonard Marquardt approved of that. He approved of his friend, dead or alive. He'd been a bit bothersome, that was all, and anyone who said different ought to go to hell.

Probably some of them had gone there, too. Jack Hudson maybe, on account of his drinking. But Jack Hudson was the very man who settled up the ancient matter of the culvert that did, or did not, run through Liedtke's property. That Irishman maybe, Pat O'Brien, who ran the telephonic exchange out of a room in his hotel down in Combermere. Not Will Boehme. Leonard had been married in a suitcoat cut by Will Boehme, the same coat he wore to the baptisms of his children, and the burials of three of them when they caught the fever. That other fellow, Murphy, from out Rockingham, probably he'd go to hell. Leonard Marquardt realized he was condemning a man to hell for no reason except that he lived all the way over the other side of the county.

He glanced around the valley. They were all scattered in township graveyards now, like this one; Mrs. McWhirter, who had propped herself up on crutches for a quarter century and stood in at Jane Prince's birthing and Leo Knechtall's birthing, too. Tom Delaney. He was barely old enough to smoke, lived his life in a fever for playing baseball, and had been taught by Mrs. Hudson to sign his name on a chit. He was dead, and so was Aaron. That was the worst of it. Aaron who had good land already bought, up north far away. He remembered with some clucking noise, or a chattering of teeth, how Aaron had walked thirteen miles to stand in at third base up the pitch at Hardwood Lake after Honos Cruikshank had his knee smashed by a mare. Now he was drowned, washed up into the arms of his father. That was something; to find your son like that.

One of those travellers was dead too, a city man. His body still wasn't found. People claimed they'd seen him buck-naked in the woods — all the way from here to Calabogie, people were saying that.

Leonard Marquardt shuddered in the cold facts of what had happened on that night. Something had come to an end. That's what it felt like; an empty hole in the world where all those people had been before. Cleared out, like trees, to make room for something new, all nine of them. He didn't know what that something new was, and didn't care. It would turn out to be no good for anything. That was for sure.

Three paces away was the grave of the other fellow. He attempted the name, carved in ornate letters on the grey stone, but had no way of pronouncing it. *Robert Pachal.* He'd never seen a name like that, a stranger's name. A man who, for a time anyhow, had married Elizabeth Anne.

Of the seven Brown girls, it was her Leonard kept a hard eye on, back when he did such things, in the days of being a bachelor. She was back now, with the little girl. He'd seen her in the stores at Schutt buying cloth. He did not speak to her. You did not speak to a woman like that; she was shut up into a block of ice and could not so much as aim her eyes at anyone. All she did with those eyes was cast about, looking for the fellow she'd been married to. He was here now, buried toe to toe with Herman, and he wasn't married to anyone, anymore.

Robert Pachal . . .

A stranger's name. Down at the sawmill Ray Hearne was saying for a fact that Mel Craftchick told him that Chris Hudder found out from Dougal Gates that they'd discovered the poor bugger floating against the back end of Gull Island with his arms stretched out in front of him, like he was still groping after Herman's dead body. That's how far he'd come with it. It made Leonard cringe to imagine a man travelling so far only to end up buried in hills that had not a flinch of feeling for him, did not even know who he was. They would not transport him back, either. They were not stupid here. You didn't go tempting God when you'd already done it once before. Not twice you didn't.

He shook his head. It was cold and he had work to do. Before turning away he tangled once more with the meaty words on the headstone, reading slowly with only a slight betrayal of moving lips —

Robert Pachal
No Pain, No Grief, No Anxious Hour
Can Reach Our Loved One Lying Here.

Acknowledgements

This book was made possible by other books, letters, stories, maps, texts, newspapers, journals, reports, oral histories, rumours, and the fundamental desire to put things down on paper. I am indebted to all of these records, to the men and women who created them, and who maintain and preserve them. I am indebted to the Saskatchewan Archives Board, the staff of the Archives of Ontario, the National Archives of Canada, the Barry's Bay Library, and the Toronto Public Library System. I also thank those remarkable people known as "amateur historians." My thanks also to Mrs. Billings for putting up with my questions. My thanks and gratitude to the Ontario Arts Council and the Canada Council for the Arts for supporting this project. Thanks to Deborah Clipperton, to Dave Sloan, Eden Guidroz, and Duncan Armstrong. My thanks and appreciation, in particular, to Jennifer Barclay of Westwood Creative Artists, and to Marc Côté, of the Dundurn Group.

I wish also to acknowledge the many sources that found their way into *Nine Bells for a Man*. These include: *Madawaska Valley Memories Vols. 1 and 2* (oral histories published by the Barry's Bay Library); *The History of Killaloe Station*, Martin Garvey; *The Shanty*, Bernie Bedore; *Shanty, Forest and River: Life in the Backwoods of Canada*, Joshua Fraser; *Booze*, James Gray; *New And Naked Land*, Ronald Rees; *Spirits of the Little Bonnechere*, Roderick MacKay; *Over the Hills to Georgian Bay, The Ottawa, Arnprior and Parry Sound Railway*, Nial MacKay; *"Hello Central?" Gender Technology, and Culture in the Formation of Telephone Systems*, Michele Martin; *The Saga of the Kashub People in Poland, Canada, USA*, Aloysius J. Rekowski; *A Pictorial History of Algonquin Park*, Ron Tozer, Dan Strickland; *Algonquin Logging Museum*, Dan Strickland; *Whitney: St. Anthony's Mill Town on Booth's Railway*, Brian Westhouse; *The John R. Booth Story*, C. F. Coons; *Names of Algonquin*, Technical Bulletin No. 10; *Early Days in Algonquin Park*, Ottelyn Addison; *Your Loving Anna: Letters from the Ontario Frontier; Finnigan's Guide to the Ottawa Valley*, Joan Finnigan; *Where the Heck is Balaheck: Unusual Place-Names from Eastern Ontario*, Michael Dawbee; *The Age of Light Soap and Water: Moral Reform in English Canada, 1885-1925*, Mariana Valverde; *Timber Wolves (Greed and Corruption in Northwestern Ontario's Timber Industry 1875-1960)*, J. P. Bertrand; *Dance With Death*, Frank W. Anderson; *Sinking of the Mayflower*, Stephen Weir; *Wolf Willow*, Wallace Stegner; *Harvest of Stones*, Brenda Lee-Whiting; *Historical Bells*, Verna Stasiuk Freed; *Twenty-Seven Years in Canada West*, Samuel Strickland; *Information for Intending Settlers on the Ottawa and Opeongo Road and its Vicinity*, T. P. French, Land Agent; *Geographical Names of Renfrew County*, Alan Rayburn; *William Lyon Mackenzie*, Charles Lindsey; *A History of Cory County*; *Large Forest Fires in Ontario*, Dept. of Lands and Forests, A. P. Leslie; *Kinsmen*, B. J. Cooney; and to the many others whose names, scribbled on scraps of paper, are lost now in a jumble of notes, and time.